A NARROW POINT OF VIEW

When a devout Christian is found murdered in his home — his body callously set alight — DI Hillary Greene and her team face their most puzzling murder. It seems impossible to find anyone with a motive strong enough to want him dead. Then, as Hillary unearths avaricious business partners and an estranged son, her focus is diverted when a new team member is targeted by a vicious criminal gang and Superintendent Brian Vane actively seeks ways to stab her in the back. Hillary begins to question her position at Thames Valley HQ . . . but where will she go from here?

Books by Faith Martin
Published by The House of Ulverscroft:

A NARROW ESCAPE
ON THE STRAIGHT AND NARROW
NARROW IS THE WAY
THROUGH A NARROW DOOR
WITH A NARROW BLADE
BESIDE A NARROW STREAM
DOWN A NARROW PATH
ACROSS THE NARROW BLUE LINE

FAITH MARTIN

A NARROW
POINT OF VIEW

Complete and Unabridged

ULVERSCROFT
Leicester

First published in Great Britain in 2010 by
Robert Hale Limited
London

First Large Print Edition
published 2011
by arrangement with
Robert Hale Limited
London

British Library CIP Data

Martin, Faith.
  A narrow point of view.
  1. Greene, Hillary (Fictitious character)- -Fiction.
  2. Policewomen- -England- -Fiction. 3. Christians- -
  Crimes against- -Fiction. 4. Detective and mystery
  stories. 5. Large type books.
  I. Title
  823.9'2–dc22

  ISBN 978–1–44480–521–5

Published by
F. A. Thorpe (Publishing)
Anstey, Leicestershire

Set by Words & Graphics Ltd.
Anstey, Leicestershire
Printed and bound in Great Britain by
T. J. International Ltd., Padstow, Cornwall

This book is printed on acid-free paper

1

David Merchant woke that morning at his usual time, just a little before 6.30. He didn't really need his alarm clock, but he was a creature of habit, so he waited patiently for it to ring before turning it off and rolling over on to the edge of his bed.

He still slept in the double bed he'd shared with his wife of nearly twenty-eight years, who had died of cancer just over three years ago. Not for the first time his strict Methodist upbringing made him wonder if he should get a single bed now, since it seemed such an unwarranted luxury to have a double all to himself. And he knew only too well how even the smallest of indulgences could help erode a man's character.

He'd have to think about it, maybe see if he could find any relevant Bible passages to help him decide, and then he would act.

That small problem out of the way, he rose and went through to his bathroom. Although he lived in a fairly modern, small detached house right on the outskirts of the large village of Kidlington, he hadn't had central heating installed, and both his bedroom and the bathroom were icy. Determinedly ignoring his own shivering, he set about briskly brushing his teeth and having a wash. Luckily, the coal fire in the main living room was also used to heat the water in the tank, so it retained just enough warmth to be pleasant.

Back in his bedroom he dressed quickly in dark-grey trousers, warm vest and a plain white shirt, then added a dark-green, hand-knitted pullover, one of the last items his late wife had made. Plain black socks and a pair of serviceable lace-up black shoes completed his outfit. Only once he was properly dressed, did he pull back the curtains and look out.

He deplored some of his neighbours' habits of dressing and undressing in their bedrooms, with their curtains left undrawn and lights blazing. He'd brought it up at the last parish council meeting, but the meetings were so sparsely attended nowadays that he might as well have saved his breath. None of those he'd wished to censure was even present. Apathy, David mused angrily, was now becoming the norm.

It was mid-February, and a sharp frost limed the countryside, turning the bland green and browns to a white-rimmed winter wonderland. In the distance, the rooftops of the nearby hamlet of Hampton Poyle gleamed in the silvery light of a full moon. The ~~very~~ first glimmerings of dawn were prompting an early robin to sing uncertainly. Unlike many of the houses in his cul-de-sac, David Merchant's house didn't have double glazing, so he could hear it distinctly.

It pleased him. Of all God's creations, David appreciated birds especially.

Downstairs, he set about boiling the kettle and pouring a bowl of bran-based cereal, then collected the morning paper from the porch. Ever since he'd complained to the small newsagent he used, the lazy paperboy had had to rise at a decent hour.

With his sparse breakfast cutlery washed, wiped and neatly put away, he went into his main living room, which had long since been converted into an office.

Here he lit the fire, carefully raking out the ashes first, and using plenty of kindling, before banking it up with anthracite. The room was carpeted in hardwearing beige carpet, and a dark-brown leather settee faced a large wooden desk, which housed neat piles of paper. Both the sofa and desk were between-the-wars utility, and solidly built. The wallpaper was woodchip and painted a neutral magnolia. Charity-shop paintings of the English countryside hung on the walls,

3

and a large goosefoot plant grew lushly in a modest bay window. But by far the most eye-catching features of the room were the two floor-to-ceiling bookshelves that lined the largest walls.

These were packed with mostly hardback, grimly educational-looking tomes ranging from old 1930s' leather-bound editions, to more modern hardbacks in primary colours. In such old-fashioned surroundings, the computer on the desk — although more than twelve years old — looked apologetically space age.

It was a quarter to eight on the dot when David Merchant sat down at his desk. A writer of theological tomes and a publisher of many years standing, he didn't even need to check his watch.

He had no idea then, that this would be his last morning on earth. And even if he had, it was debatable that he'd have done anything differently.

★　★　★

At just gone nine o'clock that same morning, Detective Inspector Hillary Greene got a parking ticket from the machine at the John Radcliffe Hospital in Headington, a large sprawling suburb of Oxford, that looked

4

down on the dreaming spires from its lofty hill.

She shoved the ticket into her pocket, shuddering at the cost she'd have to pay when she fed it back into the greedy barrier as she left, and walked briskly towards the maternity unit.

She glanced at her watch as she did so. DCI Paul Danvers, her immediate superior, knew that she was taking this hour to visit her ex-sergeant, now DI Janine Mallow, but still felt absurdly guilty as she got into the lift and punched the button for the third floor. Missing work, even when there was nothing particularly serious on her desk at the moment, left her feeling wrong-footed.

She was, in fact, already generally feeling uneasy and distinctly out of sorts, which was probably not all that surprising. The last time she'd seen Janine had been just after her ex-sergeant had shot and killed the man who'd murdered her — Janine's — husband, Detective Chief Superintendent Phillip Mallow.

Since then, the preliminary inquiry into the killing of Clive Myers had concluded that Janine Mallow had lawfully killed the man in the execution of her duties, and to prevent the murder of a second police officer, DI Gregg.

The facts had appeared to be clear cut and, since more and more evidence against Clive Myers had been coming in thick and fast over the last few months, most of the brass at HQ were finally beginning to breathe sighs of relief. And it was now confidently expected that when the final report came in, probably sometime in the summer, no charges against anyone, anywhere, would be in the offing.

Only Hillary knew that their relief might well turn out to be premature.

Naturally, she'd been ordered to keep clear of her sergeant until the preliminary inquiry had been concluded, which she'd been only too happy to do. In spite of the fact that 'Mellow Mallow' had been Hillary's greatest friend and biggest ally for nearly twenty years, didn't mean she was best friends with his wife.

But when she'd got the news last night that Janine had given birth to a healthy, seven-pound baby girl, she knew she couldn't put off the reunion any longer.

The lift opened, and she stepped out. A man, waiting to enter the lift to go down, watched her as she turned and walked towards a set of double doors. He saw a woman with a distinctly curvaceous figure, dressed in a plain black skirt and jacket with sensible heels, and wondered what had made him give her an automatic double take. She must have been in her forties, which was usually too old to attract his interest, but her skin had been good, her eyes wide and brown. Perhaps it was her hair — a shade of dark chestnut that caught his eye. He'd always had a soft-spot for red-heads.

But in the next moment she'd disappeared, and he got into the lift quickly, before it could shut.

Hillary found she was on the wrong ward, and was pointed back to the other side of the building. As she walked, she checked her purchases. Peaches were Janine's favourite, but she suspected, this far into February, they'd probably be of the forced and, ergo, tasteless variety, but it was the thought that counted, wasn't it? She'd also bought a few pricey women's magazines that she wouldn't be caught dead reading, but that she thought Janine might appreciate.

She found the nurses station, was brightly told by a young girl that Mrs Mallow was in room 22, and was pointed in the right direction.

'She's decided to call her baby Phillipa Janet — after her husband and her mother. Isn't that nice?' the nurse added quickly.

Hillary smiled. It was the nurse's way of probing whether or not she knew of Janine's recent widowhood, and she quickly introduced herself as a police colleague. The nurse, thus reassured, watched her go.

Hillary, her heart sinking the closer she got to her destination, finally paused outside the door, and took a long, slow, breath.

Then she forced a slight smile on to her face and knocked briefly, before pushing open the door and going inside.

★　★　★

It was a quarter past nine when the doorbell rang, ripping David Merchant from his engrossed reading.

His company, Merchant & Coe Publishing, specialized in children's secondary education books and religious volumes. He'd been trying to follow the rather esoteric ramblings of a would-be author about the legitimacy of St Swithin's beatification, and glanced up with a frown.

The doorbell pealed again, and he reluctantly marked his place in the manuscript with a slight pencil dot, then walked out into the chilly hall. Through the frosted glass he could make out the slender figure of a woman with a mass of pale-blonde hair.

Instantly he scowled and quickened his pace. He flung open the door and glared at his visitor with hard, implacable eyes. He wasn't a particularly tall man, maybe five feet ten or so, but he stood so stiffly upright that it made him look taller. His greying, sandy-coloured hair gleamed dully in the weak winter sunlight filtering in through the glass, and his boiled-gooseberry eyes became cold.

'What do you want? Do you have to come here, where all the neighbours can see?'

His visitor smiled, or rather grimaced, her mouth, heavily coated in red lipstick twisting into an ugly line. 'The neighbours are either all at work, or couldn't give a damn about your private life, you stupid old man. Haven't you figured that out yet?'

The voice was husky and flat with loathing, and David's normally pale features flushed with anger.

'Do you have to blaspheme every time you open your mouth? I'm used to you insulting me, but do you really have to — ' He broke off with a sigh of exasperation, and looked around the cul-de sac with quick darting glances. But he could see no one taking any interest. Nevertheless, he made up his mind quickly. 'You'd better come inside. Although what we have to talk about, I can't imagine. Unless you've had a change of heart?' he asked hopefully.

His visitor stepped inside with a distinctly

9

unlady-like snort. She was wearing a long, belted, dark-blue cashmere coat, cut to make the waist look cunningly narrower than it actually was, and calf-length soft grey leather boots with a two-inch heel. She wore matching soft leather gloves and a grey handbag slung over her right shoulder. Her make-up was heavy and apparent, as was her perfume.

David Merchant looked away from her, as if the sight of her hurt him. Which it did.

'I'm working,' he said heavily, leading the way back to his office-cum living room, and his visitor followed slowly.

'Still keeping up that good old work ethic, huh?' she mocked, glancing around and grimacing at the uninspired décor.

David walked to his desk and glanced down at the manuscript, his mind still on the author's argument. He thought the author was probably a history student, since he'd got his period detail remarkably accurate, but his theological arguments were rather wild, and very flimsily researched. The premise was interesting rather than accurate, he felt, which was, unfortunately, a common mistake with authors nowadays.

'You might at least look at me,' his visitor said, her husky voice petulant now, but with a hint of real rage lurking inside it.

David glanced at her quickly, then away again. 'I'd rather not. You're an abomination. And if you've come to try and talk me round about the money, you're simply wasting your breath.'

He glanced at the small pencil mark he'd made on the manuscript, then at a pencil holder in the middle of the desk, just to make sure that he had a pencil with an eraser on it. He had a feeling that he'd be rejecting this manuscript, and he wanted to send it back in a spotless condition.

And it was this simple action that caused him to die.

Because his visitor realized that with that simple dismissive gesture, he wasn't even thinking about her at all. Worse, he wasn't even going to give her a fair hearing. And how could this religiously bigoted, narrow-minded dinosaur ever be made to listen to reason, when he wouldn't even pay attention?

The answer, of course, was blindingly obvious. He wouldn't. Not ever. And in that instant, all her hope vanished. She could talk until she was blue in the face, but she'd never get him to change his mind. All her dreams for the future withered inside her, turning her cold, numbing her mind, leaving room for nothing but despair and a curiously calm, overwhelming rage.

And in that moment, she wanted nothing more in the whole wide universe than to see him dead.

The blonde woman looked around savagely and saw the heavy brass fire irons beside the banked fire. It took her only a few steps to her right to reach them, then she bent down and picked up the heavy brass poker. It felt hefty in her hand, almost as if it had been made for the purpose and had been poking about in fires only as a way to pass the time.

A sudden thought, deliciously ironic, made her smile and almost laugh out loud. The old bastard's cheapness in failing to install central heating was going to be the death of him.

Now just how appropriate was that?

Hysteria, so close to the surface, almost made her collapse into giggles. Instead, she lifted the poker high above her head, and whacked it down. She wasn't even conscious of giving her brain the actual order to move, so intense and all enveloping was her rage and despair.

David Merchant was still thinking about St Swithin when the first blow struck his skull. And although that blow was enough to kill him, the blonde woman hit him twice more once he was on the floor before she stood still and then finally let the poker drop beside his body.

She blinked, and stared down, and then gulped hard. Sudden fear for her own safety made her look out of the window in trepidation, but the window in this room looked out across flat open fields, and the only living things that might have seen what she'd done were some dark-faced sheep grazing nearby.

She glanced next at her hands, and gave a small sob of relief to see the gloves. Then she glanced down, grimacing at the small flecks of blood on her coat. But they were only visible to her because they were wet, and she was looking right down at them. From a distance, she knew they wouldn't be visible against the dark-blue material. If she was careful, and didn't get near anybody on the way home, she should be OK. Shouldn't she?

Of course, she'd have to get rid of the coat — burn it or something. She'd seen all those CSI shows, and knew you had to get rid of all the evidence you could. But it was such a pity about the coat. It had been the find of the month to discover it at a village jumble sale, of all places. It had cost so little and was real cashmere. And now it was ruined.

And all because of him.

Again! He ruined everything. Everything! All the time, even dead, he was nothing but a despoiler. An obstacle. A cold, hard-hearted,

self-righteous, blood-sucking, *life*-sucking para-
site.

The cold calm rage that had guided her so
far suddenly ignited, like a bush fire finding
dry tinder. It raged in her mind, making her
literally shake with rage. Any coherent
thought melted in the heat of it.

Suddenly, the room itself became an insult.
All those shelves and shelves of dry, boring,
worthless words. Masses and masses of
words, all spouting the same sanctimonious
worthless rubbish as this stupid dead old
man!

She began to feverishly search the shelves
for the worst offenders. She began to throw
them on the floor — all those bearing his
name as the author first. Then the holier-
than-thou pious prattlings that nobody ever
read. The books that derided Darwin's
theories, the poetry that was supposed to be
uplifting, and exhorting the sinner to
repentance.

Without thinking, she began to pile them
up into her arms, carrying them out into the
compact garden and piling them into the
centre of a neatly trimmed lawn. She went
back inside, laughing over the high, neatly
clipped hedges that cut her off from view of
any neighbours. She knew he'd probably only
grown them that high for privacy. As if

anyone cared what he got up to!

Then she began a more personal trawl of the room. The little articles that she knew he'd always treasured. All the mementoes that appealed to his narrow-minded philosophy. Every outrage that needed to be burned out of existence. She gathered them all, tirelessly carrying them out into the garden and piling them on to the heap.

When she was finished, she found yester-day's newspaper — carefully stored in the recycling bin, of course — and set light to the lot. Some items didn't want to burn, and for a while, she had to rip the books viciously, straining and sobbing to pull the well-made, heavy tomes apart. She didn't stop until her arms ached so much she could rip and tear no more.

The flames soon came, a lovely shade of orange and, with them, some soft grey smoke.

The killer paused, considering the combi-nation. Orange and grey — they looked beautiful together. Perhaps she could com-bine them in an outfit sometime? Clothes and fashion and art were her life's blood.

Yes. Orange might suit her.

She sobbed then, and realized she was thinking such gibberish. Rubbish. She was in shock. She'd just killed . . .

The thought stopped there, abruptly, as if

her mind had run into a cold hard rock barring her way.

She had killed.

She backed out of the garden on legs that felt numb and alien beneath her, then walked unsteadily through the hallway and back out to the front door. There she stepped outside and shut the door behind her, leaving chaos behind.

The cul-de-sac was deserted. As she'd confidently told David Merchant not long before — and yet a lifetime before — everybody who lived in this relatively well-to-do area of Kidlington, was either at work, or else busy doing other things in their own homes. Who cared, nowadays, what happened in other people's houses?

The killer shut the garden gate carefully and quietly behind her and walked away.

★ ★ ★

Janine Mallow glanced up as the door to her room opened. She'd been given a small side room all to herself, mostly, she suspected, to help the staff keep the reporters away.

Ever since she'd killed Clive Myers, the sniper who'd shot and killed her husband, she'd been periodically plagued by the press, who couldn't seem to make up their minds

16

whether she was the hero or the villain of the piece.

As far as Janine could see, it depended on which paper you read.

As a pregnant widow of a murdered policeman, the majority of public opinion seemed to be on her side. Especially when it emerged that Clive Myers had killed not only her husband but a teenage boy, and had been about to kill another police officer as well.

The only fly in the ointment was the man himself, Clive Myers. Ex-army and war hero, his daughter had been raped and traumatized into a mental institution by a gang of teenage louts. DI Gregg had been in charge of the case, and had quickly found the culprits and brought a case against them. A technical error, however, had led to their acquittal. An error that had been laid — rightly or wrongly — at the door of the police, and at her husband's door most of all, since he was, again technically, in overall charge of the case.

Clive Myers's wife had committed suicide, and the man had snapped, turning vigilante, and killing both Mel, and then the leader of the teenage gang and chief rapist of his daughter. Gregg had been next on the list.

And therein lay the rub.

If Myers had simply been a villain, a wrong

17

'un and a menace to society, they'd probably have given her a medal.

As it was, there was sufficient public sympathy for the man to tarnish Janine's actions just enough to make your average man-in-the-street look just a shade worried. What had she been doing there, on that street behind Gregg's house, when she hadn't even been on the Myers case? How, heavily pregnant, had she managed to kill an ex-soldier, armed with a rifle, hand-gun, and numerous knives? Why had her old boss, DI Hillary Greene, been the ~~very~~ first one on the scene?

As the head of the team brought in from Wales to oversee the investigation had put it, if she hadn't been pregnant and a recent widow, things would have looked very bad for her indeed. And if the evidence against Myers had not come piling in, she might even have been looking at jail time.

As it was, both Janine and Hillary's story had checked out, and she was not going to be prosecuted, and that was the best she could hope for. Left unsaid, was the prediction that her life in the Police Service was, to all intents and purposes, over.

She'd been granted extended maternity leave, plus time for counselling, and compassionate leave. Nobody had yet said it to her

18

face, but she knew her bosses back at Witney would be relieved if she never came back at all.

The trouble was, she'd worked out of Thames Valley HQ in Kidlington for most of her career, and had only recently moved to Witney when she'd married Mel. It meant she'd had no real time to acquire allies there, allies who'd fight her corner for her.

Now, as she looked up and saw the familiar face of her old boss, DI Hillary Greene, she wasn't sure whether she wanted to laugh or cry.

Hillary hesitated in the doorway, watching Janine, trying to gauge her mood.

Hillary's first thought was that she looked exhausted, and it was odd to see her without any make-up on. But then childbirth was no picnic, or so she'd heard. Although she'd been married for many years to the corrupt and now thankfully late Ronnie Greene, Hillary had never had children of her own, or wanted them. Her stepson Gary, from Ronnie's first marriage, was the closest she'd ever get to motherhood, but nowadays they rarely met up.

'I brought you some peaches and magazines,' Hillary said, walking slowly across the grey floor towards the hospital bed. 'How are you feeling?'

'Sore. I've got stitches in places you wouldn't believe,' Janine shot back, then, for some reason began to laugh.

Then cry.

Hillary stood helplessly beside her bed and wished like hell that Mel wasn't still dead.

★ ★ ★

Back at Police HQ, Detective Constable Mark Chang looked up from his desk, and wished that DI Greene would come back soon. He found the super-efficient sergeant Gemma Fordham an unsettling boss to work for, and every time he caught DC Keith Barrington's eye he sensed trouble.

Not that Barrington wasn't friendly — he was. Helpful, cheerful almost, and all that. Yet underneath, every now and then, Mark caught a whiff of something festering.

He'd been assigned to DI Greene's team not quite two weeks ago. Before then, he'd graduated in the top five per cent of his class at the Police Training College and was on the home stretch towards gaining his BA degree from the Open University in Criminal Psychology.

Everyone was anxious that he should do well. His old sergeant on the beat had been his main sponsor, pushing him to get out of uniform and into plain clothes. He wasn't so naïve that he wasn't aware that his Chinese origins pleased the top brass, who always had one eye on improving their ethnic require- ments and his degree was bound to help earmark him for 'fast track' promotion.

And it was this, he suspected, that accounted for Keith Barrington's attitude. Mark Chang worried that he was jealous.

At twenty-two, he had his Chinese father's black hair and eyes, but his English mother's lithe and willowy figure. He was, although he tried hard not to let it affect him, rather startlingly good-looking, and women knew it. And perhaps this was yet another affront to the red-haired, sometimes clumsy and not particularly handsome Barrington?

There was something else going on with his fellow DC that he hadn't yet been able to pin down, but he had no doubts that his boss, DI Greene had him all figured out.

When he'd been told that he'd been assigned to DI Hillary Greene's team, Mark had been genuinely delighted.

Everyone knew that with that waste of space, DS Frank Ross finally booted out of the force, there was an opening on her team, but he'd never, in his wildest imaginings, thought he'd be put up for it.

Hillary Greene was something of a

mini-legend at HQ. Her husband, DI Ronnie Greene, had been spectacularly bent, and rumour had it that he'd salted away millions somewhere before being killed in a car crash. His wife, Hillary, who'd been in the process of divorcing him, had come under scrutiny from the inquiry that had confirmed Ronnie's role in an animal parts smuggling operation. She'd been cleared on all counts of any complicity of course, a result that had never been in doubt from either the rank and file or the brass at HQ. Everyone knew that Chief Superintendent Marcus Donleavy really rated her, and she was popular with colleagues and uniform alike.

Although she'd gained an English Literature degree from a non-affiliated Oxford college, she'd come up through the ranks, and had an arrest and conviction rate second to none. So far, all nine murder inquiries that she'd headed had been solved, and had resulted in convictions. She was also a hero cop, taking a bullet for her boss, and best friend, DCI Phillip Mallow a couple of years ago, and had been awarded a medal for bravery.

And then had come the shooting of Mellow Mallow and the whole media circus concerning his wife. As a humble PC, Mark Chang had, like the majority of those at HQ, formed his opinions on the whole Clive Myers thing by a kind of communal osmosis.

It was generally believed that there was more to the story than the inquiry had uncovered. And most of it centred around the fact that Janine had been on the scene at all when Clive Myers had set up his rifle with the intent to murder DI Gregg.

And if many people wondered why she'd called her ex-boss, DI Greene, and not her own station house at Witney when she found herself in the shit, most then conceded that it was probably the smartest thing she'd done that day.

Oh, everyone applauded her for bringing down Myers before he could kill Gregg. But nearly everyone also believed that it was Hillary Greene who'd saved her bacon afterwards.

Exactly how, was not clear. But the why was obvious: DI Greene stood by her people, even if they had moved on. She never squealed on her own, and when faced with pressure from the brass became a damned rock. Poker-faced, polite, and word-perfect when discussing what happened that afternoon when Myers had died, she'd sailed through the inquiry with aplomb.

The fact that it was generally believed that Hillary had stuck her neck out to save Janine

Mallow only cemented her status at HQ — both with your everyday ordinary copper, who appreciated loyalty more than anything else, and with the top brass, who were grateful to her for saving them from a potentially nasty and damaging scandal.

Well, at least a worse scandal than there had been.

Now the newspapers had finally moved on to something else and the heat seemed to be dying down; everyone was beginning to feel as if they'd weathered the worst of it.

And so to be assigned to DI Hillary Greene's team had been like winning the World Cup to DC Mark Chang. Her interviewing techniques alone were a thing of beauty, and he had not been disappointed on meeting his new boss in person.

He'd seen her around, of course, and knew her by sight. But even though he'd only been assigned to her team for less than two weeks, he felt as if he was on a learning curve that made his OU degree look like a picnic in the park.

'Chang, you got those ram-raiding figures?' Gemma Fordham's voice broke into his thoughts, and he quickly plunged into the 'Out' pile of his tray, and found the folder she wanted.

Over at his desk, Barrington shot him a

thoughtful look, as if disappointed by his quickness.

Mark Chang sighed and wished, once more, that Hillary Greene was back at her desk, giving him something to do.

★ ★ ★

Outside, on the street opposite, two men sat in a car, having watched the newly created DC Mark Chang go inside.

Both were oriental, both second-generation Chinese. Both worked in Oxford and were members of a fledgling gang. In spite of all that they had in common, however, the two men were vastly different.

One of them was older, nearly forty, and was a born enforcer, a man of little intelligence and few needs. So long as he was fed, was allowed his pick of the girls who worked the streets for free and had a roof over his head, he was content. He was known simply — and with much chuckling by his masters — as Ooo Yuck. He'd earned this nickname after uttering this phrase after accidentally kicking someone to death, and stepping in his victim's voided bowels.

His companion was a man called Eddie Lee. Younger than Ooo Yuck, he was far more intelligent and already ran the gambling operation for his gang. He'd decided to Anglicize his name simply because it made life easier, although his parents still called him by his Chinese name.

He had been assigned Ooo Yuck as muscle for when they put the bite on Mark Chang.

For the young Chinese man's elevation in the police ranks had not gone unnoticed. The son of shop-keepers, Chang was a virgin when it came to gangs.

But that was all about to change.

'We going to do him or what?' Ooo Yuck asked, without any real curiosity. It always surprised people to hear him speak without the trace of any accent. Wide-bodied and very oriental-looking, people tended to forget that he'd been born and raised in Blackbird Leys.

'Not yet. First we soften him up,' Eddie said. Unlike his companion, he did speak with a very slight Chinese lilt. But only because he thought it made him more exotic. When he swore, it was in pure Anglo Saxon.

2

Mrs Vivienne Chard was one of those women who liked to work from home one day a week. Her bosses at the small advertising firm in Abingdon where she worked, were willing enough to go along with this arrangement, since her work as a graphic artist could just as easily be accomplished on her home computer as easily as the one in her office.

Not only did this allow her a respite from the daily commute, which she was beginning to find more and more onerous, but it also allowed her time to catch up on all the little chores that stacked up at a phenomenal rate. So at nearly eleven o'clock that morning, she was just stepping out across her lawn, preparatory to hanging out the family's weekly wash, whilst at the same time wondering if she could really get away with a singing lemon to sell washing powder in this day and age. Even with a catchy modern pop tune, didn't it just reek of the 1950s? Maybe she could persuade her boss that retro was in, she mused, with a wry grin.

As she bent down to hang up the first item in her basket, a pale mint-green tablecloth, the grin suddenly turned to a grimace, however. She glanced down at the family cat, a fat, contented tabby that had followed her out, and was currently rubbing her furry cheek against Vivienne's leg.

'What a stink!'

The cat, whom her children had named Familiar, during one of their 'witch' phases, didn't seem to take offence, and rubbed her white-cheeked face even more enthusiastically against Vivienne's leg.

A forty-two-year-old mother of three, Vivienne was no stranger to bad smells, but the reek wafting across her garden fence was something new, even to her.

Abandoning her laundry basket and the cat, she walked to the neat hedge separating her garden from that of her neighbour's, but couldn't really see through the tall dense thicket that David Merchant kept so scrupulously neat and tidy.

But she could definitely hear the crackle of a fire and, glancing up, she could see that the wind was taking a large amount of smoke more or less away from the direction of her garden. So she could only wonder what the stench must be like for the next house down, which must be catching the brunt of it.

Then she realized that Molly and Trevor were probably both at work, and their daughter Stacey at school. Which was just as well for all of them. They would have been gagging had they been at home.

She frowned, as she walked back to her washing, and stared down at it. If she hung it up now, it was bound to reek by the time she brought it in. Sighing, because the cold February day was just sunny enough to have dried her washing if she'd left it out all day, she began to fold down the rotating line into a neat umbrella shape. Her basket still annoyingly full, she turned and walked slowly back to the house, the cat on her heels.

But something was bothering her.

She knew that late autumn or winter was the obvious time for garden bonfires, of course, but she'd never known David to indulge in them. He composted nearly all his garden rubbish and, she thought rather cynically, ever since he'd complained about Molly and Trevor's bonfires last year, she'd doubted he'd have the brass neck to light one himself now.

She didn't much care for her neighbour, since she always felt as if she was being weighed up, judged and found wanting whenever they happened to meet and exchange a few words. But she'd known him long enough to realize that the good opinion of others mattered to him. She vaguely thought that this had something to do with his religious beliefs, but she'd never been interested enough to think about it seriously.

But she was sure that doing something so anti-social as to light a stinking bonfire was distinctly out of character for the publisher.

And that stink was really awful! It smelt chemical, like burning plastic or rubber. And underneath it there was another layer of scent, almost pleasantly sweet, like roasting meat.

Something about it made her gag.

Quickly she walked into her house, shutting the door gratefully behind her, then walked to the telephone and rang next door. She kept his number in her small private phone book, mainly because he was a member of the Neighbourhood Watch, and you never knew when it might come in handy.

It was not a number she had often dialled, but this time David did not pick up.

And that worried her even more. She knew that he worked solid office-hours from his house, only making a few short business trips to an industrial estate, where his books were actually physically printed.

So he should be answering. Unless he was at the printing works. Or on the loo. Really, there could be any number of very good reasons why he wasn't answering.

For a few moments she dithered, absent-mindedly stroking Familiar's head. The cat began to purr loudly.

Her unease grew. She wasn't one of those women who could 'just tell something was wrong'. She laid no claim to such a thing as women's intuition or anything else her old dad would have called claptrap.

But she knew herself well enough to know that unless she did something, she'd only drive herself up the wall obsessing about it and probably not get any work done, staring out of the window hoping to catch sight of her neighbour.

Thinking that she was probably making a right twit of herself, she nevertheless picked up the handset again and dialled those spine-chilling famous numbers.

Nine, nine, nine.

★ ★ ★

Less than ten minutes later, PC Mick Gregory parked neatly at the kerb, and looked around the small suburban cul-de-sac with a jaundiced eye. He was nearly fifty, and lived in a similar house — albeit a semi — on a similar estate in the village of Bladon. In truth, he secretly longed for a big farmhouse, or a converted water mill, or even a barn conversion. Of course, all of those were out of the question on his budget, but he and the wife could dream.

Beside him, his young partner, PC Dave Ricks, who had yet to find even a modest bedsit that would allow him to move out of his mum and dad's council house in Woodstock, looked around Poyle Crescent with real envy.

'Very nice,' he said.

Mick grunted and checked the number. 'OK, this is number eight.' As he spoke he opened the door to his patrol car and sniffed. 'Bloody hell, the old girl who reported it was right. What a stink.'

'Go around the back straight to the garden?' Dave asked, and Mick shrugged.

'You do that — I'll ring the doorbell, see if anyone's home.'

The two separated, Dave finding a latched wooden garden gate at the side of the house and quickly disappearing. Mick pressed the bell on the front door and waited.

Then heard a distinct shout. Young Dave without a doubt. His heart giving a nasty skip, he quickly left the doorstep and shot around through the still open gate, and then skidded to a halt. His gaze first sought out and found that of his partner, who was bent over some neatly trimmed shrubs being quite spectacularly sick.

Seeing that he wasn't in any immediate danger of being attacked, he felt himself instantly relax. Next, and very cautiously, he approached a smouldering fire that was burning, rather incongruously, in the middle of a neatly mown and edged lawn.

One part of his mind took in the fact that the garden, even in winter, looked carefully maintained and kept. 'The bloke who owns this garden isn't going to be very happy to find someone's lit a bloody great bonfire in the middle of his immaculate lawn,' he called across to his mate, trying to sound matter-of-fact and reassuring.

But he'd already seen what his young partner had seen. And the fact that the charred leather shoes sticking out at one end of the fire were emitting puffs of smoke from the holes in the toes, rather as if somebody's feet were enjoying a quick fag, made him want to sit down. Quickly; because the shoes were attached to limbs, which were, in turn, attached to the rest of a charred body.

He walked carefully to the house wall and leaned against it, carefully keeping his eyes averted, and took a breath. But, as he felt the rancid air from the fire invade his lungs, he gagged automatically, only just managing to stop the reflex from going any further.

'I'm going to radio it in,' he said gruffly. 'Don't touch anything. And for Pete's sake, come away and sit in the car.'

Moaning a little, young PC Dave Ricks followed his partner from the garden and staggered gratefully to the vehicle.

★ ★ ★

DCI Paul Danvers was sitting in his little cubby hole, laughingly called his private office, when the phone rang.

'Danvers.' He was a tall, blond, good-looking man, who'd spent most of his working life in Yorkshire. Several years ago, however, along with another, more senior officer, he'd been 'volunteered' to look into the corruption charges against Ronnie Greene, and had come down reluctantly to Oxford.

And found that he liked the area.

He promptly came to realize that he also liked Ronnie Greene's widow a whole lot more. He'd breathed a sigh of relief when it became apparent that she had nothing to do with her soon-to-be-ex-turned-late-husband's business dealings, and when the inquiry had wound up, he had transferred down from York.

The fact that he'd ended up in charge of

Hillary Greene's team had been a mixture of sheer good luck plus a bit of careful manoeuvring on his part.

Alas, although he'd managed to wangle a few pub meals with her, she'd made it very plain that she had no intention of reciprocating his interest. But he'd hung in stubbornly, and not even her short-lived affair with an officer from the vice squad in St Aldates had put him off his dogged pursuit of her. He'd always believed that if he could just keep going, he'd eventually wear her down.

He wasn't sure if it was the fact that she was a few years older than himself that bothered her, or the fact that he was now her boss that made her reluctant to take him up on his subtle offer. He'd even considered transferring out of HQ to maybe Banbury or even Swindon, but he wasn't confident enough that even that would improve his chances with her.

But then something had happened recently, serious enough that even Danvers couldn't ignore it. And for the last few weeks he'd been wrestling with the consequences of it before finally arriving at a decision that had the dubious merit of being sensible. Even clever. Even so, admitting defeat wasn't coming easy.

He knew he'd have to take the ultimate

step soon, but he kept putting it off and putting it off. The interruption of the telephone made him sigh angrily, but, as he listened to the voice on the other end of the line, he sat up a little straighter in his chair.

'Yes, sir, understood. I'll assign it immediately.'

He took down the relevant details, such as they were, then hung up, rose and walked to the glass door of his cubicle. Outside, on the second floor of the main office, a vast open plan area sprawled in all directions. In here, mainly plainclothes officers lived, work, swore and got on with the daily grind.

He moved across this maelstrom to a group of tables pushed up near one of the large windows overlooking the car-park, his eyes skimming across the small group.

Gemma Fordham was wearing her usual trouser suit and upmarket trainers, maybe not the usual outfit for a DS, but her training in martial arts let her get away with it. With her short crop of silver/gold hair and damaged, husky, sexy voice, she was, he knew, many a copper's — and a villain's — secret fantasy.

Beside her, working diligently on the computer, was the red-haired Keith Barrington, who was the first to spot him coming.

The new man, Mark Chang, dark, too

good-looking not to be in films or on the telly, was talking on the phone. He seemed to be doing OK, so far. One thing was for sure — he couldn't do worse than Frank Ross, the man he'd replaced. Ross had been the last of Ronnie Greene's corrupt cronies still on the force and, ironically enough, on Hillary Greene's team, before he and Hillary had all but forced him into retirement.

But it was to Hillary herself that he gravitated. He knew she'd visited Janine Mallow that morning and, in other circumstances, would have taken a few moments to ask how she was. Public opinion about Janine might be fickle and flow first one way then another, but amongst her own she demanded loyalty and respect. As did Hillary Greene for standing by her.

'Hillary. We have a suspicious death. Want it?' he asked rhetorically, already handing over the note.

'Where?' Hillary looked up quickly, and Paul thought he sensed an air of relief about her. She still missed Mel like crazy, he knew, and work was her way of keeping the gremlins at bay.

'Right here in town. Poyle Crescent; know it?'

'Not off hand. But with a name like that, I expect it's out somewhere near Hampton

Poyle way?' she took the piece of paper from her hand and looked at it briefly.

Paul shrugged. Why ask the man from York?

'Got a map, guv,' Gemma, ever helpful, reached into her desk and drew out a large fold-up map.

'OK. Let's get cracking then,' she said. And catching Mark Chang's startled but hopeful gaze, smiled grimly. 'Yes, that means you too, Chang,' she said with a smile. It would be his first murder case, she realized.

'Guv,' he said gratefully.

★ ★ ★

When they arrived at the cul-de-sac, it was looking rather cramped. Two fire engines and two police cars blocked most of its turning curve, and Hillary smiled as she recognized the sporty little MG that was parked up in somebody's empty driveway.

Steven Partridge, the police forensic surgeon had obviously already arrived.

She nodded to herself, knowing that that could save them some time. Unlike most medical men who operated in the death industry, Steven was willing to at least share his preliminary thoughts and guesses with Hillary. Most, she knew, wouldn't say a single word until the full autopsy, just in case they should be caught out making a mistake or false assumption.

'OK, Gemma you start with the house itself — it's this one, number eight — I want a full search, and start compiling a file on the home owner.'

'Are we sure the vic and the home owner are the same?' Gemma asked reasonably.

'Nope, we know very little as yet. But even if he or she isn't, the body's in their back garden and we'll need to know everything about them, right down to what brand of toothpaste they use.'

'Guv.'

'Barrington, Chang, start on house to house,' she said, turning to look around the neat, uninspired little estate. 'Although you'll probably find most of the people are out. Spread the network wider, target the houses with a view to this one first,' she added, nodding away to the other estates surrounding and overlooking it.

Barrington felt himself sigh wearily, and quickly cut it short. He hated to admit it, but just lately, the day-to-day grind of police work was beginning to get him down. If only he had a ten pound note for every door he'd banged on, and every unhelpful answer given to every question he'd ever asked, he'd be richer than his lover.

And that was saying something.

Since unexpectedly coming into control of his father's fortune, Gavin Moreland was a very rich young man indeed.

'Guv,' Barrington said flatly.

Hillary, catching both the tone and ennui, glanced at Keith thoughtfully. Unless she missed her guess, Barrington was heading for some sort of crossroads, and she needed him sharp and alert.

She'd have to keep an eye on him. With Chang still finding his feet, now was not the time for slacking.

As she walked up the path to the door of the house — currently being guarded by a rather green-around-the-gills young PC, she heard Barrington divvying up the assignment with Chang.

'Ma'am.' the PC on the door recognized her at once. Even before the Janine/Clive Myers incident, her face had been a well-known one. Now she almost enjoyed celebrity status.

She nodded. 'Report?'

The constable swallowed hard, but had no need to refer to his notes as he gave her a concise and largely accurate report on his activities that morning.

'The neighbour who reported the bad

smell — this side?'

She held her hand out to her left, but the PC shook his head. 'No ma'am. I think that one's empty. At least, nobody's come out to see what's going on. It's this one.' He nodded to the right.

Hillary glanced around, and saw only three onlookers loitering curiously in the street outside. And most of them, she guessed, had been attracted by the sight of the fire engines.

'Right. Is someone with her?'

'Yes, ma'am. A WPC.'

'She hasn't been told anything, I hope?' Hillary said sharply, and the PC shook his head.

Hillary nodded. 'Right — I'll interview her later.'

She slipped little rubber overshoes over her own sensible brown leather boots, and donned a pair of thin rubber gloves. Then, following the line of wooden boards that had already been laid down by the SOCO team, she walked around the side of the house and into the back garden, which was swarming with white-suited scientists.

Ignoring the bustling scene of activity, she looked around her, slowly and carefully, knowing how important first impressions could be.

And the first thing she realized was how

private this back garden was. The garden hedges at the side were thick and much taller than the norm. She could also hear very little traffic, which meant that this side of the house probably overlooked fields. It made for a perfect, private place in which to kill someone, Hillary thought with a heavy sigh.

A man in a white bodysuit, hood up, went to go past her, and she politely made room on the wooden walkway.

Slowly, she turned 180 degrees and let her eyes range over the house. No double-glazing. That was something of a surprise nowadays. And a small amount of smoke was issuing from the chimney pot — so there was at least one useable fireplace inside. Apart from that, it looked like a neat, unprepossessing little house.

Slowly, her gaze returned to the centre of activity in the lawn. Like PC Mick Gregory before her, she thought it was an odd place to have a bonfire. Most keen gardeners had bonfires on bare earth, or in a large oil can, not in the middle of a lovely little lawn.

She saw Steven Partridge spot her and beckon her over. As she approached, he murmured quietly to the police photographer snapping away over the body, 'The SIO's arrived.'

As senior investigating officer, Hillary was,

theoretically at least, top of the pecking order, but she knew better than to interfere with SOCO, and was careful not to get in anyone's way.

Instead, she looked down at the charred, blackened outline that was instantly recognizable as human, and felt her gorge rise. There was always something about seeing the human form made twisted and alien by fire that always made her want to scream.

Determinedly, she shut the inner noise of protest away, and glanced at Steven.

'Well, you and I know that most people don't let themselves get burned to death without putting up a fight,' she said flatly, and glanced at the scene in front of her. The outer ring of the fire looked undisturbed. 'So he was either dead or unconscious before being put on the fire? It is a he, I take it?'

Partridge nodded. 'And he was more likely to be dead, I think, than merely incapacitated. But don't quote me.'

'As if I would. Are those books?' she asked curiously. Several large, rectangular blackened blocks surrounded the body. Steven nodded.

'Yes, I think so. Other stuff has been burned as well, some glass, a few man-made plastics maybe, but it mostly seems to be paper. That's why the body's barely been consumed. Even if the killer had used wood and coal and what have you, you'd still need to create fire of terrific intensity and heat to actually consume a human body — which is mostly water, remember. Just ask someone who works at a crematorium.'

Hillary nodded. Although the body looked black and thoroughly burned enough to her, she supposed it was all relative to someone with an expertise such as Steven's.

'I think when we get him on the table, we'll still be able to find plenty to keep you happy,' he confirmed.

Hillary sighed heavily. 'Lovely thought, Doc.'

Steven grinned briefly. He was a small, dapper man, who liked good clothes and the company of his pretty wife. He shot her a careful look, the physician in him noticing her pale face, the dark shadows beneath her eyes, and some weight loss. She was still grieving over Mel, of course, and the fiasco with Janine and Clive Myers wouldn't have helped.

'You need a holiday,' he said flatly.

Hillary ignored him.

'Any idea of cause of death?'

'There's another crime scene inside,' Steven said, and saw her head swivel sharply towards the house. 'Looks like he was hit with a poker. It's still lying there on the floor, with blood and what looks like human hair and brain tissue still on it. Although I won't be able to tell you how many times he was hit until I've had his skull x-rayed of course.'

Hillary nodded. 'Whereabouts in the house?'

'In his office. Well, the main living area, a sort of combined living room and workspace. He must do most of his work — whatever that is — from home.'

Hillary nodded. More and more people were doing so these days, she knew. Chance would be a fine thing, as far as she and her particular profession were concerned though.

'Any sign of a break-in?'

'Not my department,' Steven said at once, then shrugged. 'But from what I've overhead from the lads so far, it doesn't look like it.'

It wouldn't take her long to find out, she knew. 'So. The most likely scenario is this — our victim admitted the killer into the house. Which suggests that the victim probably knew him or her, or had no reason to be wary of their presence in the house. Then for some reason he turns his head and — '

She broke off. 'You said he was hit with a poker? So did the killer bring it with him, in which case it must have been premeditated?'

45

She was speculating out loud, more than really asking him a question, but he surprised her.

'I think you'll find it belongs to here. I noticed there was a real fire going in the room, and that the poker on the carpet matched a set of fire irons and little shovel hanging on a brass stand in the fireplace.'

'I'll have to start calling you Sherlock,' Hillary said, genuinely impressed.

Steven shuddered theatrically. 'Anything else I can do for you?'

'Don't suppose you can name the killer, or give me his address?' she asked sweetly.

Steven said something very impolite and reached down for his black leather case.

'Well, Detective Inspector Greene, I can confirm that your victim is dead,' he said, with a little bow. Which was, at this point, all he was actually required to tell her. 'As ever, once I've got him on my table, we'll both know a lot more.'

'Thanks, Doc,' Hillary said, and stepped aside to let him pass.

'And I meant it about the holiday,' Steven Partridge said quietly, as he left.

For a few moments, Hillary stood silently at the scene. Forensically, it was a bit of a mess, even she could see that. She noticed the ground away from the boards was sodden, and supposed the firemen had doused the bonfire with their hoses. No wonder most of the SOCO team were muttering direly as they went about their business. What with their big booted feet, and their lavish use of fire hoses, they'd have destroyed a good deal of whatever forensic evidence had existed before their arrival.

'Just marvellous,' she said flatly, and saw the police photographer shoot her a sympathetic look. With a brief nod at him, she turned and made her way into the house.

★　★　★

Mark Chang rang the doorbell of his third house, and couldn't believe it when nobody answered. Didn't anybody stay at home any more? Where were all the mothers with a sick child off school, or the OAP with a good pair of binoculars and an avid curiosity in her neighbours' comings and goings?

At this rate, he'd never find out anything interesting to take back to Hillary Greene.

He sighed, and walked down the path and on to the next house. Outside, in the street, two uniforms were talking. One, Mick Gregory, watched Chang pass with thoughtful eyes.

'He's the one took over from Ross,' he said

47

to the uniform next to him, who was partnered with the WPC currently talking to Vivienne Chard.

'Oh yeah? Lucky sod, then, ain't he?' He was a heavily built rugby-mad individual, who had no ambitions to ever get out of uniform, or patrolling the streets. 'It was high time she got rid of Ross.'

'Had help giving him the old heave-oh mind,' Mick agreed, with a savage grin. 'Donleavy backed her up, didn't he? And that Yorkie Bar.'

Yorkie Bars was the nickname given to Paul Danvers and his partner when they'd come down to investigate Ronnie Greene's activities, and the not-so-affectionate label still clung.

Mark, who'd caught most of this exchange, felt a small shiver of warning ripple up his spine. It was a timely reminder not to get on his boss's bad side. She could obviously be ruthless when she needed to be.

'Still, most people are surprised she put up with him for as long as she did,' Mick said. 'Let's face it, she was the only one who could stick him.'

'I used to dream about meeting him on the rugby field,' his companion confided. 'You know, giving me a chance to get the boot in, all official and above-board like.'

Mick Gregory laughed. 'Now that's what I call having sweet dreams.'

★ ★ ★

Inside the house, Hillary was careful to keep to the hard plastic sheeting laid down, and made her way to the now empty main living room.

She wasn't surprised to see Gemma already there.

'Guv. The home owner is one David Merchant. I've found lots of files relating to a Merchant & Coe Ltd, a publishing company. Also, several royalty statements to him as the author of what sound to me like churchy books.'

'Churchy?' Hillary repeated, with a wry smile. 'I think the word you're looking for is ecclesiastical.'

Gemma smiled grimly. 'Not all of us are OECs, guv,' she shot back. OECs or Oxford-educated cops weren't all that thin on the ground at Thames Valley.

'I thought you went to Reading Uni?' Hillary countered mildly. 'Didn't they have dictionaries there?'

Gemma grinned reluctantly. There was little point, she'd fast learned, in arguing with Hillary Greene.

'Guv,' she conceded. 'Point is, I can't find any books with his moniker on them. Odd that, don't you think? I mean, most authors are vain enough to keep their own books on their book-shelves, surely?'

Hillary frowned. That was odd. 'There were burned books on the bonfire, along with the body. Go take a look, see if any of them have escaped the fire enough for you to make out the name on the dust jackets.'

Gemma went a little pale and glanced outside. The fact that she was reluctant to look at a burnt corpse was the first sign of weakness Hillary had ever been able to detect in her usually super-efficient and competent sergeant. Since they'd been working together for over a year now, that was some achievement.

'Guv,' she said unhappily.

Hillary wouldn't have been human if she hadn't had to give a small smile as her sergeant left.

Slowly, as she had done outside, Hillary let her eyes wander around the room, taking it all in. If, as seemed likely at this point, the corpse out there belonged to David Merchant, then this room belonged to the victim. Here he had worked and lived. And a room could tell you a lot about the person who occupied it.

The first thought that struck her was the old-fashioned décor and feel of the place. 'Brown furniture' was always thought of with a derogatory sneer nowadays, but perhaps Merchant appreciated the old and solid? The second thought that came to her was there were no radiators anywhere. Although the fire gave off a steady heat, she imagined the rest of the rooms must be chilly.

She looked down at the poker in the middle of the plain carpet and grimaced. Her gaze went from the fireplace, where there was indeed a poker missing from the fire irons, then to the book-shelves. Here, she could plainly see, volumes were missing. She would have bet a fair amount of her salary, that whoever worked in a room like this had a neat, orderly, old-fashioned mind. The sort that wouldn't leave gaping holes on the shelves, allowing books to fall down and lie flat on the wood.

A paler square on the already pale magnolia wall caught her eye next, and she walked up to it, careful where she put her feet, and realized that there was a small nail at the top of the pale patch.

So something had once hung there.

Hadn't Steven said something about there being glass in the fire? Had a photograph once hung there, and been taken from the

51

wall and tossed on to the fire, along with the books and, ultimately, a human body?

She heard Gemma come back, and frowned in thought.

'Can't tell the titles of any of the books guv,' she said flatly. 'But it shouldn't be hard to get a list of his own work. I doubt, being a publisher himself, he'd get another company to publish his own efforts.'

'No. It reeks of vanity publishing, in a way, doesn't it?' Hillary said vaguely.

Gemma, who had no idea what vanity publishing was but wasn't about to say so, grunted noncommittally.

'You know, I think there's a lot of rage here,' Hillary said at last.

'You've got to be in a bit of a snit to throw someone on the fire, guv,' Gemma said, less than impressed.

Hillary, whose mind was obviously busy grappling with something else said something like, 'Hmmm?' then frowned.

'No. I mean yes, that, of course, but something more. Whoever did this didn't just burn the victim, did they? They built a bonfire in the middle of his lawn and burnt his books on it. And probably other stuff personal to him as well. Notice the bare spots on the walls?'

Gemma hadn't but now saw what her boss

meant. 'We're going to need a list of contents then,' she said flatly. 'See what else chummy might have burnt. Come to think of it, the neighbour who called us in said something on the fire was stinking.'

'Probably his leather shoes,' Hillary said. 'Or something plastic.'

Gemma swallowed hard. She knew it would be many weeks before she'd be able to wash the scent of charred human flesh out of her memory.

Her father and all her brothers were in the fire service, and had been a little surprised when she had joined the police force. Although she'd never told them so, it had been just because she wanted to avoid situations like this that she'd done so.

She could only hope Hillary Greene wouldn't assign her to cover the autopsy.

* * *

It was a lovely day in Birmingham. The same pale but welcome February sun that shone in Oxfordshire shone on Britain's second largest city.

It even shone on the city's gaols.

In one of them, however, a man sat in his cell, and didn't even see the light flooding through the small square window in his cell.

His silver hair, once a source of pride, was now lank and unwashed, and clung to his sweating forehead as he stared down at the sharpened plastic fork in his hand.

It had been Lenny the Twist who'd showed him how to make it. Taught him how wrapping it in clingfilm, then setting light to it, and shaping it as it burned, helped to make a good, strong, sharp edge. Of course, Lenny had been paid well. 'His Lordship' had happily handed over his last packet of fags for the lesson.

Naturally, Lenny had thought His Lordship wanted the weapon for protection. Why else?

Sir Reginald Moreland, who had been convicted for fraud and sentenced to four years, had repeatedly told everyone who would listen that he had been created a peer for his services to industry, which meant that he was not a lord at all, but merely a 'Sir'.

But this had only induced gales of cruel laughter in everyone, who insisted on maintaining the nickname. And Kipp Robson, a vicious, armed-robbery specialist, insisted on it more than most. For some reason, this shaven-haired, tattooed bruiser had taken an instant dislike to the newest inmate.

The fact that His Lordship was rich, dressed well, talked well, and was used to ordering servants about probably had a lot to do with it.

Raised by social services and mostly drunken foster parents, Kipp had lived for all of his life in the arse-end of Brum. And now it was his chance for a little payback. All those times Kipp had watched the rich ride around in fancy cars and then had to hop on a bus himself. All the times he'd been eating takeaway curries whilst walking past fancy restaurants. All the beautiful women, wearing jewellery, walking beside men uglier and older then himself. Every slight he'd suffered, every dirty rotten unfair thing that had ever happened to him, was now going to be avenged. This one man, His Lordship, epitomized it all.

Hell, Kipp jeeringly told his mates, the judge who'd sent him down for his latest stretch probably belonged to the same clubs as His Lordship. They'd probably rubbed shoulders during Henley bloody Regatta week, or bet on the same horse at Cheltenham.

It was rare indeed that the likes of His Lordship got caught and sent to jail, and Kipp was not one to look a gift horse in the mouth.

He'd started his campaign against His Lordship the moment he became aware of his existence. Sir Reginald's food was regularly spat in before being served to him. His things were stolen the moment they were acquired. A sly nudge had sent him falling down the stairs twice now. And always the prison guards seemed to be looking the other way.

During the weeks he'd been in jail, Kipp had watched avidly, gleefully seeing Sir Reginald's bluster deflate, his personal hygiene suffer due to fear of the showers, the well-padded weight from all that good food melt away from his frame. Until finally, he'd beaten the man down until it was time for the ultimate humiliation.

And then he'd put the word out.

Although most of the felons preferred young meat, His Lordship was going to become the wing bitch.

The word, of course, had inevitably reached the ears for which it had always been intended. And it had been, as Kipp had hoped, the final straw.

Now, Sir Reginald slowly rolled up the sleeve of his shirt and clenched his fist. He would never see sixty again, and his veins popped up obligingly, blue and prominent.

He didn't seriously intend to kill himself, of course. He just wanted to give a cry for help loud enough so that those in charge could no longer ignore it. For Moreland, who knew how hierarchies worked, had accurately guessed that the wing governor probably didn't even know about his difficulties. But if a prisoner was found with slit wrists, the repercussions couldn't help but reach even to his lofty heights.

If nothing else, Moreland reasoned, he'd be put on suicide watch — segregated or put in isolation — where they couldn't get him.

The idea of being raped by sweating, brutal animals simply wasn't a thought he could let enter his head.

So when he slit first one wrist then the other, he was careful to make the cuts long and vertical, and running with the vein, and not horizontal. He knew that this would impress a shrink, who was sure to point out that it was a serious attempt.

As his blood flowed on to the floor, Sir Reginald was weighing his chances of being transferred out of this jail, maybe into an open prison somewhere. Or at least of gaining a long stay in the hospital wing, where he could at last get some peace.

Not being a medical man, he didn't really realize just what a fine job his carefully placed cuts did on draining his blood. He hadn't, either, taken into account the fact that, being targeted by Kipp, meant that nobody would be coming by his cell to just idly chat or check up on him.

So when he was finally missed, and a guard sent to check on him, Sir Reginald Moreland's suicide attempt had, in fact, become a very successful one.

3

Vivienne Chard looked pale and composed, but a slight redness around her eyes made Hillary wonder if she'd been crying. And if so, did it indicate that she and her neighbour might have had something going together?

'And you went outside to hang the washing out at what time, would you say?' Hillary asked.

They were sitting in Vivienne's open-plan living area-cum dining room, and Hillary was struck at once by the contrast of this house to that of David Merchant's. Not only was this room open plan, but was also fully double-glazed and adequately heated. The colour scheme was right up to date as well. Although the houses were similar in size, shape and construction, it struck her that the two neighbours nevertheless seemed to live in vastly different worlds.

'I'm not sure,' Vivienne said, looking worried. 'About half past ten?' she asked, as if seeking confirmation from Hillary.

She was, Hillary supposed, around the same age as herself, maybe a few years younger, but the working mother was making a determined effort to defy the years. Her figure was still workout slim, and her hair was a perfectly dyed shade of dark brown with a carefully styled cut. She was wearing an upmarket tracksuit with a pair of designer trainers. Her make-up was minimal, but cleverly applied.

'And you noticed the smell at once?' Hillary pressed.

'Oh yes. You couldn't help but notice it.'

'What did you do then?'

'I came inside and rang David's number but nobody answered. I was surprised by that — he works from home almost exclusively.'

'But he could have popped out to the shops or something,' Hillary pointed out reasonably. What she really wanted to know was why this woman had felt compelled to call the police so soon. Normally people didn't want to get involved. So when they did, there was usually a specific reason. And if something had subconsciously aroused Vivienne Chard's suspicions, she wanted to find out what it was.

Of course, Chard herself was also very much on the suspect list, and Hillary was weighing her every word carefully.

'Well, not really. David, although he worked from home, kept strict office hours,' Chard explained now.

Hillary let her eyebrows rise slightly. 'Really? I think, like most people who have to actually physically go into an office every day, I rather suspect that those who work from home tend to skive off more than most.'

Vivienne, guilty of just that offence, felt herself flush, then smiled wryly. 'But not David,' she said, with just a hint of asperity. 'Saint David, as Pete always calls him. Pete's my husband. He writes religious books you know. David, I mean, not my husband.'

'Oh. So would you say that Mr Merchant is one of the rare ones who practises what they preach?' Hillary pressed.

'Yes,' Vivienne said, after a moment's thought. 'You have to give him that. He's as strict on himself as he is with others.'

Hillary didn't miss the slightly grudging restraint that had come into her voice. 'You didn't really like him, did you?' she asked, careful to keep her tone non-judgemental. Although she hadn't yet confirmed that a body had been found at number 8, Hillary sensed from the moment that she'd first introduced herself to the witness, that Vivienne fully realized the gravity of the situation. Was she just very sensitive, or by nature pessimistic? Or did she know Merchant was dead because she herself had done the killing?

Now she fiddled nervously with her wedding ring, looked at Hillary closely, as if seeking permission to tell the truth then sighed.

'No. I suppose I didn't,' she admitted finally. 'But David had many good qualities.' Hillary noted the sudden switch to the past tense, but didn't interrupt her. 'He gave regularly to all sorts of charities. He collected relentlessly for the poppy appeal, and some cancer charities, and all that. He volunteered at a lot of churches too, I know — organizing fêtes and fundraisers, and that sort of thing. He spent some time working in certain charity shops too. I'm sure he did a lot of good.'

Hillary nodded. 'But personally?' she asked gently.

Vivienne shrugged helplessly. 'He just wasn't the sort of man you could like.'

Hillary didn't get the feeling that Chard was lying to her, so mentally put the idea of an affair between the two of them on the back burner. For now. 'Would you say he was actively disliked?' she asked flatly.

To her credit, Vivienne didn't immediately leap to an answer, but thought about it fairly, before saying cautiously, 'I wouldn't say he was *disliked*, but I would say he was unpopular. He had this habit of complaining about things if they weren't up to his standard. It made for some bad feeling here and there. But, to be honest, I don't think people really took him seriously. He was a bit of an anachronism. I tended to feel sorry for him, when he wasn't irritating me.'

In other words Hillary thought, hiding a smile but getting Vivienne's message loud and clear, he didn't bother her enough for her to have a reason to kill him.

Or so she said.

Ideally Hillary would have liked to be able to take Vivienne Chard's clothes away for forensic tests, but that was just a fantasy. Unless she could find any hard evidence or motive for this woman to have killed her neighbour, a warrant would be out of order.

She didn't even, at this point, know for sure if the victim *was* David Merchant or not. The charred body was unrecognizable, and would probably have to be identified by dental records.

'Do you know who Mr Merchant's next of kin is?' she asked curiously.

'I imagine it would be his son. Blast, I can't think of his name. Something old-fashioned, I think. His wife died a few years back. Mind you, I haven't seen his son for even longer. I think they had some major falling out when he was in his late teens. But with a father like that, it's hardly surprising, is it?'

Hillary smiled. 'No. I suppose it isn't.'

'Is he dead?' Vivienne finally plucked up the courage to ask outright.

'We're not sure yet,' Hillary said, and carried on smoothly, 'Did you notice anyone calling at the house this morning?'

'No. But then, I work from a small office out at the back. And you can't see over the hedge.'

Hillary sighed. 'Do you know of anyone Mr Merchant had argued with recently?'

Vivienne shrugged. 'I'm not really very nosy, Inspector Greene. Sorry. Live and let live is my motto. I don't really care what my neighbours get up to.'

Hillary gave a rather strained smile. Unfortunately, that attitude was far too prevalent for her taste. Give her a nosy old busybody any day. 'Do you know the exact nature of the falling out between father and son?'

'Heck no.'

'Did Mr Merchant only have the one child?'

'I think so.'

'Do you know anything about his publishing company?'

Vivienne gave a graphic shrug. 'Sorry.'

But Hillary didn't get the feeling she was

being deliberately obstructive. With a mental sigh, she forged ahead. 'Have you ever noticed if Mr Merchant wore anything that could be easily identified?' she asked next, but without much hope now. 'A watch, a wedding ring, a belt with an unusual metal buckle? Anything like that?'

Vivienne frowned. 'I can't say as I ever thought about it.'

Hillary nodded, hoping that the rest of her team were having better luck, and ploughed on with her questions. And when she left, nearly half an hour later, she thought she had a good outline of life in Poyle Cresent, and a rudimentary sketch of David Merchant.

A man of strong moral and religious convictions, obviously. One whose house indicated someone with no interest in physical comforts or worldly pleasures. Although Vivienne had carefully avoided saying so, Hillary got the impression that the victim was also possessed of a narrow mind and rigid, unbending character.

The sort of man, she thought grimly, that any number of people might want to kill.

She thought again of the sense of anger she'd picked up on in Merchant's living room, and wondered who it was that he'd pushed too far this time. And just what the killer's sin had been.

For she was fairly sure now that David Merchant had seen things in perfect black and white.

★ ★ ★

Back at the murder scene, Gemma saw her boss returning, and stepped outside on to the porch to greet her.

'There's no other sign of ransacking in the house, guv,' she said at once. 'I don't think, despite some things being obviously missing, that this is a burglary gone wrong.'

Hillary nodded. 'No. I've got a feeling that when forensics are through we're going to find all the missing items are on the bonfire. There's a son, apparently. Find out who, what, where — the usual. He might be able to identify the body, but I doubt it. At least he might be able to help in pointing out just what items are missing.'

'Guv.'

'You got an address for the business? They must have an office somewhere.'

'Yes, guv.' Gemma consulted her notes, and peeled off the address. It also was in Kidlington, in an industrial complex out near the small Oxford airport.

'Right.' Hillary dialled Barrington's number and ordered him back to the house. Sensing

Gemma felt that she was being kept out of all the best bits, she threw her a bone. 'According to the neighbour, the son and his father had a bad falling out some years ago. I want to know what about. Sometimes things can take a while to fester.'

As expected, Gemma perked up. 'Right. Wife?'

'Dead.'

'So she's off the suspect list then?' her sergeant said laconically.

* * *

It was just about opening time by the time Mark Chang had worked his way through the neighbouring estates to the local pub, The Black Bull, on a busy main road.

Although he drank very rarely, he pushed his way inside, not surprised to find it still largely deserted. He walked to the bar and ordered an orange juice, glancing around.

The pub wasn't particularly old, but it was furnished in dark panelling, with low mock-beams that made it seem dark and poky. A bank of gaming machines flashed orange and red lights from one corner.

Mark paid for his drink and headed for the only table occupied, where two old men were sat, not speaking and each reading a

67

newspaper. By the similarity of their features, Mark suspected they were brothers — maybe even twins.

'Good morning,' Mark said politely. 'I'm sorry to bother you.' He put his drink down on their table, then reached for and displayed his police identification, noticing how it tweaked their attention. Nowadays, you never knew how anyone was going to react when they learned what you did for a living.

'I was wondering if you knew anything about a man called David Merchant?'

'Sit down, then,' one of the men said. Both were sporting well-worn, none-too-clean trousers, checked shirts and hand-knitted v-neck sweaters. They had the look of retired farm labourers about them, with thick necks, lean but muscular-looking builds, and thinning grey hair. Both had similar Roman noses, and milky grey eyes.

'You mean the holy roller?' one of the men said. 'I'm Ron, that's Robbie. My brother.'

Mark smiled. 'Live around here then?'

They named an area of council bungalows, built mainly for old folks, and Mark nodded. 'Holy roller?' he asked, taking a sip of his juice. And wondered. Should he offer them a pint each? Or would that be considered bribery in reverse?

'You know, a Bible basher. Wouldn't be

seen dead in a place like this, I can tell you,' Robbie spoke up. 'A den of sin and iniquity this place, eh, Mike?' he suddenly raised his voice, making Mark jump, until he realized that the old man was calling across to the bartender, who merely snorted and carried on cleaning some pint glasses.

'We only know about him 'cause of the dauber, see,' Ron continued.

Mark, rather confused but pleased to have finally found someone who seemed to know something about their victim/suspect, reached for his notebook.

'Er, the dauber?' he prompted.

'The painter. That Whitey fellow,' Ron said, slurping his ale.

Mark blinked. Were these old sods being racist, or what?

'Whitey?'

'Not Whitey, you daft sod,' Robbie put in scornfully. 'Whyte. With a 'Y' not an 'I'. Very particular about that, Frank is.' And he nodded sagely.

'Frank Whyte?' Mark said, catching on. 'He knows David Merchant, does he?'

'Bound to. Landlord, ain't he?' Ron said. And took another slurp of ale.

Confused again, Mark looked across to the pub landlord, who grinned. 'Not me mate,' he called back.

'You ain't being clear, Ron,' his brother chided. 'See, Frank's a painter who rents a cottage off of the holy roller.'

'Oh, I see. Mr Merchant is Mr Whyte's landlord,' Mark said, finally getting the point. 'Do you know where this cottage is?'

'Oh yers.'

Mark waited, pen poised. When neither of the men spoke, he said softly, 'The address?'

'Oh, dunno the address,' Robbie said.

'But you said you knew where it was.'

'Ah, so I do,' Robbie said. 'You go out past Sturdy's Castle, see, and takes the next turn off towards Tackley. But the cottage ain't actually in the village itself, but just before you get towards it. Don't know the name of the road, or the number of the cottage like.'

'Bound to have a name, not a number,' Ron pointed out. 'It being all on its own like. And the holy roller being a snob. Probably called it Glebe Cottage or some such.'

'Why's that then?' Robbie asked.

'It's a name to do with churches, innit?' Ron stated, in a tone that clearly said he was going to accept no arguments.

'Want us to draw you a map, then, youngster?' Robbie asked, taking pity on Mark and then draining the last of his ale and putting his glass down with a distinct click.

Mark caught on. He smiled. 'Can I get you

70

two gentlemen another pint?'

Ron almost choked himself emptying his still half-full glass.

★ ★ ★

Merchant & Coe Publishers Ltd, rented space in a sixties-built building that looked remarkably like a Portakabin without actually being one. Painted a particularly vile shade of turquoise, it looked out on to a small gravelled courtyard, intersected with large bushes that probably looked pretty in the spring, but now only looked brown, dying and depressed.

Keith Barrington looked around and shivered. And into his mind flashed an image of Cannes. It probably wasn't an accurate image, since he'd never actually been to Cannes in person, but he'd seen it on the telly once or twice, usually when they were reporting on the film festival. And it was where Gavin would be playing a charity tennis tournament in two weeks' time.

In his mind he saw blue seas, palm trees, chic French cafés and elegant gulls. Gavin, of course, wanted Keith to go to France with him. But then Gavin had been waging an ever more savage campaign to get Keith to leave the force since the moment they'd met.

But only recently had Keith felt any sense of temptation. Now, looking around this bleak little hole, with the drone of light aircraft perpetually overhead, he was beginning to understand why Gavin was so scornful of the Thames Valley. A Londoner born and bred, Keith had only transferred here after an unfortunate incident with his sergeant back in the Smoke had left him with no other choice.

But he'd never felt at home here, and even after nearly two years, still didn't feel as if he belonged.

'Are you still with me, Constable?' Hillary's sardonically amused voice made him stiffen and look across at her.

'Sorry, guv,' he said miserably. 'I was miles away.'

'I noticed. Think you can concentrate on our burned body, who he is, and who might have killed him?'

Keith blushed. 'Sorry, guv,' he said, genuinely contrite. He knew she needed him to be on the ball, and the fact that he was finding it harder and harder to concentrate on the job was as worrying to himself as it was obviously becoming a worry to his boss.

He'd thought that with Frank Ross gone, things would get better. But now he was beginning to think he was only fooling himself. His growing discontent had nothing to do with his work colleagues, but felt distinctly internal.

'Right then. Who's the business partner again?' Hillary asked crisply.

Before they'd left Poyle Crescent, Gemma had filled them in on all the details about the publishing company she'd been able to find, and now Keith flipped back through his notes.

'A Mr Martin Scraggins, guv.'

A somewhat unfortunate name, Hillary thought briefly. 'He a relative of the 'Coe' part of the company?'

'Yes, guv. Grandson — maternal side.'

'Right. Well, let's see what he has to say then.'

Keith grunted. 'It would be something if we walked in to find David Merchant alive and well and not happy to find that rumours of his death have been grossly exaggerated.'

'It would, Constable, indeed it would,' Hillary agreed, but didn't think it likely. 'But if we did, he'd then have some serious explaining to do about the unusual bonfire in his back garden.'

* * *

Inside, all was beige floor tiles and buttercup yellow walls. It made Hillary feel faintly nauseous. The receptionist-cum-general dogs-body quickly disappeared on being shown their ID, and was back within a few moments, looking wide-eyed and trying her best to sound disinterested.

'Mr Scraggins said to come right in,' she parroted, standing to one side of the door and opening it wide. She looked to be about eighteen, and was wearing a business suit in charcoal grey that wouldn't have looked out of place on a candidate for 'The Apprentice'. Hillary suspected that this was her first job after leaving school, and the suit was a present from her proud mother.

'Thank you.' Barrington smiled at her as they passed. Inside, the room was square and, thankfully, white. Posters of past publications lined the walls — most of them uninspiring volumes of what looked like school text books, self-help books of the more worthy sort, medical and theological tomes.

Strictly no racy romances, sexy thrillers or cheap paperbacks need apply here, Hillary mused.

'Mr Scraggins?'

Behind a functional desk, a small man nodded briskly. Hillary guessed he wouldn't stand much over five feet tall, which was almost certainly why he'd elected not to stand. His hair was too black to be anything but dyed, and he wore a dark-blue business suit and pearly pink tie.

'Yes. Samantha said you were police? There hasn't been another spate of burglaries on the site, I hope? Last month, the timber yard opposite lost a load of very expensive cherrywood, I believe.'

'No, sir. This is about your business partner, David Merchant. He is the 'Merchant' part of Merchant and Coe, I assume?'

Martin Scraggins looked astonished, then blinked rapidly, and tried to look merely affable again.

'Yes, he is. And I must say, he's the very last person I expected to attract the attention of the police. He surely can't have been caught speeding or littering!' He gave a brief laugh, but his eyes, Hillary noticed, weren't smiling.

'No, sir. We have cause for concern for his safety though,' she said carefully. Until the dead body was confirmed as being that of David Merchant she had to be wary of her wording.

Martin Scraggins stiffened slightly, and for a second she saw a flare of something flash across his face, before he smoothed it over once more and replaced it with a very good facsimile of concern. But what had it been? Surprise, maybe. Relief? Certainly something coming down on the side of joy rather than grief, Hillary thought.

'Oh? I hadn't realized there was anything wrong. Of course, David is more of the author/editor side of our business. He rarely comes into the office. I'm more of the accountant/money man. I practically live here.'

So that's how the firm was divided, Hillary mused. Interesting. So, had Mr Scraggins been fiddling the books? And if so — and he'd been found out — she suspected that David Merchant, with his strict moral code, wouldn't condone it. And for some reason, she doubted that Merchant's Christian code would be of the turn-the-other-cheek variety. From what she'd learned of his character so far, he'd probably feel morally bound to make sure that his business partner felt the full weight of the law.

Reining in her flights of fancy, she smiled briskly, and said pointedly, 'Do you mind if we sit?'

Scraggins flushed. 'Oh no, sorry. You rather took the wind out of my sails. Please, by all means . . . ' he indicated the standard office chairs lining the room, and both she and Barrington pulled one up and sat in front of the desk.

'When was the last time you heard from

Mr Merchant?' Hillary asked, as Keith took meticulous notes.

'Oh, probably last week sometime.'

'In person?'

'On the telephone.'

'Did he seem much the same as usual?'

'Yes. Not depressed or worried or anything like that,' Martin said quickly. 'That is the kind of thing you want to know, right?'

'Yes, sir, that's very helpful,' Hillary said with a smile. And thought that he was being far too helpful. There was something that was making Mr Scraggins very uneasy, she would have bet money on it.

'On good terms were you, sir?'

Martin blinked. 'Of course we were. Good grief, Merchant & Coe have been going for nearly a hundred and fifty years. Both our great-grandfathers started the company, and we took over from our own fathers when we left uni. David was a little older than me, of course,' he added automatically.

Hillary smiled, but doubted it would turn out that their murder victim was *that* much older.

'Do you know much about his family life?' she suddenly changed tack.

'No. He was a widower, of course, had been for some time.'

'And his son?'

'Never met the lad. Although . . . well, David never seemed to like to talk about him. I dare say he didn't measure up to David's standards.'

'From what I've been learning about him, sir, I'd imagine that most people didn't,' she said mildly.

But Martin Scraggins didn't take the bait.

'We always got on very well,' he reiterated firmly. Again, Hillary mused, too firmly. They'd probably had a row recently.

'Do you know if he had any enemies, sir?'

Martin shifted on his seat. 'You know, this is beginning to sound really serious. Is David dead?'

'Possibly, sir. We're still investigating. So, had he told you of any threatening phone calls, hate mail, or anything of that kind?'

'Good grief, no! David spent all his spare time volunteering at charities and such like. He even went to church three times a week — I know, because he had to practically shop around to find that many services to go to. Nowadays most churches only do Sundays. And some not even then.'

Hillary nodded. 'Well, sir, thank you for your time. If by any chance you should hear from him, please let us know.'

Martin Scraggins blinked, then nodded. He

watched the two police officers leave and sat for quite some time in his chair, thinking furiously.

Outside, Hillary walked slowly towards her car, an ancient Volkswagen Golf she called Puff The Tragic Wagon — because it was.

'Keith, I want you to hang around here and see if the secretary takes a lunch break,' she said, glancing at her watch. It was nearly noon. 'I want you to get her on her own and pump her about life in the publishing business. Find out if there'd been any recent falling out between Merchant and Scraggins, or if there was some sort of friction between them.'

'Personal or business?'

'Either,' she said, surprised that he should ask.

Keith sighed heavily, realizing the stupidity of the remark even as he made it. 'Yes, guv,' he said firmly.

She shot him a quick look and shook her head. 'Start pulling your weight, Constable,' she chided gently. 'You'll have to get the bus back. I need to report in to Danvers.'

Keith watched her car pull out of the car-park and thought once more about Cannes. Being the South of France, did that mean it was warm enough to swim in the sea, even in February?

★ ★ ★

Mark Chang also used the bus to return to Police HQ, and waited patiently whilst Hillary was in with the DCI. But as soon as she emerged, he got to his feet.

From across the crowded and noisy room, Hillary could see at once that Chang was excited. Although he was physically still, she got the feeling that mentally he was hopping about, like a puppy which had found an interesting trail.

It was nice to see such youthful enthusiasm after Keith's moping, miserable face.

'Mark?' she said, as she reached him. Although it was early days yet, she was beginning to feel pleasantly pleased with this latest edition to her team. He was still very green, of course, but he was bright, willing to learn and work, and possessed a calmness that was rather soothing on her nerves.

'Guv,' he said, and quickly related his tale of the two brothers in the pub. 'The thing is, guv,' he finished, 'it seems that this painter, Whyte, was in the pub last night moaning about Mr Merchant. Apparently they'd had some sort of a row. Neither Ron nor Robbie were able to get to the bottom of it — it appears Whyte was quite drunk, a not unheard of thing, apparently, and he was also

80

going on about being 'grassed up' by some busy-body or other. It sounds interesting.'

Hillary smiled. 'It certainly does. You have an address for this Whyte character?'

For some reason, this seemed to catch the young, good-looking constable on the raw. He visibly hesitated and then said rather cryptically, 'Not as such, guv, but I've got a good idea where it is. Ron drew me a rough map.'

'Right then. Let's go.'

Mark Chang, who'd been hoping to get in on the interview, breathed a careful sigh of relief and reached for his coat.

* * *

The cottage just outside Tackley did indeed have a name — Peony Cottage, to be exact. It was a small, square, red-brick cottage with a dark-grey slate roof. In the stark February sun, it was hard to tell whether or not the small, unkempt garden had ever been planted with peonies or not.

Hillary noticed that the garden gate was well oiled, and had recently been fitted with a new bolt. The front door, too, had new-looking locks fitted, and the guttering had obviously been replaced in the not-too-distant past. She suspected that David

81

Merchant would have taken his responsibilities as a landlord seriously. She would have bet the inside had smoke alarms fitted, and any gas appliances would have been regularly serviced.

She rang the bell and waited.

Nothing stirred.

She rang the bell again, and was rewarded by the sound of a window opening above her.

'Sod off! I'm not in!' a disgruntled voice yelled.

She stepped back just in time to see an upstairs window close.

Smiling, she leaned on the bell and left her finger there. Eventually she heard a muffled swearing and thumping as someone came downstairs, and she stepped back as the door was thrust open.

A tall, stoop-shouldered man with longish, wispy, pale hair and large grey eyes glared back at her. His face had a whitish stubble, and he was wearing, of all things, an army greatcoat. His feet were bare, long and bony. And just slightly blue.

'What the hell do you want?' he asked, but Hillary sensed the belligerence was more for show than anything.

'Police sir,' she said flatly, holding out her card. 'And we want a word. You are Frank Whyte?'

'Francis Whyte actually,' the artist responded bravely, with a smile and a mock bow. 'But nearly everybody but the cat calls me Frank. You'd better come in then — unless you want to cuff me and haul me off?'

Hillary smiled. 'Not just yet sir,' she said, deadpan, and had the satisfaction of seeing him give a double-take.

But she had the measure of him almost at once. This was the sort of man who liked to play the role of larger-than-life Bohemian and almost certainly misunderstood artist. He'd probably never married, never accrued much wealth, probably didn't drink as much as people imagined, and had almost certainly been raised in a happy, middle-class environment.

'Go on through to the lounge there,' he waved vaguely, and Hillary stepped out of the tiny hall through the first door. It was a small lounge, with a large sofa, over which a garishly coloured, crocheted throw had been tossed. 'Here, let's light the fire,' Frank Whyte said, shuffling around Mark Chang and igniting the gas fire.

When he straightened up, he glanced at Hillary, then gawked at Chang. 'Bloody hell, mate, you ever thought of doing nudes?'

Mark Chang's face didn't flinch by an inch.

'Sir?'

'I'd like to paint you. What do you say?'

'No, thank you, sir,' Chang said politely and Hillary hid a grin.

She eyed the artist warily, suspecting that the man himself was nude under the greatcoat. Sleeping naked probably went with his self-image — as did the replacement of a towelling robe with a reject from the Army & Navy Stores.

'So, what can I do for the plod? Sorry, can't offer you coffee, but I'm out. Probably out of milk too. My model, the lazy cow, was supposed to do the shopping yesterday, but didn't.'

'Don't you know what the inside of a supermarket looks like, Mr Whyte?' Hillary asked calmly, and again earned a double take and a reluctant grin from the artist.

'I can see I'm going to have to watch you,' he said, letting his eyes run over her. 'Nice curves. I like a woman with a Junoesque figure. Don't suppose *you* fancy being painted in the nude?'

'What? *Again?*' Hillary said, sounding bored in the extreme and this time Francis Whyte guffawed out loud and held out his hands in a gesture of submission. They were, she noticed, big, pale and sensitive. And she wondered if his canvasses were any good.

There were certainly no signs of his work on the walls, which were all bare.

'OK, OK, pax,' Whyte said. 'Now, what can I do you for? I don't own a car, so I can't have failed to renew my tax disc or what-the-hell ever. I own a push bike — better for the environment.'

'Good for you, sir,' Hillary said, not one whit impressed. 'Now, what can you tell me about your landlord?'

Whyte, who was standing with his back to the fire, the backs of his bare legs beginning to turn red from the heat gave a theatrical start.

'What? Mr Holier-than-thou-by-light-years? Why, what's he done?'

Hillary smiled. 'How long have you been living here, sir?'

'Oh, four months or so. I signed a six-month lease with him back in the summer sometime.'

'So it's up for renewal soon?'

Frank Whyte gave a genuine start this time, and smiled slowly. 'No flies on you, are there?'

'And would I be right in thinking that Mr Merchant probably wouldn't have been likely to give you a second lease, sir?'

Frank Whyte was already nodding. 'Bang on the nose, my lovely Juno. No, he wouldn't.

I conned the old fart into thinking I painted nothing but landscapes. Unfortunately some sneaky bastard, probably as narrow-minded as Merchant himself, squealed on me.'

'Nudes?' Hillary grinned.

'Nudes,' Frank Whyte agreed. 'Although I do turn my hand to the odd landscape now and then. Just for the sake of variety, you know.'

Hillary glanced around the bare walls silently, and Whyte laughed. 'I know what you're thinking, but that's a good sign actually. When an artist hasn't got any paintings on his walls, it means they're all at a gallery, or an exhibit, or have been sold.'

'So you're doing well?'

'I don't complain.'

Hillary noted that that wasn't quite what she'd asked him, but let it pass. 'When was the last time you saw Mr Merchant?'

'Oh hell, I dunno. Week before last, I think. I saw him in town and dodged into a shop. Pet shop, actually. Got sworn at by a sulphur-crested cockatoo. The language somebody had taught that bird! If I'd had the dosh handy, I'd have bought the foul-mouthed little bugger on the spot.'

Hillary nodded, fighting back a sudden rush of ennui-laced irritation. 'Let me rephrase the question then. When was the last

86

time you talked to Mr Merchant?'

'Oh not for ages. A month maybe? I tend to post off my rent cheques. The less I actually had to talk to him, the better. He was so good and righteous he actually gave me headaches.'

'He hasn't then, confronted you in person about your, er, canvases?'

Whyte smiled widely. 'Not yet. But I'm expecting him anytime soon. I received a very polite letter from him you see, requesting a meeting about the renewal of the lease. A mealy-mouthed little missive that made it pretty clear he no longer considered me to be the kind of tenant he was looking for. That's how I knew someone had squealed on me.'

'Do you still have the letter?'

'Good grief, no. I recycled it in the paper bin. It got collected yesterday, I think. Or was it the day before? Time tends to blur.'

'And did it make you angry?' she asked curiously, but the artist was already shaking his head and grinning.

'What, the prospect of being evicted from this place? Hardly. I paint in the upstairs north-facing bedroom, but it's hardly ideal. Besides, I like moving from place to place. I was thinking of heading for Cornwall for Easter. Maybe St Ives. Dunno.' He shrugged. 'Why?'

'Thank you for your time, sir,' she said and

smiled widely again.

'You know, you're something of a smasher,' Francis Whyte said. 'All that Titian hair. I could do something with you.'

'I'm too much woman for you, sir,' Hillary said, deadpan, and could still hear Whyte laughing as they let themselves out.

Outside, she could sense Chang's disappointment.

'Did you notice anything odd about that interview, Constable?' she asked quietly, as they walked back towards Puff the Tragic Wagon.

'Odd, guv?' Chang echoed, frowning. 'Not really. The suspect didn't really appear to have any motive. Nor did he seem to bear any real animosity towards the victim. In fact, he seemed to regard him as something of a joke.'

'His sort see all of life as being a joke, Constable,' Hillary agreed mildly. 'But when you've conducted as many interviews as I have, you learn that everyone always wants to know the same thing.'

Chang stared back at the small, featureless cottage, thinking furiously. And coming up with nothing. Taking pity on him, Hillary said quietly, 'They all want to know what's happened. But apart from asking that one, rather rhetorical question about why we were interested in Merchant, he didn't seem all that curious, did he?'

Mark Chang thought about it, then slowly shook his head. 'No, guv, he didn't.'

'And I always find a lack of interest very, very interesting, Constable,' she said flatly. 'So, after you've attended the autopsy on our victim, I want you to find out all you can about our Mr Francis Whyte.'

Chang nodded.

And if the thought of attending his first full autopsy worried him, he didn't show it. But Hillary doubted if that he'd come through it without either fainting, or losing his breakfast. And probably both.

4

Keith Barrington waited at the bus stop nearest the small industrial estate, gambling on the fact that the secretary would probably prefer to go into town for lunch. He also thought it a fairly good bet that the girl didn't have a car of her own yet, and at five past one, he was proved right. She emerged from the gated entrance, walking without looking where she was going, since she was delving into her bag, probably searching for her purse.

She turned automatically along the pavement, but when she did finally look up she recognized him at once, of course. As she approached the bus stop her footsteps faltered for a few moments, before she smiled at him uncertainly.

'Hello. Don't worry,' Keith said cheerfully. 'The boss needed to take the car somewhere and so left me to catch the bus. You look like I'm about to arrest you.' He grinned widely, knowing it made him look goofy and was almost guaranteed to help her relax.

The young girl smiled back. 'That's a relief.'

Keith noticed the red and blue bus turn the corner down the road, and nodded at it. 'Good. I hate having to hang around.'

'Me, too. It really eats into your lunch hour if it's late,' she agreed, young enough to be intrigued by a visit to her boss from the police and inclined to be friendly.

'Have you found a good place to eat in Kidlington?' he asked, making his voice sound amazed, and she laughed.

'Not really. I usually go to the pub — near the traffic lights at the top end of the main shopping street?' She made it a question.

Keith shrugged. 'Don't think I've ever been in,' he said, truthfully enough. 'I'll give it a try though. I haven't got to get back to the office until two.'

He paused, waiting to see if she was going to object to him tagging along with her, but by then the bus had reached them and she clambered on board, giving the driver the correct change, and any awkwardness was allowed to pass.

He sat behind her on the bus, leaning forward and chatting casually. He quickly learned her name — Fiona Lewis — and that she lived in Woodstock with her parents. She was, as he suspected, saving for her first car, and the job at Merchant & Coe was her first job.

'I saw it advertised in the *Oxford Mail* and thought it sounded glamorous. You know, publishing?' she gave an exaggerated eye roll. 'It had to be better than being in an estate agent's or accountant's or something like that, or so I thought. I tried for a job at a travel agency, but didn't get it.'

'Hoped to get half-price holidays, huh?' Keith said, sympathetically.

They were still chatting amiably as they entered the pub. Keith ordered a baked potato and coleslaw, Fiona — predictably — a salad baguette. Keith guessed she'd leave most of the bread, and she did.

'So, what's he like to work for then, your boss. Is he Coe or Merchant?' Keith asked, hoping that his supposed lack of knowledge about her boss's real name would lull her into a false sense of security.

'Neither. His name's Martin Scraggins,' she giggled. 'Aren't you glad you don't have a name like that?'

Keith, who'd heard far worse, grinned. 'Little bit of a squirt, isn't he? Is he a bit of tyrant? They say short men are the devil to get on with — because they develop some sort of inferiority complex or what-have-you.' And he wrinkled his nose as he added salt to his spud.

'Oh, he's not all that bad,' Fiona said, a

shade reluctantly, Keith thought. 'At least I don't work for that Mr Merchant,' she added, and shuddered.

'Oh?' he prompted. So Martin Scraggins hadn't confided to his secretary that Merchant was the source of a police investigation. If he had, she wouldn't have been so casual about mentioning him.

But then, he didn't really read anything into that. Fiona was new to the job and young. Why would he discuss important matters with her?

'He gives me the creeps a bit,' Fiona confided now. 'Whenever he comes into the office, which isn't often I'm glad to say, he always looks at me funny.'

'Funny? Aye-aye.' Keith deliberately seemed to misunderstand, and gave her the wink. 'One of those sort, is he? Wandering eyes and hands to match?'

Fiona shuddered. 'Oh no, just the opposite in fact. The girl who had the job before me warned me that he was one of those devout kinds. And not the all lightness-and-love-and-forgiveness kind, but the real fire-and-brimstone sort. You know, the miserable ones who think everything is a sin, and unless you're unhappy, you're not living right. Every time he saw me, I swear he checked to see that my skirt reached over my knees. And he sniffed if I wore lipstick. Honest! I swear that's what caused it. I saw him looking at my mouth once, and I was only wearing some Avon Peach, but it made me feel like Jezebel.'

'He sounds like a riot,' Keith said, grimacing. 'And I suppose, sod's law being what it is, he's the one with all the power at the company, right?'

'Well, I don't know about that,' Fiona said thoughtfully. 'I heard him and Mr Scraggins arguing just the other day, and Martin was definitely giving as good as he got. Not that I blame him mind. All that money! And he promised me I'd keep my job if the take-over went ahead.'

Keith kept his face bland and barely interested. 'Take-over, huh? That sounds ominous. I'd be wary of any shake-ups if I were you. They never seem to bode well.'

'Oh, I don't know,' Fiona said, relaxing more and more as she sipped her Coke. 'I thought so too at first, but then Mr Scraggins explained that the new company would be publishing other stuff, besides the dull stuff we do now. I can't tell you how boring it is — sociology text books, mechanical engineering manuals and all this stuff about religion. Even typing letters about it is boring. Mr Merchant gave me a whole load of the religious books we publish and I took 'em home, to be polite like, but not even Mum can read them. And she reads a lot! But if we get taken over, we might start publishing, oh, I don't know, romances maybe. Or even cook books. They'd be an improvement, I can tell you,' Fiona gushed, sounding youthfully optimistic. 'But I like crime books best. You must read a lot of them, being a policeman like,' she added ingenuously.

Keith, who read almost exclusively horror, smiled. 'So, what were they arguing about?' he asked, and saw from the way her smile dimmed that he'd been a bit abrupt. 'You know, you said your boss and his partner were arguing.'

'Oh that,' Fiona said uncertainly, suddenly twigging to the fact that she was being interrogated. From the conflicting emotions crossing her face, Keith could tell that she was torn between being alarmed and being thrilled. But it was too late to backtrack now: the cat was out of the bag.

'Don't worry, I'm not interested in industrial espionage!' he said theatrically and grinned.

Fiona shrugged uncertainly, but supposed, on thinking it over, that it was all right to talk. He was, after all, the police. And she'd been raised in a household that respected the law.

'Well, Mr Merchant was against the

take-over, and Martin was all for it. I know it means a lot of money for both of them if it goes ahead, but Mr Merchant isn't the sort to care about profit and all that. It was one of the things Martin was shouting at him — that just because he didn't care about money, didn't mean that Martin felt the same way.'

She paused and absently twiddled her glass of Coke. 'Is something wrong? I mean, all these questions . . . My mum won't like me working where there was something going on.'

'Oh well,' Keith said vaguely, leaning back against his chair and picking up his half of shandy. 'We're not sure yet. Let's just say we're concerned for Mr Merchant's safety,' he said, with massive understatement.

Fiona's eyes grew wide. 'You mean he's missing?'

'Possibly.'

'Oh shi — I mean, oh my. Oh, but I'm sure Mr Scraggins had nothing to do with it. Mr Merchant was so much bigger than him for one thing!' she said, then unexpectedly burst into nervous giggles.

Keith, deciding not to push it any further, finished his meal, and they parted amiably, Keith to walk back to HQ, and Fiona to ride the bus back to her 'glamorous' job.

***

In his cottage near Tackley, Frank Whyte got dressed. His hands shook as he donned a pair of paint-specked ancient denims, and, as he searched for a clean pair of socks, he tried in vain to convince himself that he wasn't scared witless.

Socks found, he slipped his feet into an old pair of steel-capped work boots, and pulled on a T-shirt, then a loose dress shirt with a grey pinstripe and, on top of that, a large, chunky, knitted sweater. He tended to feel the cold. Then he stepped across the tiny landing into his studio and stared at his latest canvas blankly.

On it, a naked woman leaned against a windowsill, looking out. Her breasts were flattened against the pane of glass, and he'd painted the window next to her as half-open, allowing her reflected glories to be clearly visible. It was tantalizing, cheeky and erotic without being pornographic. It had the potential, he thought, to be very good. Far better than the dross he'd been churning out for the past eight months.

He hated painting junk, just to pay the damned rent and put food on the table.

He sighed as he stared at the painting, but knew better than to pick up his brushes. In his present mood, he'd only ruin it.

The model's face in the painting was seen in two-thirds profile, staring down at something below her. What, was left to the viewer's imagination. An outraged female neighbour, or appreciative male passer-by perhaps? Maybe her dog, that she was watching playing in the garden? It could have been anything.

The half-painted face of Lori Dunne, his current muse and bedmate seemed to mock him. How she'd laugh if she knew what a mess he was in.

Or would she?

Sometimes, Frank thought he caught a cold, hard glint in her lovely eyes that warned him that she was not quite the free spirit she seemed. That there was something else lurking beneath that supposedly free-spirited and devil-may-care youthful exterior.

But she was so bloody lovely.

If only he hadn't called on that dozy, narrow-minded old git this morning. Why couldn't he have stayed away? What he'd told that clever-eyed woman copper just now about not caring about being evicted had been more or less the truth after all. If it hadn't been for his growing dependence on the lovely Lori, he could have simply given David Merchant the old two-fingered salute.

But as it was . . .

Frank sighed heavily. He'd totally lost his head. Even now the stupidity of what he'd done refused to sink in.

He stared at the beckoning canvas and felt the pull of the siren, even now. If he had any sense, he'd pack up and start hitchhiking somewhere. Anywhere away from here.

For all her sauce and apparent good-will, that woman copper, DI Greene, was as sharp as a tack. And, unless his instincts were letting him down — and they rarely did — she'd taken a heavy blow recently. She had the look of someone who'd been recently pole-axed by this merry-go-round called life. And everyone knew that a wounded she-bear was far more dangerous than a contented one. She'd be out for blood over this David Merchant business. And he was directly in line for it.

But still he stood in his studio, staring at the unfinished painting, and he never did get around to packing.

* * *

Keith was glad to have something positive to report to Hillary Greene for once. He was well aware that his stock with her was low at the present and, as she listened to him relating what he'd learned from Fiona, he felt a tiny wave of relief and satisfaction to see her nod in approbation.

When he'd finished, she nodded. 'Good, well done, Keith. Follow it up. Find out all you can about it, without letting Scraggins know we're on to it if you can. Pump the secretary again — confide in her just enough to get her on side. I want to have facts and figures when I tackle Scraggins again.'

Keith nodded, but even as he did so, he felt a small tug of resentment that surprised him. Always before, winning Hillary Greene's approval had warmed him. Now he felt just the tiniest bit resentful: he felt like a good little doggie getting a pat on the head.

He knew that it wasn't because his attitude towards her had changed. She was still the best damned guv'nor he'd ever worked for — dedicated, loyal to her team, clever and fair. No, it was he himself who was changing. And he was not sure he liked it.

This was the best time in a murder inquiry — when you began to get leads and chase down facts. You never knew when you'd stumble on the one thing that would catch a killer. As he settled down in front of his computer, determined to do a good job — and like it — he waited to feel the familiar thrill of the chase.

But it never came.

*　★　*

In Birmingham, his lover, Gavin Moreland, stared at the governor of one of the city's prisons, trying to take in his words.

He'd been called away from Moreland Imports, his father's company, where he had been working as titular head since his father's incarceration five weeks ago.

An 'incident' had occurred at the gaol concerning his father, the woman secretary had said. Could he come at once? And no, she was not at liberty to discuss details over the telephone.

So he'd driven up the motorway from London, and had begun to feel a cold creeping unease the moment he'd arrived and been ushered straight to the governor's office. The man who'd met him had lawyer/lackey written all over him. His first thought was that they'd found something else to charge his father with, but he'd quickly dismissed that idea. If that was so, surely he'd be at the police station now, and not here?

When the governor had met him gravely, and proceeded to pour him a sherry, the cold unease had frozen around him, settling in a

101

hard tight knot in his stomach.

But even then he'd not been prepared for the actual words that had been spoken.

Now, he heard himself repeat them. 'Dead?'

The governor, a slim, grey-haired man who had the look of an academic about him, cleared his throat, and said softly, 'Yes, Mr Moreland. I'm very sorry. There will of course be a full inquiry.'

Gavin blinked. 'But how? I mean, was it a heart attack?'

'No, I'm afraid not.'

Gavin blinked. 'He wasn't attacked by someone, was he? When I last visited him he told me some men were making his life hell. Some man called — '

'No, Mr Moreland, there's no question of that,' the governor intervened hastily. Beside him, the lawyer/lackey stirred, as if sensing the threat of a lawsuit. 'I'm sorry, Mr Moreland, I know this is going to come as a shock to you, but sometimes, the inmates have a very hard time adjusting. Your father, I'm afraid, because of his background and . . . well, he was not able to adapt to the way of life here. It came as such a shock to his system you see. Not that he gave us any cause for concern. If he had, I assure you, we'd have put him on suicide watch.'

Gavin felt the word slide over him, like the many-legged caress of a spider. 'Suicide?' he heard himself repeat helplessly.

'Yes. I'm sorry, Mr Moreland, but your father has killed himself,' the governor said quietly.

★　★　★

In Thames Valley Police's Headquarters in Kidlington, Superintendent Brian Vane stared at the memo in front of him. It was an innocuous enough looking missive, and was resting in a pile of many other documents, ostensibly awaiting his signature. He spent many hours reading, initialing, and passing on such paperwork.

Normally, he worked in a continuous easy flow, but this one had stopped him cold.

On the face of it, it should have brought a smile to his face because it foreshadowed promotion. True, it was a sideways sort of promotion, bringing with it a posting to Hull, which was not a place Brian Vane had any particular wish to visit, let alone live.

But he could read between the lines with the best of them, and he knew what this 'offer' to chair the latest sub-committee meant. It might be the latest 'baby' of the chief constable, but it was without doubt a poisoned chalice. Whoever took it would be sidelined almost permanently. Usually such outwardly prestigious postings went to near-retirement age, upper management personnel who wanted a quiet pasture to graze in for their remaining few years.

Vane was not yet fifty-two.

Technically, of course, he could turn it down. But he knew the powers-that-be at Thames Valley wouldn't like that. They wanted him out — quietly, without fuss, and with honour on both sides. And if he should kick up a stink, well, they had ways of making their displeasure known.

Vane let the memo drop and walked slowly to his window, looking out across his uninspiring view of the large car-park. He'd been given Phillip 'Mellow' Mallow's job after Mallow had been gunned down by the rampaging vigilante, Clive Myers.

At the time, it had been understood by everyone that he was to have the post for a few years, add it to his CV, then move onwards and upwards.

But he'd seriously mismanaged the whole débâcle that had developed when Mallow's widow had killed Clive Myers.

And he knew why, of course. It was because of the involvement of Hillary Greene. If it hadn't been for her, he wouldn't have been so blindsided. But it had seemed such a heaven-sent opportunity to get rid of her, that he'd acted without thinking.

During his younger days, Hillary Greene, then a fairly new recruit, had been assigned to one of his cases, and found out that he'd planted evidence to get a conviction. Oh, it had been a righteous bust — the man who got sent down deserved every year he'd served. And since then, he'd committed other, similar, crimes and was probably serving time now for some other offence.

And Greene, to give her credit, had not shopped him. But even so, finding himself her new boss all these years later had made him uncomfortable in the extreme. He didn't like the look in her eyes whenever she saw him, or enjoy the feeling that he was somehow beholden to her.

He wanted her moved on, somewhere, anywhere, off his patch. So when she'd gone to the aid of her ex-sergeant, breaking more rules than you could shake a stick at, he'd leapt at the chance to come down on her.

Since then, of course, it had slowly dawned on him just how stupid he'd been. He'd played right into her hands by openly calling into doubt her actions on the afternoon Janine Mallow shot and killed Myers. In wanting to put Hillary firmly in the shit, he'd only landed himself there instead.

He'd always known that the chief super, Marcus Donleavy, really rated Hillary's detective skills, but he had seriously misread the amount of loyalty Greene commanded from the Kidlington nick as a whole.

His only chance of salvaging something rested with the inquiry into the Myers shooting finding something to Greene's detriment. Or if Janine Mallow had taken the fall, she might have taken Hillary with her, or, at the very least, seriously harmed her reputation. But it hadn't panned out like that — not surprising, really, when so many people needed it to play differently.

And now that the fuss was at last dying down came this: the clever little knife in the back, the warning to get out, and go quietly.

Well, all right. He knew he couldn't fight the system — he would go. To bloody Hull. Take the small pay rise and go from committee job to committee job. Take early retirement on a full pension the moment it became an option.

But Vane didn't want to go without leaving Hillary Greene a farewell present she'd never forget.

★ ★ ★

106

Lin Chun Chang and his wife, Lui, were stacking colanders in the back of the shop when they heard the explosion of glass. It was six o'clock and nearly closing time, and Lui, a small, rounded woman with long grey hair pulled back in a pony-tail, gave a little scream of fright and surprise.

The Changs, who'd moved from Northampton several years ago, had bought the kitchenware shop in the Oxford suburb of Summertown, and had never regretted it. For all the years that they'd owned the shop and lived above it in a small but tidy flat, they'd never had any trouble, and they didn't think for one moment that they had any now.

As they both hurried forward, Lin Chun was thinking that perhaps a car had crashed into the big plate glass window of 'The Kitchen Sink'. Or maybe something had fallen from the roof of the shop opposite, which had had scaffolding all around it for the past week. He knew workmen could sometimes be careless.

As he headed for the front of the shop, Lui went straight to a customer who had been studying some clever 3-D place mats, new in, and who was now staring out towards the street, wide-eyed and uneasy.

'My what a noise!' Lui said with a

107

determinedly cheerful smile. 'You are not cut, I hope?'

'Oh no,' the woman said, then glanced down at herself with an angry scowl. 'Not that that isn't due to more luck than judgement. Bloody vandals.'

It was then that Lui felt her stomach tighten in fear. She left the customer, who trailed after her to the front of the shop, where the remains of the large glass window lay shattered on the floor. A display of floor mops lay scattered willy-nilly, and Lui felt her heart sink to see a whole rack of drinking glasses had been toppled, and now lay shattered and ruined, only adding to the mess and danger on the floor.

'Oh please, be careful where you tread, ladies,' Lin Chun Chang said anxiously, staring down at the ruins of his shop front.

'It was two Chinese men,' the customer said flatly. 'A big fat one and a smaller one. They used a sledgehammer, I reckon. My husband used to have one — he was in construction, so I recognized it.' She was a pleasant-faced woman, in her fifties, but Lin Chun and his wife stared at her in horror.

'You mean someone did this on purpose?' Lui cried.

''Fraid so,' the customer said, and nodded implacably.

'We must call the police,' Mr Chang said next. Then added to the customer, 'We have a son in the police.'

'Oh but he's in CID,' Lui added proudly. 'So he won't be called out on something like this.'

The customer tut-tutted about what the world was coming to, as a gathering crowd of sightseers gathered outside. When she left, she'd bought a set of six 3-D place mats with a fishy motif. Lui Chang thought sadly that she'd only bought them because she felt sorry for them.

But, even as they got on to their insurance company, called out a glazier to temporarily secure the building, and began on the long back-breaking process of clearing up the mess, it never occurred to them that this had been anything other than a random act of mindless violence. Just another of those horrible things that sometimes happened.

But their son, Mark, would soon learn differently.

★ ★ ★

When Keith Barrington finally left the office, it was nearly seven o'clock and pitch black. Officially, his shift had ended at 4.30, and he knew he wouldn't be getting overtime.

Hillary Greene had still been at her desk, although Chang had left, and so had the sarge. Gemma Fordham lived in a very large, white-painted house on the prestigious Woodstock Road, in North Oxford. It was owned by the man she lived with, a blind Oxford music don, and they'd been together now for coming on to three years.

Idly, as he drove towards his tiny bedsit in Botley, Barrington wondered if Gemma Fordham ever thought of getting married and settling down. He knew the martial-arts expert was ambitious, but nowadays women coppers could have it all.

This made him think of the state of his own messy love life, and he smiled grimly. He left his car in its usual spot in a vast Do-It-Yourself shop car-park, situated at the back of the Victorian villa where he, and half the student population of the city seemed to live. He tramped wearily up the street of similar bedsits to a narrow-fronted doorway where he let himself in.

The hall smelt of takeaway curries, and was booby-trapped by the usual pile of bicycles. He mounted the stairs, hearing the old lino crackle beneath his feet, and finally put his key in the door.

The moment he stepped inside the room, Keith saw him.

Gavin Moreland had always been able to make his heart rate do silly things. Dark, good-looking, fit, Gavin was the very antithesis of himself. Born with the proverbial silver spoon in his mouth, he'd gone to the best schools, where he'd learned and become very proficient at tennis. It was his dream to turn pro, but all that had gone on hold when his father had taken a fall for smuggling. Elegant, sophisticated, bitterly funny and with a talent for living the good life, Gavin had probably been as horrified as Keith had been when they met and fell in love.

After all, a gawky, red-haired plod could hardly have been Gavin's choice of an ideal lover.

But somehow, through all the break-ups, make-ups, tantrums and soul-searching, the two men couldn't seem to either live together or live apart.

Keith shut the door behind him and leaned heavily against it. 'Not now, Gav,' Keith said flatly. 'I'm knackered.' For all that the sight of him had instantly lifted Keith's depressed spirits, he didn't think he could cope with Gavin right now.

But for once Gavin had no sharp come back. He simply sat, leaning against the headboard of Keith's rather narrow, mean little bed, and stared at him.

111

Keith frowned. 'Have you been drinking?' he asked flatly.

'Not yet. But I'm planning on starting,' Gavin said, with a wide, white smile that made Keith's chest hurt.

'What's wrong?' Keith whispered.

'Oh, nothing much. It's just that my old man killed himself this afternoon, because he couldn't take it in the nick. Where your lot put him.' Gavin reached behind him and extracted a bottle of whisky, which he proceeded to unscrew. 'To British Justice!' he toasted Keith bitterly and took a long hard swallow.

Wordlessly, Keith went to the bed, and held him whilst he drank, and raged, and cried, and then drank some more.

Somewhere near one o'clock in the morning, Gavin finally fell into a drunken stupor, but Keith continued to stare, dry-eyed at the stained wall of his bedsit.

For the first time in their tumultuous relationship, Gavin needed him. For once, Gavin's money would not be able to help him. His fickle friends had already mostly deserted him when Sir Reginald had first fallen from grace. And Gavin's brittle, defiant nature alone wouldn't be enough to sustain him during this sea-change.

No. Gavin needed him — Keith.

And Keith wasn't sure whether that thought thrilled him or terrified him.

★ ★ ★

The next morning, Hillary Green came into her office, and found a note from Steven Partridge. Their victim had been identified from his dental records: it was definitely David Merchant.

Hillary went to Paul Danvers' office to report in, surprised to find it empty. She shrugged and returned to her desk. Now at least, there was one less ambiguity to worry about.

Mark Chang had come in, bright and early as usual, and he nodded at her as she took her place. Gemma had also just pushed through the door when her phone rang.

She picked it up, surprised to hear Keith Barrington's voice on the other end.

'Guv, it's me. I need to take the day off.'

Hillary watched her sergeant shrug out of her winter coat, revealing her usual trouser suit, sensible boots and cap of short silvery-pale hair.

'Oh?' she said neutrally.

'It's a family crisis, guv. There's been a death in the family.'

'All right. I'm sorry. Will you be in

tomorrow, or do you want longer?'

'No, guv, I'll be in tomorrow. I just need the one day.'

'All right. Let me know if there's anything you need.' When she hung up, she noticed that both of the others looking at her curiously.

'Keith won't be in today. Death in the family. Right, the ID on the victim is confirmed. It was David Merchant. Gemma, how far are you along on his details?' And, as they settled down into their second day of the murder inquiry, Hillary wondered if they were in for a hard slog — or if the case would be a relatively easy nut to crack.

She hoped the latter. She could do with an easy ride for once.

But she wasn't going to get it.

5

Keith Barrington glanced across towards the passenger seat as the white chalky cliffs bordering the motorway sped past the windows. 'You all right?' he asked softly.

It was a misty, murky morning, dull and depressing and typical of February, and the moment the words were out he wished he could have retracted them.

Predictably enough, Gavin Moreland sighed heavily. 'Of course I'm not bloody all right. Why would I be all right? I'm going back home to make arrangements to bury my father. He was only fifty-eight you know. If you bastards had just left him alone, he'd be alive now.'

Keith changed lanes to pass a trundling lorry, and considered his response. He needed to be tactful, but on the other hand, he knew he just couldn't let the challenge pass. If he did, Gavin would assume that Keith was accepting liability on behalf of the whole establishment. And would use it as leverage sometime in the near future.

'He was caught breaking the law, Gavin,' he said mildly. 'And most people caught

115

breaking the law do go to gaol, you know. Your father might have thought he'd be an exception — a lot of people like him do.'

'People like him?' Gavin repeated, his voice ominously bland.

Keith took a long slow breath then let it out again. 'Look, let's not discuss it now, all right? I'm driving and you're still in shock. Logic and grief don't mix.'

'Are you even sorry he's dead?' Gavin suddenly snarled, and Keith felt himself pale.

'Gav! Of course I'm sorry. He was your father. And it was a bloody nasty and rotten way to go. I wish it hadn't happened. You must know that?'

He peered ahead, praying for an exit ramp, but, of course, there wasn't one. He steered back into the slow lane and eased his foot off the brake. Then he glanced over once more. 'Damn it, I wish I wasn't in this car,' he said grimly. Gavin was pale and shaking, and needed to be held.

A crisis was imminent and Keith could clearly feel its approach — and its nature didn't really centre around the death of Sir Reginald Moreland at all.

'Let's just get back to London,' Gavin said savagely, turning his face to the window and staring out at the bleak passing scenery. 'Once I've sorted out the funeral arrangements, I need to see old Godfrey Purbright. Dad's main legal man. I'm going to sell the company,' he added flatly.

Keith took another long slow breath. 'You know, they say you shouldn't make any major decisions until at least six months after bereavement. They reckon you're not thinking properly until then. Maybe you should wait a while, huh?' he coaxed gently. 'See how things pan out. You never know, you might feel differently then.'

Gavin Moreland slowly leaned his head back against the headrest on his seat and closed his eyes. 'How long have I wanted to play professional tennis?' he asked quietly.

Keith's hands tightened on the wheel. 'Ever since I've known you.'

'And that's more than three years. The reason I never did is because Dad would have had conniptions and because, deep inside, I was always scared that if I tried, and failed miserably, he'd laugh at me. Well, now he's gone. I know he's left everything to me, so it's not as if I won't have the money to support myself until I get good enough for the prize money and sponsorship deals to kick in. So you tell me — what's to stop me?'

Keith felt his heart sink, because he realized the answer to that. 'Nothing at all,' he said flatly. Which meant Gavin would leave, and this time it would be really over. During the course of their stormy relationship, Gavin had often threatened to leave, and twice had followed up on the threat. But he always came back. This time, Keith knew it would be different. And something of his misery must have sounded in his tone, for Gavin shot his lover a searching gaze that gradually softened into something very close to satisfaction.

'Exactly,' Gavin said softly. 'So I'll tell Purbright to sell, and then I'm gone. I'll start in Australia — if I can train in the heat and achieve some real stamina, I'll know whether or not I can give it a serious go. Besides, Australia's a good place to pick up a first class coach. And I play better on clay than on grass at the moment, so after that, I can concentrate on the French Open.'

'Sounds good,' Keith said flatly.

'Oh it will be,' Gavin said grimly. 'I'm going to make bloody sure it is. If this thing with Dad has taught me one thing, it's that life's too bloody short. I'm going to tour the world, work like a navvy and play just as hard, while I'm still young. I'm going to enjoy myself for once.'

An unsaid offer, bordering on an accusation hung, in the air.

Gavin looked across at his lover, noting the white knuckles that clenched the steering wheel so hard, the tight line of his jaw, and the grim, flat concentration of his driving. Good. He was hurting. It would help, later on, when he finally asked Keith to come with him.

Deliberately he turned his face back to the window and let the man he loved suffer in silence. He was playing hard ball now. And just as he knew he had the killer instinct on the tennis court, now was the time to find out whether he had it when it came to his private life.

And getting what he wanted.

★ ★ ★

Hillary and Gemma drove to Park Town, a largely genteel part of north Oxford, where Gemma parked only semi-legally beneath a large, now bare, horse-chestnut tree.

They found the offices of Burbage, Baines and Yates in a converted Edwardian terraced house overlooking a large playing field. Now, just a solitary dog-walker braved the damp chilly open air, and Gemma, wrapped up in a long, warm winter coat, hoped Guy wouldn't change his mind and get a seeing-eye dog. She knew who'd end up mostly walking it.

Hillary walked up three well-maintained steps and rang the discreet buzzer. A pleasant woman's voice asked for details and, after Hillary gave them, the door gave a little chirrup, rather like a surprised sparrow, and clicked off the latch. Hillary pushed, and the two women walked into a warm, wooden-floored vestibule. A woman appeared from a door set back from a corridor leading off to the right, and smiled briefly.

'Inspector Greene?'

Gemma had made the appointment with Arthur Baines yesterday, before the identity of the victim had been established. She liked to be efficient — just to remind Hillary Greene that she was indispensable.

'Please, follow me.' The secretary was one of those seemingly ageless ash-blondes with a figure that novelists would invariably describe as willowy. Hillary, whom those same novel-ists would describe as having a Junoesque, or maybe hour-glass figure, disliked her on prin-ciple. Gemma, tall, lean, fit and strong, simply dismissed her.

'The police officers, sir,' the woman spoke after opening a door, and standing to one side. Once inside, Hillary noticed at once that a pleasant room had been forced to suffer a bad partition. A single, large window looked disconcertingly off-centre as did an original fireplace on the facing wall. Wainscotting simply disappeared halfway along, and the ornate ceiling rose almost ran into the central, newly installed plasterboard wall.

A large, florid-faced man rose from behind a desk, nodded a wordless 'thank you' to his secretary, and watched Hillary and Gemma approach with curious pale hazel eyes. 'Inspector Greene.'

On receiving the request for an interview yesterday, Arthur Baines had very quickly run down a mental list of his clients, seeking for one who might have fallen foul of the law. Needless to say, he couldn't think of that many. His firm hardly ever touched criminal law, and if the majority of his clients sometimes tended to cut things a bit fine in the pursuit of corporate profit, most of them were far too canny to get caught.

'Please, would you sit down? I took the liberty of having tea brought in just before you arrived.'

Hillary, who'd have preferred coffee, smiled and let him pour out two cups.

'Milk, lemon, sugar?'

'Milk and one sugar for me please, Mr Baines,' Hillary said.

'Just lemon for me,' Gemma said, her gravelly, sexy voice making Arthur Baines look at her again. He'd briefly registered a trouser-suited, short-haired, blonde woman and immediately classified her as not his type.

But that voice now — that was very distinctive, and very sexy indeed.

Almost as if reading his mind, Gemma accepted her tea cup — a genuine Spode — with a cool smile. And the solicitor quickly looked away.

'Now, Inspector?' Arthur, to whom time really was money, raised an enquiring eyebrow, anxious to waste as little of the precious commodity as possible.

'It's about one of your clients, sir. Mr David Merchant.'

'David!' Arthur couldn't help but exclaim. Then he smiled ruefully. 'Sorry. Not very tactful, I know. It's just that, of all the people I thought might have reason to come to your attention, David is the very last I would have picked. He's not in serious trouble, I hope? I mean, our company isn't really very experienced in criminal law, you see. And if he needs representation — '

'He doesn't, sir,' Hillary cut in quickly, not willing to chance hyperbole this early on in the interview. 'Mr David Merchant was murdered at his home, sometime yesterday.'

With the ID only just confirmed, there had, as yet, been no mention of it in the press, apart from the briefest of outlines, and Arthur Baines looked genuinely shocked.

'David? Someone murdered David? Well

. . . Yes . . . I suppose I can see — ' Suddenly he broke off, and laughed uneasily again. 'Sorry. Once more, not very tactful of me.'

Hillary smiled briefly. It was nice to disconcert the professional classes once in a while. 'By implication, Mr Baines, you seem to be implying that David Merchant is the kind who *would* get himself killed?'

'Oh no, I wouldn't say that. Well, not in so many words. But when you said he'd been killed . . . well, it did occur to me that it wasn't all that surprising. Not really. I mean, David was an inflexible sort of man. Uncompromising. And people with deep convictions do tend to get on other people's wicks, I find.'

Arthur Baines managed a smile and then shook his head. 'Oh dear. I really shouldn't have said that either. Poor David. The poor chap didn't deserve that. Oh, this is really terrible.'

And indeed, the man's face had gone from florid to rather pale. He looked, now, more like fifty years old, rather than the forty or so she had at first assumed him to be.

'What can you tell us about his financial arrangements sir?' Hillary asked casually, taking a sip of her tea. It was one of those smoky, flavoured teas that came with a fancy name. Hillary had some difficulty swallowing it and hastily put her cup back down on the desk.

Gemma, who was rather enjoying hers, noticed and bit back a smile.

'Oh his will. Yes, I have it. Just a moment, while I . . . ' He indicated the intercom on his desk and pressed down a button. 'Janice, will you look out the David Saul Merchant file for me?'

He leaned back in his chair and regarded Hillary grimly. 'I have to say, Inspector, this is really shocking news.'

Hillary, after a moment's thought, was prepared to admit that for Arthur Baines it probably was. She doubted that many of his wealthy, comfortably upper-middle class clients ended up as murder statistics.

'Did you like Mr Merchant, sir?' she asked.

'Oh no,' Arthur Baines said at once, then looked surprised. Then he smiled ruefully. 'I'm afraid David wasn't the sort of man you liked. You could admire him, if you so chose. Or sneer at him, if you preferred.'

'But you couldn't ignore him?' Hillary guessed, and had the satisfaction of seeing the solicitor give her an appreciative nod.

'I see you have the measure of the man already,' Arthur said, then looked up as the door opened, and the ash-blonde came in with a large, pale-blue folder, tied up with a dusty looking red silk ribbon. All reliably old-fashioned, Hillary thought. She bet it impressed the clients no end.

She waited while the blonde wordlessly sailed away, and Arthur quickly reacquainted himself with the wording of David Merchant's will.

'Yes,' he said after a short silence. 'It's just as I remember. He's left the lot to charity.' Arthur looked up and smiled. 'Not too surprising, given the man. Fully half of it goes to the Salvation Army. The rest is given over to various church restoration projects, soup kitchens in deprived areas, that sort of thing.'

'Nothing to the son?' Hillary asked bluntly.

Arthur Baines sighed and leaned back. 'Victor? No. Nothing to Victor I'm afraid.'

'Was the son in the previous will?' Hillary asked cannily, and again the solicitor gave her an appreciative glance.

'He was mentioned in the previous will, yes. He got half, with the rest subdivided as we see here,' he splayed his hands over the documents. 'But just over four years ago, David came in to change it to this.'

'Did you try to dissuade him?'

'Not likely!' Arthur Baines almost snorted. 'I knew better than to try that. David knew his own mind.'

'But you must have had some thoughts on

the matter?' Hillary pressed.

'Well, yes. I assumed there'd been some massive estrangement, obviously. I heard later, in a roundabout sort of way, that the lad had left home after some sort of big flare up. David was radiating disapproval and disappointment I can tell you. But then — Victor was a bit of an odd lad. Not surprising, perhaps, given such a strictly religious and regimented upbringing. Rebellion was almost inevitable I suppose.'

'Yes,' Hillary agreed with a sigh.

'I rather thought that later on, when he got older and more mature, young Victor might make it up with his old man. You know, come to his senses, and see which side his bread was buttered and all that. We usually all do, in the end. Even the rebels.'

'Oh? It was worth having then, his father's estate?' Hillary asked sharply.

'Oh, well, he wasn't worth a fortune, you understand — not by today's standards anyway. But even so, it comes to a tidy sum. His house, even in today's market, will fetch a good figure. Then there's his half of the business — various stocks and bonds and so forth. And the cottage in Tackley, of course. Oh yes, Victor could have expected to get his hands on something close to a million pounds sterling. Maybe a little less after taxes and so on,' he added regretfully. 'David never would countenance anything that smacked of trying to avoid paying the Chancellor of the Exchequer his due. 'Render unto Caesar the things that are Caesar's' he used to quote to me. Made me want to take him by the throat and give him a good shake . . . well, never mind,' he finished hastily.

Hillary gave a brief smile. 'An aggravating man,' she said. 'Do you know what the argument with his son was all about?' she persisted.

'No. And he wouldn't have discussed it with me even if I'd asked. Which I assure you, I didn't. He guarded his reputation keenly, you see. He wouldn't want strangers to notice his family's dirty laundry.'

Hillary nodded. 'Are you aware of any enemies he might have had, Mr Baines?'

'Oh no.'

'Did he ever speak to you of someone making threats, perhaps? Poison pen letters, nasty phone calls, stalking, anything like that?'

'No.'

'I see. And is there anything you can add that you think might be relevant to our inquiry?'

'I'm afraid not, Inspector. If there was, believe me, I would tell you. Like I said, I might not have liked David all that much, but he was a man who did a lot of good. And in death, too, a lot of people will benefit from his generosity. He didn't deserve to be killed, Inspector.'

Hillary couldn't have agreed with him more. 'Well, thank you, sir. If anything comes up, we'll get back in touch. Oh, do you have an address for Victor Merchant?'

'No, well, not an address. But I heard that he was living in a council house in Cowley somewhere. Up near the big round-about I think.'

Hillary caught Gemma's eye, who nodded back.

They took their farewells of the solicitor and, once back in the car, Gemma opened up her laptop and busily tapped some keys.

'This must be him. Victor Timothy Merchant — an address near The Grates, I think. I've got an aunt who lives over that way. I should be able to find it.'

'OK. 'Lead on McDuff',' Hillary said wryly.

Gemma filed the quote in her memory and vowed to ask Guy what it meant when she got home that night. He was bound to know.

★ ★ ★

The council house semi had, in fact, been turned into four tiny housing association flats. The massive car plants that had once made Cowley famous still produced the odd Mini or two, but there was no hint of industry or prosperity at 13B. The house was grey pebble-dash, the windows single-glazed and pitted with rust. The tiny patch of front garden consisted mainly of dead grass and parked, disreputable-looking bicycles.

Gemma detected the acrid stench of dog mess and wrinkled her nose as they walked up the cracked concrete path.

'If the old man was worth nearly a million, the son was certainly on his uppers.' Hillary echoed her sergeant's thoughts as she rang the bell to flat 13B. Suspecting that it was broken, she rapped hard on the front door.

A timid Indian woman, dressed in a gorgeous lime-green sari, came from one of the bottom floor flats and let them in. She seemed to speak no English, and merely stared at their ID cards blankly. Gemma glanced at the two doors, marked 13, and 13A and said, 'It must be on the upper floor, guv.'

Hillary, smiling a reassurance at the Indian woman, climbed the stairs behind her sergeant. As the woman returned to one of the bottom flats, she heard a child wail.

How many rooms could there be in a quarter of a council semi, she wondered? And how many people could you really ask to fit into one? The answer made her shudder.

Although she lived on a narrow boat, where space was also limited and — well, narrow — she'd never felt claustrophobic, as she was beginning to feel now.

At 13B, Gemma rapped briskly on the door.

After a long moment, they heard the sound of someone fumbling with the doorchain, and then a tousled blonde head peeked through the gap.

The woman couldn't have been more than five feet four. On spotting the two police cards held up towards her, she held open the door for them, and both policewomen were struck at once by the colourful effect the woman radiated.

'Oh, rozzers! Nice to be wanted, as they say. Better come in then, before you cause a stir with the neighbours. You'll be hearing toilets flush all down the street when word gets around you're here!'

Hillary didn't doubt that a lot of cannabis would be flushed, but it didn't bother her.

The little peacock of a woman in front of her spoke in a high, little-girl pitch, but her smile was wide and seemed genuinely amused. Hillary could see at once that she'd had a lot of work done on her teeth, which were too shiny, white and aligned, not to have been capped.

'Better come in. This is it, I'm afraid.' The room she showed them into had obviously once been the house's main bedroom. A sofa pushed to one wall obviously pulled out into a bed. A dog-leg partition probably concealed a shower cubicle with no room to swing even the tiniest of cats and a cramped loo, whilst a two-ring gas burner and an old-fashioned sink over by the single window made pretence of being a kitchen.

'Take a pew,' the woman said. She was dressed in high-heeled, pale-pink mule slippers, with a cheery nest of silvered feathers on the uppers. She was wearing bright turquoise leggings that clung to fairly muscular-looking calves, and a pink flounced tutu-like skirt that perfectly matched the slippers in shade. On her skinny chest resided a T-shirt with a sequinned rainbow taking up much of the material, and her smooth bare arms ended in a pair of long, silk, cream-coloured gloves — the kind worn by movie stars in the 40s and 50s. Around her neck she had wound and wound a mass of chiffon scarves in all the colours of the rainbow. They completely hid her neck and

131

cascaded over her front, no doubt in an effort to draw the eye away from the paucity of her breasts.

She had a large mass of blonde hair, in a style that Farah Fawcett had once made famous so many moons ago, and her make-up was as bright and garish as her clothes would lead you to expect.

'Had a good look, have you? By the way, my name's Vickki. With two ks and an i. And I don't mind you looking, by the way. That's my thing see — I'm a fashion designer.'

Gemma, who still hadn't stopped blinking, would have bet her last penny that no fashion house had ever bought one of Vickki's creations. Not unless they were colour blind.

'We were told Mr Victor Merchant lived here,' Hillary said, and Vickki nodded amiably, yawning widely then heading over to the gas rings, where she filled a battered kettle.

'Timbo? Right, right. He does live here. Well, sort of. When he isn't camping out somewhere, or dossing down at a friend's place, or gracing the local YMCA with his presence.'

'I take it Mr Merchant isn't here now?' Hillary asked drily. It had probably been too much to ask for.

'Timbo hasn't been here for nearly a week.

132

I started calling him Tim when we first met, because, let's face it, you can't be a couple and be called Victor and Vickki, can you? I mean, Vic and Vik? Victor and Victoria? It's just too . . . ' And she pantomimed sticking two fingers down her throat and being sick. 'But he didn't like Timothy, or Tim either, so I call him Timbo. Mind you I'm the only one who does, but I like that. It makes me special, you know?'

Gemma, sensing the lack of self esteem behind this remark, wondered just how many girlfriends Timbo had, and whether he liked them *en masse*. He'd certainly done something to make this weird little woman want to stand out from the crowd.

Hillary glanced around the room, trying to figure out what was 'off'. Something was pinging her radar, but she couldn't seem to place it.

'What does Timbo do?' she asked casually. 'From the way you talk about him, it doesn't sound as if he has a regular job.'

'Oh no. He's creative, like me. Only with Timbo it's photography. He likes to think he's gonna be the next David Bailey. Whoever the hell he is.'

'A famous photographer who made his name in the sixties,' Hillary responded automatically, and saw the blonde head turn

133

her way. Big baby-blue eyes regarded her with a steady, unimpressed gaze.

'Oh right. Well, whatever. Timbo's got his first gallery show next month — a little bastion of the arts in the metropolis that is Witney. Anyway, he's all in a lather about it 'cause he reckons some big-wig critics and art-writers from London might show up, and he wants to put together his best work. Reckons the muses will be kinder to him if he suffers for his art, so he sods off, in all weathers, hitch-hiking around the country and taking pictures of whatever he sees that takes his fancy. Silly sod will probably come back with pneumonia and shots of a foggy motorway service station. Still, it keeps him happy. And out from under my feet. As you can see, there ain't a lot of room here.'

That was an understatement, Hillary thought. Every inch of wall space was taken up with pastel drawings of clothes and accessories, whilst textiles piled up in every corner. There was not, Hillary noticed, a single photograph on display. Obviously Timbo deferred to Vickki's creative efforts when it came to decorating the home.

Which begged an obvious question. 'Has he got a studio somewhere, Vickki?'

'Huh? That's a laugh. Can't afford a studio. Besides, you don't need all those smelly chemicals and stuff and a dark room and what have you nowadays. Ever heard of digital?'

She made her coffee and brought it back towards them. It had either not occurred to her to ask them if they wanted one, or she was putting on a show of how little the law intimidated her. Or maybe, Hillary thought, she simply couldn't afford to give away such precious resources as sugar, milk and coffee.

'All he needs is access to a computer and paper. And he's got a friend who does all that for him. Does the framing, too, I think.'

'His name and address?' Gemma asked briskly, pen poised over her notepad.

'Sorry, luv, no idea. You know, you've got the figure for a model. Tall and beanpole thin. Nice hair too. Pity about the voice. I mean, just because you wouldn't get to use it,' she added hastily. 'Models are seen not heard, and that gravelly voice sounds so great, it would be a pity. You ever think of doing voice-overs for commercials?'

'I've already got a job, thanks,' Gemma said wryly, and Vickki shrugged her coat-hanger thin shoulders.

'Suit yourself.' She sat down on the sofa and crossed her turquoise-clad legs. She blew delicately on her coffee, the outlandish, cream silk gloves giving her a curiously vulnerable, and somehow ridiculously glamorous look.

She certainly had style, Hillary thought. But what kind? She had the feeling that the woman used it to hide behind. It seemed to her to be more of a disguise than a statement.

She gave a mental head shake, refusing to let her curiosity get the better of her. She was here for information about David Merchant and his son. 'So, how long have you and Timbo been together?' she asked casually.

'Oh heck! Nearly three years now,' Vickki said, surprising both the older women. Hillary, for some reason, had assumed that the relationship was fairly recent, and Gemma simply couldn't understand how any man could put up with a woman like this for that amount of time.

'I see. So, have you met his family?' Hillary asked cunningly.

'Hasn't got any. Not really,' Vickki said promptly. 'His mum had died not long before I met him, and he was still cut up about it. He hasn't got any brothers or sisters, and if he has any aunts, uncles or assorted cousins, he hasn't mentioned them.'

'What about his father?'

'Oh, him! The Saint. No, Timbo said he was going to keep us well apart. He said I'd probably give the old man a heart attack. Then he'd laugh, and say maybe that wasn't

136

such a bad idea, and he'd hold me back as a final resort.' Vickki's girlish giggle suddenly split the air. 'Cheek! Still, from what he said, the old man was someone it was better to avoid, so I didn't mind.'

'No love lost between them then?' Hillary asked, and Vickki frowned over her coffee cup.

'Here, why all the questions? I mean, Timbo isn't in any real trouble, is he?' There was genuine nervousness in the voice now, but Hillary wondered why it had taken her so long to get around to asking what should have been an obvious question.

But then, the girl seemed to be incredibly self-absorbed.

'So you never met David Merchant?' She ignored the appeal for information, and smiled brightly.

'No.'

'You never went to his house?'

'No.'

'Would you know him if you saw him? I mean, did Timbo have a photograph of him?'

'No. Only of his mum. He always said she died just to get away from the old man. Divorce being so out of the question and all. Timbo said he just wore her down and wore her down until she became a splodge and died. That was when he was drunk, mind. He gets a bit maudlin and silly when he's had a few.'

Gemma made a note. Young Timbo sounded like a very bitter man to her.

'Do you have his mobile number?' Hillary asked, and wasn't surprised when Vickki instantly shook her head.

'No. He doesn't take it with him when he's out 'looking for inspiration'. Besides, he can't afford to top it up until he sells something at this gallery showing. Like I said, he tends to cadge a lot.'

Hillary got the sense that the young man was more like a vagrant, seeking hand-outs from charities and relying on the kindness of strangers. It seemed a weird way for him to live. The bedsit might not be much, but it was warm, dry and even came complete with a bed partner.

Hillary suddenly wished that she had some of Victor Merchant's photographs to look at. She had a feeling they would either be very very good or very very bad.

'Do you have any idea where he might be on a certain day? Doesn't he arrange to phone you or anything like that?' she persisted.

'No. Well, he phones, of course, from time to time, but I never know when. And he probably wouldn't tell me where he was if I asked him. He gets very protective of his solitude when he's in an artistic mood,' Vickki said flatly. She was beginning to look and sound resentful now. 'Look, what's going on?'

'Timbo's father is dead,' Hillary said flatly. 'He was murdered at his home yesterday.'

'Oh shit.'

'So you see, we need to contact him.'

'Yeah. Yeah, I get you. But honestly, I don't see how it can be done. I mean, when he next phones, of course I'll tell him to get his arse right back here, but that's all I can do. I swear. And he might not ring for ages.'

Hillary nodded, getting to her feet. 'Well, do what you can. We need Mr Merchant to tell us all that he can about his father.'

'Well, I doubt if he can be of that much help,' Vickki objected, rising with her. 'You know he hasn't seen or spoken to the old man in years.'

'Yes. Do you know what the rift was about?'

'Not really. Timbo just said that he couldn't stand living with the joylessness of the man any more and, as soon as he was old enough to stand on his own two feet, he legged it.'

Hillary sighed. 'Well, somebody hated his father enough to kill and set fire to him.'

'*What!!!*' Vickki squeaked, and beneath the

layers of her make-up, Hillary saw her go suddenly ashen-pale. 'What do you mean? Did his house catch fire?'

Hillary looked at her closely. Was she worried that her boyfriend's inheritance had gone up in flames? Did she not know that Timbo wouldn't be inheriting the house anyway, under the terms of his father's will? Or was she just genuinely shocked at the amount of brutality that a burnt corpse indicated?

Vickki's pupils contracted abruptly, and Hillary was convinced of her genuine shock. 'I'm sorry,' she said softly. 'I shouldn't have just sprung it on you like that. Do you want to sit down? Have you got a friend we can call?'

'Huh. What? No, no, I'm fine. It's just . . . it's so horrible.' The little girlish voice did nothing to detract from the simplicity of the words, and Hillary nodded.

'Yes. I know. Well, here's my card.' She was deliberately brisk, forcing the little blonde to become the same.

'Oh, right.' Vickki nodded determinedly and took the square of paper. Her hands though, in those ridiculous gloves, trembled visibly.

'When Timbo calls, tell him to call me immediately. And tell him that he must come home,' Hillary reiterated firmly. 'It's vital that we interview him.'

'Yeah, OK,' Vickki said faintly.

It was only when they got outside that Hillary realized that they hadn't got Vickki's last name. She shrugged, knowing she would probably be interviewing the brightly plum-aged girl again soon. She would get it then.

★ ★ ★

In the car, Gemma checked her phone and frowned at a text message. 'Guv, you mind if I make a quick call home?' she asked rhetorically, already climbing back out of the car.

'Of course not.'

Hillary watched her sergeant dial and then pace, talk, look surprised, briefly concerned, then talk and pace some more. When she returned to the car, she looked faintly nonplussed.

'Not bad news I hope?' Hillary asked.

'No. Well . . . no. Sort of. Just mainly . . . weird,' Gemma said, rather confusingly. Then she shrugged and turned on the ignition, let off the handbrake, put the car into gear and checked the mirrors.

But she drove almost mechanically.

What Guy had just told her was distinctly

unexpected and she just wasn't sure what to make of it.

Apparently, his cousin, Miles, and his only son, Matthew, had been killed in a boating accident in Switzerland. There was nothing particularly weird about that of course — people died in accidents all the time. And Guy barely knew either of them, so, although it was sad, in that vague way it always is sad when you find out that distant relations have died, it wasn't in any way a personal catastrophe.

But in this case there was more to it than that. For Miles was the family baron, and his son, Matthew, the next in line. With both gone, the title now went to the second son of the original line, which meant Guy.

Guy was now Guy, Lord Brindley.

And since he'd asked her to marry him last week, and this time she'd finally said yes, it meant that, once the wedding had taken place, she'd be Lady Brindley.

And just what the hell she was supposed to make of that, Gemma Fordham had no idea.

6

Godfrey Purbright lived up to the image Keith had conjured up for him on hearing his given name — a man with silver hair, dressed in an impeccable dark-blue suit, and wearing half-moon glasses. His office, however, was thoroughly modern and, far from sounding dry and dusty, he had a robust voice and manner.

'So, young Gavin, are you going to sue the prison authorities?' was his first sentence after greeting them, and shaking hands with both the young men in his office. The way he eyed Keith briefly and without surprise told the young police officer that Gavin had already warned him he'd be bringing him along. And that he was also aware of his client's sexual orientation seemed certain.

'I'm not sure,' Gavin said, with surprise. 'I hadn't thought about it. Do we have a case?' he added curiously.

'For lack of adequate supervision?' Purbright said thoughtfully. 'I don't see why not. We could ask why he wasn't on suicide watch. And he complained to me several times about being the target for bullying. Did he speak to you about it?'

'Yes,' Gavin said tersely. 'There was one thug in particular who had it in for him. He said the guards deliberately turned a blind eye,' he added bitterly.

Beside him, Keith stirred uneasily in his seat. He felt very much as if he were batting for the opposite side here, and although he didn't like to hear prison officers maligned, he didn't doubt either that there might be some truth in the allegations. He wished he hadn't let Gavin persuade him to come. He'd tried to point out that it was very much a family matter and, since they were bound to discuss financial matters, a private matter as well.

Gavin's response had been short and to the point. Keith was his lover, which made him family. And money wasn't going to be allowed to come between them — that had been firmly established at the very beginning of their relationship. Keith, being working class, had thought it would be easier said than done, but he'd been surprised by how little Gavin's wealth had really affected him. He never let Gavin buy him the really big stuff, like cars or expensive jewellery or what have you. And Gavin, for the most part, pretended Keith's relative poverty simply didn't exist.

Now Godfrey Purbright sighed gently. 'Well, I think it's an avenue we should at least explore. The compensation won't bring back your father of course, but it might teach the authorities to be a bit more careful of their inmates in future.'

Keith very much doubted it, but wisely kept his mouth shut.

'Well, I don't want to get caught up in a long and expensive court case,' Gavin said flatly. 'Not now. Prepare a report and then I'll decide.'

Godfrey nodded. 'Very wise. Now, funeral arrangements. You're aware of course, that there has been a full post-mortem and that there'll almost certainly be an inquiry. But I think you could count on burying your father soon.'

Gavin nodded grimly.

'Now, as to his will . . . ' He paused and looked at Keith pointedly. The red-headed young man flushed, again wishing himself a million miles away.

'Look, it's not my idea to be here,' he began, then subsided as Gavin reached out and took his hand, effectively silencing him.

'Just the gist, please, Godfrey. My father discussed the will with me when I was eighteen. I take it that it hasn't been altered significantly since then?'

'No,' Purbright agreed, and spent the next half an hour going meticulously over Sir

Reginald's assets, tax liabilities, and several complicated issues concerning bonds and interest rates that went totally over Keith's head. Gavin, though, seemed to understand it all. And that, thought Keith with a flash of resentful amusement, summed up the difference between them in a nutshell.

It was dark by the time they left the solicitor's office and drove to Gavin's apartment on the river. The view across the Thames was spectacular and, as always, it lifted Keith's heart. London, at night. The lights, the traffic, the buzz. He missed it all. The thought of going back to Oxford tomorrow made him feel depressed, and that worried him.

They were in the middle of a particularly nasty murder case. He knew Hillary and the rest of the team would be frantically busy, being a man down. And Chang was still so wet-behind-the-ears, who knew what use he'd be? He should be feeling the rush to get back, or, at the very least, guilt about not being there.

He heard a sizzling noise, and turned to see Gavin cooking them a stir-fry for dinner. Mostly vegetables and noodles, he supposed. As a soon-to-be professional athlete, Gavin was very much aware of nutrition and the needs of his body.

As the steam rose over the wok, Gavin

Moreland watched his lover by the window. The lights turned his head a fiery red, and he paced restlessly.

Gavin smiled.

Tonight, he'd begin to work on him in earnest.

★ ★ ★

The next morning, Freddie Dix awoke at his usual time and stumbled downstairs. His dog, Jilly, grey in the muzzle now, climbed laboriously out of her basket and greeted him by thrusting her cold black nose into his palm.

Freddie bent to stroke her dark head and sighed. 'Want a little bite of bacon then, girl?' He set to with the frying pan, cracking in an egg for himself, and an extra rasher for the dog.

He didn't often feed her fried food, mindful of the vet's admonitions, but it was another cold, grey day, and they needed something in their stomachs before their usual morning walk.

Freddie, nearing his seventieth birthday now, lived in a cramped terraced cottage near the big Sainsbury's store, and since his retirement as a television repair man, liked to keep to a routine.

So it was that he and his ageing but willing

dog carefully and slowly tramped their usual two-mile walk that took them to the outskirts of Kidlington, overlooking the village of Hampton Poyle and back again.

The moment they returned to the warm kitchen, Jilly made for her basket and slumped down with a satisfied sigh and Freddie put on the kettle.

Next he collected the paper, the local *Oxford Mail*, and put it on the kitchen table, ready to read once he'd got his cuppa made. After that, he'd prepare his lunch, then settle down in front of the telly to watch the horseracing.

But that morning, his routine was going to be interrupted.

★　★　★

Hillary was at her desk when the phone rang.

'Hey, Hill,' the cheerful, irreverent voice of the desk sergeant rang in her ears. 'Got a live one down here for you, I reckon. I'll put him in interview room two, shall I?'

'Sure, thanks.' She hung up abruptly. Desk sergeants tended to know what cases Hillary was working, and could generally be relied upon to sort the wheat from the chaff.

'Mark, we've got a walk-in. Want to sit in on it?'

Mark Chang did. Hillary's interview techniques were widely acknowledged to be unparalleled.

She trotted down the stairs and into the main hall, nodded a thanks across the room to where the desk sergeant was sorting through the mail, and pushed on through to a long corridor, where the interview rooms led off in rows.

Interview four had an electric light glowing above the lintel, showing that it was in use and, as she opened up the door to room two, she flipped the switch to show that this one, also, was no longer vacant.

She glanced curiously at the man rising from his seat in the centre of the room. A senior citizen, fairly well dressed, with neatly brushed white hair with a slightly yellow tinge, and red cheeks. He'd probably felt the cold air this morning, or so she hoped. The only other explanation for the high colour would be booze, and she didn't particularly want to deal with a drunk this morning.

But the man's first words quickly dispelled any such likelihood.

'Hello. I hope I've done the right thing, coming in like this. Only it was in the morning papers, see, so I thought I'd better come along.'

His voice was clear, as were his slightly

rhuemy blue eyes as they regarded her.

Hillary held out her hand and smiled. 'Thank you, sir. I'm Detective Inspector Hillary Greene. This is Constable Chang.'

Freddie Dix reached hastily for her hand and shook it, somewhat shyly. He glanced uncertainly at Chang and, when Mark held out his hand, shook it also.

'Please, sit down, sir. It's a cold day, isn't it?'

'Yes. Thank you. I've already been for my morning walk, so I'm feeling a bit tired.'

'Thank you then for coming in. Mr . . . er . . . ?'

'Oh. Dix. Sorry, Freddie Dix.'

'Thank you, Mr Dix. Now, what can we do for you?'

'Well, it's about the story in the paper this morning. About a man being killed in Poyle Crescent the day before yesterday. Is it true?'

'Yes, sir, it is. Do you know the man?' she knew Merchant had now been named in the paper, as she'd read the article herself a few hours earlier. It was unusual, since the police as a rule liked to inform the next of kin first, before any public announcement. But given their difficulties in tracing Victor Merchant, Hillary had taken the decision of releasing the victim's name in the hope of shaking loose some vital information.

'Oh, no. Well, I don't think so. I mean, I might have seen him around and known him by sight, but the name didn't mean anything to me,' the old man said. 'It was the address you see. I go by there every day. Well, the end of the road; I don't go into the actual cul-de-sac. Me and Jilly stick to our usual route.'

'Jilly?'

'My sheepdog.'

'I see,' Hillary said, careful not to let her body language change, but instantly felt more alert. 'And you say you walk past the entrance to Poyle Crescent every day? What time would this be, Mr Dix?'

'Oh, I reckon by the time we get there, it must be heading on for between ten or half-past. Depending on how much of a lie-in I have, see?'

'And so you would have been passing Poyle Crescent two days ago at around this time?'

'Yes. But I'm not sure if what I have to say will be any use, because the newspapers only gave the number of the house where the poor man was killed. And I don't know, well, obviously I don't, never having walked up that way, what house relates to what number. Do you see?'

Surprisingly, Hillary did. She reached into her briefcase and withdrew a notebook and from memory, sketched a rough draft of the houses in Poyle Crescent, and numbered them. It wasn't hard, as she'd noticed that the numbers ran in a straight order from 1–10. Mark Chang watched, fascinated.

She put a big X on David Merchant's house, and pushed the paper towards the witness.

'Does this help, Mr Dix?' she asked gently.

'Oh! Yes. So it was the one. I did wonder. She caught my eye, you see. Not just because she was a blonde,' and at this point Freddie Dix's already red face burned a deeper shade. 'I'm a bit partial to blondes, see,' he admitted shyly. 'But really, because she seemed so upset. Well, not upset, she wasn't crying or anything. She seemed more sort of dazed. Anyway, it was this house she came out of,' he said, tapping the notebook page and the big X. 'I'm sure of it.'

Hillary glanced across at Chang to make sure he was getting a note of all this. He was. Nevertheless, Hillary pressed the button of the recorder.

'I think it would be better if we had a verbatim account of this, Mr Dix. I hope you don't mind?'

Freddie stared at the recorder, then shrugged. 'I'm sure it's OK if you say it is.'

Hillary smiled. 'Thank you. Now, let's

make sure we have everything clearly. You were walking past the entrance to Poyle Crescent two mornings ago. That is the 18th. Can you tell me what time this would be?'

'Oh my, no. Not to be accurate. It must have been half an hour either side of ten o'clock though.'

Hillary nodded, not showing by so much as a sigh how such vagueness was less than helpful in establishing her time-line.

'I see. And, as you were passing, you saw someone leaving Mr David Merchant's house. That is, the house marked X on the drawing I've just shown you?'

'Yes.'

'Now, Mr Dix, are you sure she was leaving the house? What was she doing?'

'She was walking down the path and coming through the gate.'

'Did you see her actually coming from the door of the house into the garden?'

'No.'

'Do you remember hearing a door close before you noticed this woman?'

'No.'

'So she might never have been inside? She might have called at the house, rung the bell, got no reply, and been coming back down the path?'

'Yes, she might have,' Freddie said,

scrupulously honest. Hillary nodded encouragement.

'All right, Mr Dix, that's very clear. Now, can you describe this woman?'

'Well, she was blonde, like I said,' Freddie said. 'But I wasn't really paying that much attention to her. I was watching Jilly in case she did . . . you know, poops. I have to clear up after her now you know, or I might get fined.'

Hillary nodded. 'Yes, I know about that. And I'm sure you're a responsible dog-owner. So did this woman pass you?'

'Oh no. She crossed over on to the other side of the cul-de-sac and went up the road from the way we'd just come. By then, me and Jilly were carrying on in the other direction.'

'Could you remember what she was wearing?'

'A raincoat I think. Grey, or beige maybe. She had it tied tight around her. And longish boots. And a hat. It was a cold day, you see. Bright, the sun was shining and everything, but it felt chilly, you know?'

Hillary nodded. 'So you didn't see the colour of her eyes, for instance?'

'Oh no.'

'What about her size?'

'Well, she wasn't tall.'

'And build?'

'Well, sort of thin, I suppose, like girls seem to prefer to be nowadays.'

'Age?'

'Oh, now you're asking me,' Freddie sighed. 'I'm never any good at guessing things like that. It's the same with weights and what have you. I didn't think she was all that old. Not middle-aged anyway. But, like I said, I didn't really get that good a look at her.'

'No. Would you recognize her if you saw her again?' Hillary asked, with very little hope now.

'Oh no. At least, I don't think so.'

Hillary nodded. Then said carefully, 'Did you notice anything else unusual, Mr Dix? Did you notice a really big bonfire, for instance? Did you smell smoke, or see a lot of smoke, or smell something rather unpleasant?'

'Smoke? Yes, I think so. But not much, and it wasn't particularly unpleasant.'

Hillary nodded. She reached for her note-pad and drew a brief map of the area surrounding Poyle Crescent. Then she showed it to him. 'Do you suppose you could point out to me where you walked your dog when you passed the crescent sir?'

Freddie Dix did so, without much hesitation. 'We walk it every day you see. Me and Jilly. Creatures of habit we are.'

'OK. Well, thank you very much, Mr Dix. You've been very helpful. I'll just have your statement typed up and then perhaps you could sign it for us. Mark? Would you like a cup of tea, Mr Dix?'

'Oh thank you, that would be nice.'

Hillary nodded and once again shook the old man's hand. 'Mark, when you've got Mr Dix's statement, perhaps you could run him home.'

'Oh, I can take the bus,' Freddie said, but was clearly glad of the offer.

'No, it's no trouble, Mr Dix, I assure you,' Hillary said.

She left the interview room and returned to her desk, and stared at the sketch in front of her thoughtfully.

The route Freddie Dix and his dog walked took them right past the rear aspect of Poyle Crescent. If the bonfire had been going strong by then, and that awful reek was in the air, there was no way Freddie could have failed to notice it. So the mysterious blonde visitor had probably not set that macabre bonfire in David Merchant's garden. And yet, Freddie *had* smelled smoke, or so he said. But that could be put down to auto-suggestion. Or had there been a second, non-relevant bonfire perhaps?

Had she called and got no answer because

David Merchant was already dead? Or was the blonde a possible accomplice? The description was too vague to be much use. So far the only blonde woman in the case was Vickki with two ks and an i. And she'd denied flatly ever knowing David Merchant or going to his house.

Of course, she could be lying. With Timbo away, had she called around, hoping to broker a peace between father and son? Hillary thought it rather unlikely. The woman she remembered would probably have been too self-absorbed to bother.

Of course, there could be a woman in David Merchant's life. His wife had been dead for a number of years. Naturally, a man such as Merchant had been might not have been engaged in an active sexual relationship. She had a feeling he was not the hypocritical sort. But a widower might want to marry again. Which meant courting. Wooing. A proposal of marriage before legitimizing the sex — all of that. So a woman in his life was not out of the question.

But if that was the case, David Merchant had kept it very much a secret. His neighbours didn't seem to know about it, nor his business partner.

Hillary sighed, and put the mystery blonde to one side, with a big mental question mark over her head, and set to reading the first of the forensic reports.

It was nearly ten o'clock, and still no sign of Keith Barrington. Still, a death in the family meant you couldn't always watch the clock — if there *had* been a death in the family. For some reason, Hillary wasn't sure that she fully believed in her detective constable's excuse.

But when he showed up for work ten minutes later, she quickly revised her opinion. He looked pale, and had a drawn, tense look around his mouth. And his eyes had a certain bleakness to them that instantly tightened her nerves.

'Keith,' she said watching him take a seat. 'Do you want another day?'

'What? Oh, no, guv. No, there's no point. It's all happening in London, anyway. So, what do you want me to do?'

Hillary thought for a moment, then said, 'Gemma's got stacks of paperwork to go through. Help her sort through it.' She glanced across at her sergeant's empty desk, wondering where she was and what she was doing, but having no doubts that whatever it was, it would be relevant.

'Grab a handful and get stuck in,' she added, nodding at the piles on her sergeant's desk.

'Guv,' Keith sighed, and set to work. It didn't take him long to come across various correspondence from a firm of solicitors dealing with some issue for him, but he supposed that Hillary would probably have already talked to them. It was one of the first things she did.

Realizing that he needed to consult the murder book before he went any further, he retrieved the file which, as he suspected, Gemma had purloined for herself. One of the most vital jobs in any investigation was to keep a file fully updated with everyone's movements, discoveries, thoughts and inter-view notes. This meant that any one of the team could go through it and get an overall view of the case.

He read Chang's statements first, feeling a flash of guilty relief that the oriental youngster hadn't seemed to turn up anything vital. Gemma's notes were as terse and to the point as the ass-kicking sergeant herself. Hillary's were more detailed, thought-provoking, and helpful.

As he'd thought, she'd already talked to the solicitors . . . 'Hang on!' he said out loud, searched through the paperwork he'd been studying, then whistled. It wasn't the same firm.

'Something?' Hillary asked briskly.

'Guv, I've come across paperwork from another legal firm — not the one you talked to about his will. This is an outfit in Bicester.'

Hillary frowned. It was fairly unusual for a small businessman to having dealings with more than one legal firm. 'Then find out what it's all about and see if it helps us on,' she said, and Keith, happy to get out of the office, grabbed the file and was gone.

★ ★ ★

Gemma cruised the narrow streets, looking for a parking spot/ and finally spotted a lumbering station wagon pulling out a few hundred yards ahead of her. Speedily she nipped forward and parked her little hatchback at first attempt, making a Mondeo, coming in the opposite direction toot angrily.

Gemma gave him a smile and the finger. He might have seen it first, but she was quicker.

The driver shook his head and sorrowfully carried on cruising. She got out, locked the car, and back-tracked down the road to the Mayflowers Gallery.

It was a small shop, wedged oddly into a terrace of mostly houses. Only a small pet shop three doors down and a Pound-a-Go shop at the end told her that some hardy souls still dabbled a toe in commercial enterprise in this rather downbeat area of Witney.

Gemma stared at the gallery, wondering at the title. Mayflower in the singular might have referred to the ship that had carried some of North America's first settlers across the Atlantic. But Mayflowers plural? Perhaps it specialized in selling botanical prints. But when she pushed open the door and went inside, that notion was quickly dispelled.

Mostly modern abstracts lined the off-white walls, whilst one or two cleverly spot-lit bronze sculptures were scattered about the floor. A woman came out of the back room, and Gemma assumed she'd set off some hidden alarm, indicating that the front door had been opened.

It was an odd sort of place — it didn't seem to be either one thing or another. The single plate-glass window was spotlessly clean, as was the slightly grey-shaded old wooden floors. So it wasn't exactly grubby or down at heel. But it didn't seem to ooze wealth either. It seemed more functional than anything else, which rather confused her perceptions of what an art gallery should be.

'Are you just looking? Or are you interested in something particular?' the woman who spoke was somewhere in her mid-fifties, with blonde hair that was turning to silver. Her figure was just starting to run to fat, but she disguised it in a rather clever, black pants suit. Her eyes were dark chocolate brown, but her mouth had a pinched look.

'I'm looking for the owner?'

'That would be me. Mary Wainwright.'

Gemma flashed her badge, and the older woman began to look distinctly wary.

'Yes, er, Sergeant Fordham. I hope there's nothing wrong.'

'No, madam. Just routine inquiries. I believe you accept and sell work on behalf of an artist called Whyte. Francis Whyte?'

'Yes.'

The syllable made Gemma smile. So it was going to be one of those interviews was it?

'Popular as an artist, is he?'

'Well, that depends,' Mary Wainwright said carefully.

'On?' Gemma persisted with a tight smile.

'Well, he sells a lot of canvases, but not for a lot of money.'

Gemma tried to sort that out, and couldn't. She was hopelessly lost in this world, but wasn't about to show it.

'And how does that come about, Miss Wainwright?'

'Mrs,' Mary Wainwright said quickly. Then added slowly, 'You see, some artists become famous, and their works can sell for large sums. Some good artists build up a body of work over the years, which gradually acquires admirers, and their work can sell solidly, if not so spectacularly. And then there are those artists like Frank.'

'Let me guess. His canvases aren't worth the cost of the paint?'

Mrs Wainwright smiled briefly. 'Hardly that, Sergeant, no. Or he wouldn't be represented here. As I said, he sells a lot of canvases, but almost exclusively to interior designers. Nowadays, those with money but no taste hire designers to decorate their houses, and those designers need original works of art for their finishing touches, but ones that won't break the bank. Frank Whyte has become something of a favourite of theirs. His canvases are colourful, bold, and often go with the 'in' colour schemes of the moment. I sold one of his just yesterday — a large, gouache painting of hollyhocks. 'Pastel heaven' as the interior designer who bought it described it. It was perfectly professionally painted, pleasant, and inoffensive. The owners of whatever house it went to will probably keep it for as long as they keep their colour scheme — probably until sometime next spring — then donate it to a charity shop. The interior decorator bought it for fifty quid.'

Gemma nodded. 'So Frank's a bit of a factory worker — churns them out, you sell them, everyone's happy.'

'Yes. Except, I imagine, it takes a fair amount of time and patience to paint as many canvases as he does. And at only fifty quid a pop — less my commission, of course — well, you can work it out for yourself.'

Gemma could. 'Constantly short of cash, is he?'

'Constantly,' Mary Wainwright confirmed.

Gemma nodded. 'You ever hear him complain about his landlord?'

'No.'

'Did he ever say that he was having trouble paying the rent?'

'No.'

'Did he confide in you that he was thinking of doing a moonlight flit, and leaving his rent in arrears?'

'No.'

Gemma smiled tightly again, thanked her and left. In her car she wrote up her notes, and wondered if the gallery owner would have answered her with so many monosyllables if she'd introduced herself as Lady Brindley.

Somehow Gemma didn't think so.

★ ★ ★

164

Keith parked up in the car-park behind a small Tesco's and walked a narrow alleyway into Sheep Street. He wasn't ~~exactly~~ sure at which end of it he'd find Linfield & Combs, but finally located it not far from a grand, cream-painted hotel overlooking a mini-roundabout.

On the bottom floor was a range of small shops, but the legal firm rented a few rooms over the top, overlooking the centuries-old market-place. The woman who rose from behind a desk after he'd climbed the stairs and pushed through into the over-heated interior eyed him warily, even after he'd shown her his identity card.

'I need to talk to Mr Linfield. It's about a client of his, a Mr David Merchant.'

'I see. I'll just check that he's available,' she said blandly. She was one of those slender brunettes who could be any age between late twenties to early fifties. She left the room, rather than use the intercom, where her boss's replies would be overheard, and returned a minute or so later. 'He can only give you ten minutes or so, Constable,' she said primly. 'He's seeing a client at eleven fifteen.'

Keith nodded briefly. He'd take as long as he damned well needed, he thought mulishly.

But the man who rose from behind a

commonplace pine desk had a wide smile and a friendly manner, and Keith felt his hackles being smoothed down.

'Constable Barrington. Please, have a seat. How can I help you?'

He was perhaps forty, dressed in shirt-sleeves, with the cuffs rolled up to expose slightly hairy wrists. A clever cut made the most of his mouse-brown hair and rather small, unspectacular features. 'Robert Linfield, by the way. It's my father's name on the lintel, but he's sort of semi-retired.'

'Ah. It may be your father that I need, sir. Does the name of Mr David Merchant ring any bells?'

'Oh my, yes. And you're right, it was my father who set up the original trust fund for Mr Merchant's parents, but I'm fully conversant with it. My father gave me a full year of briefings before he was finally persuaded by my mother to move to Spain.'

Keith blinked. 'Trust fund? Mr Merchant's parents you say?'

'Yes. They set up a trust fund when in their late seventies for any offspring of their only child, David. They were very happy when he chose the family publishing firm as a career, apparently, but they weren't entirely convinced of its ability to provide a healthy, steady income. My father assured me that in this they were mistaken, as I understand Mr Merchant's publishing firm is a solid little business. But the senior Merchants had made a fair sum in their lifetime with several shoe factories on the side — now of course, long since sold — and they wanted to ensure the financial future of any grandchildren they might accrue.'

'I see,' Keith said. 'So, this trust fund? Can you tell me anything about it?'

'May I ask why you want to know, Constable?'

'I'm afraid Mr David Merchant was found murdered in his house two days ago, sir. We're currently going through his paperwork as you can imagine, and came across some correspondence from this firm.'

'Oh my, that's terrible.'

'Yes sir. The trust fund?'

'Well, there was nothing really all that remarkable about it. The senior Merchants set aside a lump sum of nearly ninety thousand pounds, to be divided equally between any offspring of David Merchant and his wife, when they reached the age of twenty-five. Yes, I know twenty-one is considered more the norm, but the Merchants were very careful characters. My father called them old-fashioned, even for the times. This would have been back in, let me think

— oh must be the mid-1970s.'

'I see. Mr Merchant has only the one son, I believe.'

'Yes.'

Keith wasn't sure of the son's age, and wished he'd paid more attention to the murder book, or at least stayed to take more preliminary notes.

'So he will inherit a considerable sum?'

'Well, first my father, and then myself, have carefully invested it over the years. The Merchants were adamant that it must be invested via perfectly safe methods — Government bonds, National Savings Certificates, that sort of thing. So we haven't really been able to do anything really clever with it. But good solid steady returns over nearly thirty years mounts up. I don't think, you know, Constable, that I can really go into details without the consent of Mr Victor Merchant.'

'No,' Keith said gloomily. And was amazed he'd got as much out of the solicitor as he had. Then he remembered reading that Hillary was having trouble locating the wayward son and heir, and asked hopefully, 'I don't suppose you have contact numbers for him?'

But the only number he had was for the same mobile phone that Victor Merchant had presumably left behind in his tiny bedsit.

'Well, if you can think of anything relevant, sir, perhaps you'd let me know,' Keith said, leaving his card.

Robert Linfield took the card and promised that he would. Only after Keith had left, did his friendly smile fade.

He sat down in his chair, tapping his fingers thoughtfully on the desk top, then left to enter a small room, dedicated to filing cabinets, and drew out one drawer and retrieved a folder.

For fully ten minutes he studied the Merchant Trust Fund, his scowl turning thoughtful. His secretary buzzed him that his 11.15 appointment was waiting, but he told her he'd be another five minutes.

He read the latest angry correspondence from Victor Merchant, that had been forwarded to him from the Reverend Michael Crabtree, one of the three trustees named by the senior Merchants. The reverend must be in his late seventies, maybe even early eighties by now, Linfield mused.

He sighed.

This was going to get complicated. And maybe, who knows, incredibly messy as well.

He could sense trouble ahead.

Once he'd seen his 11.15, he'd better telephone all the trustees and call an emergency meeting. Now that David Merchant was dead, the situation had altered somewhat. In fact, rather more than somewhat.

★ ★ ★

'You know, walk-ins are rather like buses, Hill, you ever notice that?'

The voice that greeted her after she lifted up the receiver of her ringing phone sounded familiarly cheerful.

'Sarge,' she said crisply, recognizing the desk sergeant's sense of humour, as well as his voice.

'Wait hours for one, and nothing, then two come in all at once.' He finished the classic joke, and added, 'I've put this one in interview room four. Sorry about that,' he added cryptically, and rung off.

Hillary sighed, collected Chang, who'd just finished entering Freddie Dix's interview to the murder book, and trotted back downstairs.

She understood the reason for the desk sergeant's apology the moment she opened the door to number four. The room reeked of disinfectant. Probably the last interviewee had been sick in here — or worse — and the cleaning crew had only just finished clearing

170

up the mess. Her eyes stung with the residual blast of ammonia as she pushed open the door.

'Sorry about the smell, sir,' she said automatically, to the man who was sitting in one of the chairs.

'It's not too bad once you get used to it,' he responded, amiably enough. He was a middle-aged man, dressed casually and sporting a largely padded frame comfortably. He could have been a taxi-driver or short-order chef. He had that easy air of someone who dealt constantly with the public.

'Stan Collins.' He half rose and Hillary walked forward to shake his hand.

'Detective Inspector Greene, Constable Chang.'

'It's about David Merchant. The man in the papers who was killed the other day.'

'Yes, sir?'

'It was me day off — I drive the bus route to London from Gloucester Green.' He named Oxford's bus station. 'Anyway, I was just walking down to my local, and that takes me past the end of Poyle Crescent.'

Hillary had already set the tape recorder going, and interrupted briefly, 'This was the morning of the 18th?'

Collins thought about it, then nodded.

'Yes. I usually have Sundays off, but this time I swapped with Geoff. Yes, that's right. Not yesterday morning, the morning before.'

'And what time would this be?'

'About half eleven or so. The pub opens earlier, but I try to get there for twelvish.'

'I see. Please go on.'

'Well, I noticed there was a fire going in this garden where I had to pass by on the pavement. Bit of a stink it was starting to give off, too.'

'Yes,' Hillary agreed, feeling her stomach tighten with excitement.

'Well, as I was going past the end of the road, I saw this bloke running along in front of me. I thought it a bit odd, because he wasn't really a jogger like. You know, them prats who dress up in running togs and what not? He was just dressed ordinary, and he didn't really look the type to run. You know; he wasn't co-ordinated the way they usually are.'

Hillary knew what he meant. 'He just looked like an average Joe who for some reason was running?'

'Right.'

'Can you describe him?'

'Only from the back,' he said disappointingly, and Hillary bit back a groan.

'Well, do your best sir.'

'OK. Well, he was a bit taller than me, and thin. Had sort of longish pale hair. He was wearing a long dark coat — it was a cold day but bright. That's it, really.'

Hillary sighed. 'Did you see where this man came from? What house?'

'No. Only that he came out of the cul-de-sac. You know, where that chap was killed. I'm sure of that.'

Hillary took him through it in some detail, but at the end of it, didn't have much more to go on.

She thanked Stan Collins for his help, made sure Chang had his contact details and let him go.

'All right, Mark. Your next task. Call back at all the houses on Poyle Crescent and find out if anyone had a visitor fitting Collins's description the day of the murder or any other day. Find out if any of them know of anyone fitting the description. Or if they'd seen this man calling on David Merchant before.'

'Guv.'

When she went back upstairs, Keith was back. He told her about the meeting, and she nodded, telling him to add it to the murder book.

So it looked as if Victor Merchant was about to come into some money from his grandparents soon. There went a perfectly good motive down the drain. He certainly didn't need to murder his old man to get an inheritance.

'When you've finished that, find out just how old Victor Merchant is, will you?' she called across to Barrington, who nodded wordlessly.

Hillary looked at him for a few moments, and sighed. Something was definitely wrong there. At some point she'd have to find time to take him aside and find out exactly what it was.

But, right now, she had a particularly nasty murder to solve.

7

Hillary leaned back in her chair and rubbed a hand ruefully through her hair. It was getting too long again, and would soon have to be cut. Luckily, she'd been going to the same hairdressers in Summertown for decades, and they knew how to maintain her chestnut hair in the neat near-pageboy bob she preferred. Six good brush strokes through it every morning and it behaved itself — well, nearly — for the rest of the day. Now *that* was what she considered a decent haircut.

She sighed, and let her mind wander over what they had so far.

The second witness's description of the man seen leaving the cul-de-sac where David Merchant had died vaguely fitted that of the artist, Francis Whyte, of course. That had stuck out immediately. But the trouble with that was, there were plenty of lanky blond men in Oxfordshire. And her witness hadn't sounded all that enthusiastic about being able to identify him, and she wasn't sure of a result if they hauled Whyte in for a line-up. And, as a general rule, she preferred to be at least reasonably confident before she set up an identity parade.

Still, she made a mental note to do the follow-up interview with Whyte herself within the next day or two, although she couldn't as yet, see any realistic motive as to why the painter would want his landlord dead. Even if he was about to be evicted, she was sure in her own mind that Frank Whyte's blasé dismissal of such a possibility was genuine. People like him were natural drifters anyway. It was not as if he was about to be turfed out of a beloved home of many years.

Personal animosity seemed unlikely as well. As devout and evangelical as their murder victim may have been, a man like Whyte was far more likely to laugh or shrug his shoulders at the man and his preachings, surely? Even if he had been needled by Merchant, he was hardly likely to hit him over the head and set light to him!

Unless, of course, the victim had found some sort of vulnerable spot that had caught the artist very much on the raw. Hillary sighed. Too much theorizing gave her a headache.

For the moment, she put Francis Whyte to one side.

Could this be a religious or hate crime? Granted, Christians weren't exactly perse-cuted any more or thrown to the lions, but could their victim have got on the wrong side of another religious zealot who didn't share his particular brand of doctrine?

Hillary shuddered. She hoped not. The last thing they needed was some sort of hate, race, or religious flare-up. But it would have to be considered.

She made a mental note to keep a look-out for any signs of it as the case continued, but she wasn't really all that worried. In her experience, hate crimes were usually accompanied by graffiti or messages of some kind. Usually, the perpetrator wanted the whole world to know why so-and-so had been targeted, and what their sins/crimes were.

No, this smacked of the distinctly personal to her. Although she was more than willing to admit that whoever had done this deed had been filled with hate and rage at the time. The burning of the victim's most prized possessions reeked of that.

What else?

The visit — or, to be more precise, the maybe visit — of the mystery blonde woman.

'Still no sign of a woman in the vic's life, Gemma?' she asked her sergeant, who was busy typing up her notes and findings.

Gemma looked across at Hillary from her keyboard and shook her head. 'No, guv. We didn't really expect one, did we?'

'Oh I don't know. He's been widowed long enough for it be considered a 'respectable' amount of time,' she pointed out. 'And to a man like our vic, that would have been important.'

Gemma smiled. 'It's been my experience, guv, that the more holier-than-thou a person is, the more likely he is to be up to no good.'

Hillary smiled briefly. 'You and the Jesuits should sit down and have a conversation some day,' she said drily. 'But I think, in this case, we might be in danger of thinking in clichés. Not all religiously devout people have to be hiding hypocrisy. At least, from what I can tell, our vic practised what he preached.'

Gemma grunted. 'Well, if there was a woman in his life, I can't find hide nor hair of her.'

Hillary sighed and glanced out of the window. It would be dark soon. Spring still seemed a long way off, although she'd noticed a few snowdrops blooming along the side of the canal, where her narrowboat, the *Mollern*, was moored in the nearby village of Thrupp.

'Any luck identifying the burnt items found on the fire?' she asked.

'Yes, guv. Most of them were books. There was a rounded metal object, which I think might have been a St Christopher or something, given the vic's leanings.'

Hillary frowned. 'I wouldn't be so sure about that. I don't think medallions would have been our vic's kind of thing. More likely to have been an award of some kind. You know, dolled out to him for raising the most funds for some deserving cause.'

'Could be, guv. I reckon some of the glass we found came not from framed photographs, but from printed diplomas. One of the neighbours remembers seeing some things like it on the walls in his den. Like you said, official-looking thank yous from charity organizations.'

Hillary nodded. 'So it looks as if our killer wanted to eradicate all signs of David Merchant's good deeds.'

'Because he'd done the killer a bad one?' Gemma speculated, getting interested now, and swivelling her chair around to face Hillary properly.

'Or because he didn't do a particular good deed? A deed that the killer resented not happening maybe?' Hillary said, rather ungrammatically. 'Or maybe the killer had reason to think that it was all a front. That Merchant hid something far darker and nastier behind the façade of being 'a good man'. Or perhaps the killer just saw red. Like a kid throwing a tantrum.'

Gemma shrugged. Speculation was interesting, but it got them no further forward. She hesitated, wondering if she should tell Hillary about her decision to marry Guy and thus become, for better or worse, Lady Brindley.

But something held her back. She wasn't sure if she was afraid of ridicule — not from Hillary, perhaps, but from the others — or whether she was simply not sure that she was doing the right thing.

Practically speaking, of course, she was in the clear. With thirty looming on the horizon, if she wanted kids — and she did — she needed to settle down soon. And Guy was a good catch — well-heeled, in a secure job which carried with it a certain kudos, and he was already well-liked and accepted by her family. Her father and brothers, of course, being all hale-and-hearty fire fighters, tended to be a bit tentative around the blind music don, but Gemma rather liked that. It gave them, as a couple, another kind of kudos.

And they'd been together for nearly three years now, so nobody could say she was rushing into things.

And yet.

Gemma sighed, and returned to her keyboard and her notes.

Brian Vane parked his car at the pavement and looked around enviously. The Moors area of Kidlington was one of the most coveted, and eyeing the 'old' part of the village, he could see why. Homes with some age to them sat in large well-kept gardens. The roads were lined with trees that probably bloomed pink and white in the spring. It all sniffed of green wellies and English setters. He himself lived in a nice enough just-about detached house in Headington, but he knew he was not in this league.

Not that Detective Superintendent Phillip 'Mellow' Mallow had been in it either, he thought, with just a faint sneer. It had belonged to the rich, second wife, hadn't it? Mallow, for once, had struck a blow for male emancipation, and came out of the divorce much better off than he'd gone into it. Now, of course, it belonged to the grieving widow.

Brian straightened his shoulders and walked to the door, ringing the bell, and looked surprised to see a middle-aged woman open the door.

'Yes?'

'Oh. Hello. I'm Superintendent Vane. I've just called around to give my congratulations to Mrs Mallow. I understand she's home from the hospital now?'

'Just yesterday,' the woman said, standing back to let him in. 'So you're the man who got Mel's job. I'm Janine's mum, Mrs Tyler. I'm staying for a while, just till she's on her feet again. What with the new baby and everything.'

Brian Vane smiled widely. He was good at charming middle-aged and old ladies.

'That's nice. Nowadays, families don't stick together like they used to.'

Janine's mother, who'd divorced her father long since, sniffed. 'You'd better come on through. Jan, it's someone from the office for you,' she called through the open door, noticing Brian Vane's wince, and smiling slightly. Officious sod. 'I'll just go through and put the kettle on. Go on in.'

He obligingly followed the waved hand and found himself in a charming room, that he instantly envied. Large, comfortable furniture, cosy velvet curtains that reached the floor, and a real fire crackling away in the grate. A pale-faced blonde woman rose from the settee and, from the cot beside her, Brian heard the thin reedy call of a very young infant. He had three children of his own and recognized it instantly.

'Hello Mrs Mallow. DS Vane. We haven't met, which seems odd. I heard on the grapevine you had a lovely new daughter, so I thought I'd just drop in to say hello.'

Janine Mallow felt her face tighten, and forced a brief smile on to her face. But her mind was racing.

What did he want? What was he doing here? And it wasn't just natural resentment at the man who had taken over her dead husband's job that was at the route of her angst either. She'd heard on the grapevine that Hillary didn't like or rate her new boss, and she'd heard all about the fracas they'd had on the afternoon she, Janine, had shot and killed Clive Myers, the man who'd killed her husband.

Vane was trouble.

'Please, sit down. I expect Mum's got the kettle on.'

'Yes. And this is the new arrival?' Vane smiled expansively and looked down at the cot. Like all the very young, this one seemed wrinkly, vaguely ugly, and without any real coherence yet. He remembered his own kids had been the same. 'What's her name?'

'Phillippa. After her father,' Janine said flatly.

Vane nodded. 'That's a lovely name. I expect it'll get shortened to Pippa though. It usually does.'

Janine watched him warily, as he sat down

on the sofa and glanced around. 'A lovely room. A lovely home.'

'Yes. Mel liked it,' Janine said drily.

Just then, Mrs Tyler came in with a tray, deposited it on the coffee table, glanced at her daughter's tight face, then went across to the cot and lifted up the still grizzling infant.

'I'll take her out and change her, shall I?' she asked tactfully, pulling a face at her daughter behind the visitor's head, and nodding down at him. Janine, who had no trouble reading her mother's silent messages, couldn't have agreed more.

The man was definitely oily. No wonder Hillary couldn't stand him.

'Well, I'm glad to see things have settled down now that the preliminary findings of the inquiry have been handed in,' he said, sounding as if he was somehow taking the credit. 'I hope the PR department has been keeping the press off your back?'

'They know their job,' Janine agreed blandly. 'But there's only so much they can do. I'm either a heroine or a police vigilante, depending on editorial policy.'

Brian shifted uncomfortably on his seat. 'Yes, well. It's all blowing over nicely.'

Janine smiled grimly. 'Yes. The top brass will be pleased about that.'

It was a dig, a definite dig, and Brian felt

himself flush. Did she know that the same top brass was already getting ready to bustle him off sideways because he'd inadvertently threatened not to toe the line on the Myers/Mallow fiasco? It certainly seemed like it.

'Your old boss has got another murder case on her hands,' he said, deciding subtlety was not going to be of much use here, and only slightly changing the subject. The woman was obviously as hard as nails. Hardly surprising, since, in his opinion, she'd almost certainly killed a man with malice aforethought. And, presumably, without a qualm.

'Hillary? Yes, I wouldn't be surprised. Chief Superintendent Donleavy knows she always gets results,' Janine said, and again flashed a bright smile his way.

Vane glanced across to the flickering flames and nodded. 'Yes. She's certainly been lucky so far.'

'Oh luck has nothing to do with it. Sir,' she left a long pause between the sentence and the last word, just to stress her contempt, then leaned forward. 'Tea?'

'Oh, yes, thank you. A little milk, no sugar.'

Janine poured some out and handed a cup over. 'I understand you and Hillary had a rather public difference of opinion on the day Clive Myers died, sir,' Janine said, making

Vane almost splutter over his first mouthful. 'Word gets around, you see,' she added, pouring out her own cup.

Vane shot her a hot, tight look. 'Yes. I'm afraid I'm an old-fashioned copper, Inspector Mallow. I like things done by the book. And, well, let's face it, what happened that day was hardly by the book, was it?'

Janine poured some milk into her cup. Vane was vexed to see that her hand was quite steady.

'No, sir,' she surprised him by admitting. 'But then, the situation was rather unorthodox as well. DI Gregg was only moments away from being shot and killed, after all.'

Vane nodded, trying to look sympathetic. 'Yes. Lucky you were on hand to save him, wasn't it?' he said, with telling blandness.

Janine leaned back with her teacup. 'An extraordinary set of circumstances, yes, sir. But that only adds to what I was saying: it was hardly a by-the-book sort of scenario.'

'A lot of people wonder why you called your old boss, instead of your own team at Witney,' Vane fished mildly, and Janine smiled.

'The inquiry committee made the same comment, sir,' Janine agreed placidly. 'As I told them, really it was just instinct. I'd worked with DI Greene for many years, whereas I'd only been at Witney such a short time. And, of course, HQ was right on the spot, so to speak. If I'd called Witney it would have taken them up to twenty minutes to get there. And then I was in shock. I just called the first person I knew who was both competent and on the spot. The inquiry didn't seem to find it that unusual a thing to do,' she added flatly, a definite hint of hardness in her tone now.

And again Vane felt himself flush.

'I knew DI Greene when she was just starting out in the force, of course,' Vane said heartily, taking another sip of tea. 'She's come a long way since then.'

'Not that far, sir. And I don't think she has any ambitions to go any higher. Being a DI suits her.'

'Yes,' Vane smiled. 'But she does have the reputation for, well, shall we say, sailing a bit close to the wind. First there was that business with her husband. Bent as a corkscrew, so I hear.'

'She was completely exonerated over that, sir, as you know,' Janine replied. 'She was in the process of divorcing him anyway, and the Yorkie Bars found no evidence against her at all.'

'Oh yes. DCI Danvers is now her boss, isn't he? I must say, he seems very loyal.

Considering he was part of the team from York who investigated her.'

Janine smiled. If Vane was trying to dig for dirt there he was wasting his time.

'Yes, sir. Just goes to show, doesn't it? That the man who investigated her for corruption is more than happy to be her boss now, I mean.'

Vane nodded, then forced his lips to loosen as he took another sip of tea. 'And what about you, DI Mallow? Are you thinking of returning to work soon?'

'Oh, I've got maternity leave, sir. So I'll have plenty of time to think about my future.'

'Well, let's hope the final report, when it comes in, removes any lingering cloud that there might still be hovering over it. I understand from the chief constable that there are still one or two loose ends to be tied up.'

Janine tensed, and forced herself to shrug nonchalantly. 'I'm sure there are. But it's a good team they've got, so I'm sure it won't take long.'

Vane smiled, genuinely this time. He'd been a cop for many years and he could spot sudden tension when he saw it. And smell the slightest whiff of fear. And for all that the tainted heroine-of-the-moment DI Janine Mallow had been confident when discussing things in general, she'd definitely turned a bit green over that 'loose ends' comment.

It was the best he could hope for in the circumstances. He rose, making the usual appropriate noises, and outside in his car, sat behind the wheel for a moment or two, thinking furiously.

When he got back to HQ he'd have to go over the inquiry report with a fine tooth comb. If he could just figure out what loose end it was that was worrying Janine Mallow he might be able to pull on it, and find something useful. Something that could be used against Greene.

He started the car and pulled away from the kerb. Despite what many people thought, he knew he was a capable copper, with more than his fair share of closed cases behind him. He might not be quite the detective Hillary Greene was, but he was no slouch either. If there was something there, he was confident he could find it. After all, he'd probably be the only one seriously looking for evidence against Mallow and Greene. The inquiry team would not have been anxious to find anything that contradicted their statements, so who knew what goodies might be unearthed?

He began to hum as he returned to HQ.

Back at the house, Janine watched him go, then reached for her phone.

'DI Hillary Greene.'

'Boss, it's Janine. Your guv'nor, Brian Vane was just here.'

At her desk, Hillary straightened up in her chair. 'Shit. What did he want?'

'It was a fishing expedition, boss. Nothing more. He got nothing.'

Over the wire, she heard the older woman sigh. 'OK. Don't worry about it. I'll keep an eye on him.'

They spoke for a few more moments, then Hillary hung up. So Vane was still trying to rock the boat. The man was relentless, she'd say that for him. She didn't think he'd find anything out that the inquiry team hadn't been able to discover, but a man with a grudge could do an awful lot of damage nevertheless.

There was not much she could do but wait and watch and see what developed. She knew the areas where they were vulnerable, of course — Janine much more than herself. But so far they'd been lucky.

She could only hope their luck held and not let herself get paranoid about it.

★   ★   ★

She didn't know it, but DC Mark Chang was also feeling distinctly paranoid.

190

But in his case, with reason.

He stared at the text message on his telephone, then blinked, then stared again, as if he could magically make it disappear.

But he couldn't.

The message, unusual for text, was spelt out in full, with none of the usual clever abbreviations or electronic shorthand usually associated with texting. And no matter how many times he read them, or blinked at them, the words stayed the same.

IF YOU DON'T WANT TO SEE YOUR PARENTS SHOP BURN TO THE GROUND, MEET AT UNIVERSITY PARKS, MAIN ENTRANCE, SIX BENCH DOWN FROM RIGHT. TONIGHT, 11.30.

Mark slowly folded the phone away and slipped it into his pocket. He was still sitting in his car in HQ's car-park where he'd checked his messages after returning from follow-up interviews.

He knew all about the broken window in his parents' kitchen-ware shop, of course. He only lived a few streets away from their home in a narrow terraced house, which he shared with three other students. He regularly ate at home because it was cheaper, and when he'd arrived at his parents' shop, where they lived in an apartment over the top, he'd spotted the temporary chipboard at once.

But he'd never seriously considered that it might be the result of anything other than mindless, random violence. Yet now it seemed that someone really was out to get him. So perhaps his paranoia wasn't so surprising.

The thing was — what did he do now?

Protocol said that he report the incident at once to his superior officer — in this case Hillary Greene. But he was still so new to the squad, and he felt a distinct sense of shame that he was already bringing hassles to the workplace.

Perhaps he should go and find out what it was all about first? It might be just some kind of practical joke after all. Just a bit of nastiness that he could quickly clear up by himself, and strictly on the quiet?

Besides, he felt a bit of a namby-pamby prat asking for backup on something so simple as a brick-through-the-window incident.

No, he'd go alone, and see what it was all about.

Decision made, he got out of the car and walked into HQ. Although he still felt uneasy, it was impossible to feel alone or afraid here, surrounded by his colleagues, and aware of a sense of belonging.

He only hoped he could hold on to this feeling of invincibility tonight. When he was alone and in the dark.

★ ★ ★

Lori Dunne brushed her damp palms over the nap of her coat as she walked into the police station. She'd never been in one before, and little about the smell, sound or sight of it reassured her.

Here was authority — she could feel it; inexorable, unarguable power. It made her nervous. For a woman whose main weapon was her looks and her sex appeal, there was something about faceless, organized procedure that made her stomach cramp. After all, how could you wheedle, or manipulate, or seduce something that had no heart, loins or feelings?

She approached the front desk with a slightly sick feeling, only perking up when the middle-aged man behind the desk saw her coming, and she recognized that flash of interest and distinctly masculine vulnerability that crossed his face.

'Yes, miss, can I help you?'

Lori smiled and began to unbutton her coat. 'It's warm in here after coming from outside,' she said, letting her voice become

193

tinged with that slight breathlessness that was always so affective.

Unbuttoned, the coat revealed a long, surprisingly summer dress of cream lace with pastel embroidered flowers that was set off by the pale-green silk, full-length underskirt beneath. It seemed to float and cling at the same time.

The desk sergeant gulped audibly.

'The central heating's working well for once,' he heard himself simper, and coughed. 'This isn't a local police station you know, miss, if you have a crime to report I'm afraid you have to — '

'Oh no. I mean, that is, I'm here to talk to someone about a murder inquiry. The man who was . . . ' — she leaned forward a little and let her voice lower to a horrified whisper — 'you know, burned. In his garden.'

The desk sergeant drew his eyes back from where he could see the swell of her breasts against all that lace, and nodded briskly.

'Right. You need to speak to DI Greene then. If you'll just wait here a moment.'

He reached for the telephone and tried to keep his eyes from the woman's face. But it was hard. It was such a perfectly beautiful face. She could be one of them fashion models, he thought wistfully. Perhaps she was. Perhaps she was famous.

'DI Greene. Another walk-in — the Merchant case. Yes. I'll put her in interview room four then? Right.'

He hung up and came from behind the desk, sucking in his beer belly as he did so, and leading her down a short, not very savoury corridor. The interview room was white, square, and intimidating.

'Just have a seat, miss, and DI Greene will be with you shortly.' With real regret, the sergeant left her to return to his desk.

Lori wasted no time in slipping off her coat and hanging it on the back of the chair. This she pushed back a little and sat on it so that she was far enough away from the table to be able to cross her long, extremely good legs, and show just the right amount of calf. No thigh. That would be vulgar.

Then she reached up behind her and loosened the tortoise-shell comb that was holding up her long, pale-blonde hair, allowing two wings to fall forward carelessly, half covering her eyes. She was too young to know who Veronica Lake was, but if she had known of her, she'd have been a role model.

Lori only hoped that this DI Greene who seemed to be heading the case was as susceptible as the next man when it came to virginal-looking female charm. She was depending on his sympathy.

All her life, Lori Dunne had learned to play people. Mostly men, but not always. She'd been born, late in life, to a middle aged, middle-class couple, and had been one of those beautiful babies and children who won soap commercial auditions and child beauty pageants.

At school, she quickly became aware that other children didn't like her, so she'd learned how to charm the teachers and, after hitting puberty, could have become an absolute menace, were it not for an innate cunning that kept her — mostly — out of trouble.

By her late teens she knew exactly what she wanted: to be rich, famous, and envied.

The first blow had come when she'd done the rounds of the fashion modelling agencies at sixteen and been turned down. Oh, she was beautiful, willowy, and could wear any fashion effortlessly and all that, but that all-important love-affair with a camera simply didn't happen. No matter how feverishly the photographers, lighting technicians, make-up artistes (the male ones anyway) and directors tried, the camera simply didn't like her face.

So that route was gone.

She couldn't act, she discovered at the age of twenty, when she failed to gain a place at even the most provincial of colleges, and not even the amateur theatrical companies would take her on.

Singing lessons were a wash-out. She couldn't carry a tune. This left her, at twenty-three, feeling embittered and hard done by. It was a friend who suggested she should become an artist's model. After all, paint and canvas wasn't as critical as the camera. And the more she'd thought about it, the more she'd liked it. After all, painters were mostly men — and she knew how to handle men.

It also gave her a certain cachet — to be an artist's model. It would, or so she believed at first — also give her an entrée to a certain circle, one which rich men, who drove sports cars and owned yachts in Monte Carlo, often frequented.

If she couldn't acquire wealth, fame and fortune for herself, she'd just have to marry into it.

Alas, here again, it seemed she was doomed to failure. True, she'd been painted by quite a few artists now, but the pay was poor and so far there'd been not a sniff of a millionaire. And now she was stuck with that loser Francis Whyte and this mess he'd made.

It made her want to scream. If only . . .

The door opened and Lori Dunne wanted

to scream all over again. A woman! Worse, two women! She felt like crying with vexation. What the hell use were they to her?

She stood up quickly and changed tactics, smoothing down her dress and getting ready to play the 'misunderstood' card. Women, she knew, tended to despise her on sight. She was young, beautiful and graceful — all the things most women were not.

But, as she watched the two women take up the chairs opposite her, she felt, again, that sense of sick-making unease.

The older one, the one who had to be DI Greene was looking at her without any expression at all. What's more, she could feel neither resentment or antipathy hidden underneath the poker face. She had good skin, Lori noticed immediately, and really good hair. But she was well-padded, and although that curvy look was not currently fashionable, Lori knew plenty of painters who would have been itching to paint her.

The younger woman was more striking — lean, bony, with short almost white, spiky hair. Really good eyes. Now she probably *could* have been a fashion model, Lori thought bitterly. She'd just bet the camera would love her — all those interesting, bony angles and high cheekbones.

'Please, sit down, Miss . . . ?' The older

198

woman spoke, and Lori flushed and abruptly sat down.

'Oh. Yes. Sorry. Lori Dunne. I'm feeling sort of nervous. I've never been in one of these places before.'

She heard her voice wanting to take on that now almost reflexive sexy breathlessness she normally used and fought to hold it back.

'There's no need for concern, Miss Dunne,' the younger blonde one spoke, her voice so scratchy it was like hail on gravel. Lori's eyes widened. What a sound! Now if she'd had a voice like that, she could have made it as a singer — specializing in one of those one-off, novelty acts; it only took one hit to make a fortune or a name.

It simply wasn't fair.

'Miss Dunne?' Hillary Greene said, alarmed by the way the young woman's blue eyes became unfocused. Was she on something?

'Yes. Sorry. It's about that man who was killed.'

'David Merchant. Do you know him?' Hillary asked pleasantly. Was this the blonde woman visitor to the Merchant house that her dog-walking witness had seen?

'No. Sorry, never met him. It's just . . . oh dear, I'm not sure quite how to put this without sounding . . . I mean, I don't want to get Frank into trouble, and it's probably nothing.'

'Frank?' Hillary prompted, wondering if this scatterbrained performance was the genuine article or just for her benefit. And if she brought in Freddie Dix would he, or his sheepdog, be able to pick her out of a line up?

'Yes. Frank Whyte. He's an artist.'

'Yes, we know. We've already spoken to Mr Whyte,' Hillary said with a smile. 'You're his model?' she guessed.

'Yes. Oh that's good then,' she lied, making herself smile brightly. 'So he's already told you all about it. I could have saved myself the bother of coming in.'

She made to rise, but Hillary quickly moved to prevent her. 'Please, Miss Dunne, remain seated for a little while longer. What exactly is it that you think Mr Whyte told us?'

Or, Hillary mused with a mental smile, what did he not tell us?

Lori sat back in her chair and sighed heavily. She fiddled with her hair, which naturally, fell down, then she sighed again and made a big to do of putting it back up. Then she remembered her all-female audience, and bit her lip.

This wasn't going how she'd wanted it to go at all. She wished these two were men. She'd have had them wanting to protect her by now. Easing all this along. Ensuring that she came out of it sounding like the victim that she was. Really.

'Well, it's just that I had to tell Frank that I couldn't sit for him any more. Because of the man who was killed. Frank got kind of upset about it — well, to be honest, he got really angry, but I just couldn't have my parents upset, could I?' she opened her big blue eyes widely, looking from one to the other. 'Mum and Dad are getting on a bit, and they're, well, rather easily shocked. For someone living in this day and age, I mean. I had to protect them, see? I'm all they've got. I'm an only child.'

She sat back in her chair, generating helpless appeal. Sometimes it worked with women — and the older one was old enough to feel maternal, surely?

Hillary slowly leaned back in her chair, trying to sort through the mess. 'Let's start at the beginning, shall we? You say you told Mr Whyte that you could no longer model for him. When was this, exactly?'

'The day before St David died. Oh!' She clapped a hand to her mouth. 'Sorry. I shouldn't have called him that, should I? The poor man's dead. And really, I didn't mean it. It's just that that's what Frank always called him, and I fell into the habit. Sorry.'

Beside her, she felt Gemma stir and could almost hear her thoughts. Like Hillary, she was becoming tired of the little-girl-lost performance, but, unlike her sergeant, knew how to hide her impatience.

She smiled benignly. 'That's all right. I'm sure it doesn't matter. Now, why did you tell Frank you could no longer model for him?'

'Because Mr Merchant found out about it, of course,' Lori said, as if Hillary was being particularly dim.

'But why should that make any difference?' Hillary asked, genuinely puzzled. 'Mr Merchant was only Mr Whyte's landlord; he had no say over his artistic output. I take it you do do nude modelling?'

Lori flushed. 'Yes. Well, it's proper art, isn't it? Not porno, or anything like that.' For the first time she spoke without any artifice and she sounded genuinely aggrieved and defensive.

'Exactly,' Hillary said, a touch more gently now. 'So why did you give notice?'

'Because that Mr Merchant was waiting for me one day when I left the cottage. He gave me all this usual guff about how what I was doing was unbecoming, and God liked modest women, and I was endangering my soul and all that.'

She paused for a moment, looking puzzled,

then shrugged. 'Well, I could tell he meant well. I tried to tell him that nothing was going on with me and Frank. Well, it wasn't. Have you seen him? He's a nice bloke and all that, but he's not exactly George Clooney, is he?'

'And how did Mr Merchant respond to that?' Hillary asked curiously.

'It made him feel better, you could tell. But he still said it wasn't right. I was getting ready to try and fob him off, gently like, when he, well, sort of took the rug out from under my feet.'

Hillary nodded. She had Lori Dunne's measure now and thought she was probably telling the truth so far. 'And what was that?'

'Like I said, he told me that if I didn't stop, he thought it would be his duty to have a word with my father. He said fathers had an obligation to look after their daughters' moral welfare. I couldn't have him bothering Mum and Dad, could I?'

Hillary nodded. 'Do they know what you do for a living?' she asked softly, and Lori blushed.

'No. I told them I work on the mobile library — as an assistant.'

Hillary had to smile. It was quite a clever lie: if she'd told them she worked at Kidlington Library they could have dropped in there at any time and found her out.

'Your parents wouldn't approve,' she stated it as a fact.

'They wouldn't understand, no,' Lori said. They'd always supported her in her bid to become a model, then an actress, then a singer. After all, it only seemed natural to them — she was their little princess, always beautiful, charming, graceful. Why shouldn't the world share her? Her humiliating defeat at every turn had only been made bearable by their unfailing comfort and encouragement.

Besides, she still lived at home and was very content there and, until she snared a rich husband, didn't want anything rocking her comfortable little boat.

'So I told him all right, I would quit first thing, and that seemed to please him. So I told Frank the next day and he really blew his lid.'

Again her big blue eyes opened wide, this time Hillary thought, with genuine remembered surprise. 'He effed and blinded for ages, going on about how St David had no right to interfere and that he was a narrow-minded, miserable killjoy and he'd sort him out good and proper.'

'Sort him out?' It was the blonde sergeant who repeated the phrase, and Lori glanced at her nervously.

'Yes. But it was only a figure of speech. I

mean, he didn't really mean it. He was just letting off steam. You know how artists are. I mean, Frank isn't violent at all. In fact, he tries to play the part of this free-spirit, artistic type, but really, he's as respectable as — well, my dad. He gives blood, for goodness sake — has done for years. He's got one of those long-serving medals for it. And he knows first aid. He stopped a man from choking once, at the fish and chip shop. He knows that fancy thing — you know where he gets behind you and joins his hands together in your stomach and gives a sort of heave?'

Hillary nodded. 'Yes, I'm familiar with it. And when was it that this happened? When you told him why you would no longer be his model, I mean,' Hillary put in hastily, not wanting to hear more about the choking chip eater. Out of her peripheral vision, she could see Gemma biting her lip to stop from smiling.

'The next time I saw him after being nobbled by St David. The day before he died . . . ' She let her voice trail off. 'Look, I don't want to get Frank in trouble, like I said. It's probably nothing. But I just thought I'd better say something. Just in case, like. I don't want none of this getting back to my mum and dad, see?'

And Hillary thought that she probably did.

Lori Dunne knew which side her bread was buttered, and didn't want her particular slice of the loaf falling butter side down in the shit.

But was that all there was to it? Only a while ago she was wondering if their victim had done something to catch Whyte on the raw. And now here was this air-head, giving her the very motive she'd been pining for.

A fleeting admonition not to look gift horses in the mouth warred with the warning about Greeks bearing gifts — especially of the equine variety.

'Did Mr Whyte say exactly how he was going to sort him out?' she asked calmly.

'No.'

'Did he, to your knowledge, in fact seek Mr Merchant out?'

'No.'

'Is Mr Whyte the kind of man who likes arguments?'

'No — oh no. Like I said, Frank likes to think of himself as laid-back and too blasé to do anything as naff as to lose his temper.'

Hillary nodded. She took her through it all again, but was soon convinced she'd heard all there was to hear.

'Well, thank you for coming in, Miss Dunne. You've been very helpful.' She pushed back her chair and held out her hand.

Lori looked at her doubtfully, shaking

hands warily. 'And you won't say anything to Mum and Dad?' she pressed.

'No,' Hillary said truthfully. But if it turned out that Frank Whyte was involved in any way with the events at David Merchant's house, then she suspected they'd soon be reading all about it — and their daughter — in the papers.

When she was gone, Gemma heaved a sigh. 'Give me a break. That kind of woman makes my head hurt.'

Hillary smiled. 'We'll have to speak to Frank Whyte again though. Do you think she could be the mystery blonde visitor?'

Gemma nodded. 'I was wondering that. She seemed dead keen to drop the artist in it, didn't she? Think she could have some sort of grudge against him we're not aware of?'

'Possibly,' Hillary said. 'She's not the sort to take male rejection well. But I can't see it, somehow. I think Whyte may have been genuinely smitten with her though. She's the kind who can wrap a middle-aged man around her little finger.'

'So he could have gone steaming off to Merchant's house to confront him. Tell him to keep his pious nose out of his business?' Gemma said, with a trace of excitement in her voice now.

'Yes, but then what?' Hillary challenged

grimly. 'That might have led to harsh words, maybe even resulting in Whyte bloodying the man's nose for him. But a man like David Merchant wouldn't fight back — he'd be more likely to turn the other cheek, which would probably defuse the situation anyway. Don't forget, the killer bashed the victim over the head, then set up a bonfire of the vanities that included the corpse itself. That smacks to me of something far more deep-seated. Hatred like that isn't the kind of thing that comes from a sudden angry altercation.'

Gemma shrugged. 'If you say so. Perhaps our little Miss Breathless Big-Eyes killed Merchant to protect mummy and daddy, and is trying to frame the artist.'

Hillary laughed. 'Can you see her breaking a nail carting Merchant's body outside and dumping him in the garden?'

'Not really. And certainly not without help,' Gemma said, with a wistful sigh. 'Pity. I'd have enjoyed putting the cuffs on her.'

Hillary shrugged. 'Well, you might get the chance yet,' she consoled her sergeant. 'When you get the chance, try and get a photograph of her and show it to Freddie Dix. You never know your luck. If she was our vic's mystery visitor, she'll have some explaining to do, at the very least.'

8

It was nearly six o'clock in the evening by now, but the full team was still working.

'Keith, before I forget, I want you to thoroughly check out all the charities our vic was involved with. See if any money is missing. I'm not saying I think he was a wrong 'un,' she added, before Barrington could get too excited, 'but where there's responsibility for money, there's a possible motive for murder.'

'I can't see him collecting enough alms to make it worthwhile though, guv,' Gemma said cautiously. 'Just how much money can you possibly make nowadays calling at homes and shaking a collection box?'

'Probably not a lot,' Hillary agreed. 'But if our vic was a big mover and shaker in charitable circles, he might be treasurer of this or that. And then we might be talking more zeros.'

'Right, guv,' Keith said heavily, and with such an evident lack of enthusiasm that even Gemma scowled and glanced across at him curiously.

'And if you can muster up the energy,

Constable,' Hillary said drily, 'see what you can find out about the missing son if not heir,' she added. 'Which reminds me.'

She reached for the receiver and picked it up. A departing sergeant called out his goodnights to everybody, and Hillary glanced at her watch. She'd have to call it a night soon.

She dialled a number from her notes and saw Mark Chang glance outside. He looked tense and uneasy, and she wondered what was biting him. Were both of her constables going down with something?

'Hello?' a sunny, little-girl voice squeaked in her ear.

'Vickki, hello. This is DI Hillary Greene. You remember me?'

'Oh yes, I'm not likely to forget,' she giggled nervously.

'Have you heard from Vict — sorry, from Timbo yet?'

'No, sorry. I would have called you right away if I had. Honest injun.'

Hillary sighed. 'Perhaps you could phone around all his friends, see if they've heard from him or know where he is? I really need to speak to him as soon as possible.'

'Already done it,' Vickki surprised her somewhat by saying. 'Nobody's heard from him, and nobody knows where he's gone. But like I said, that's not unusual. When he's 'creating' he could be anywhere or gone for months.'

'I hope not. I don't want to have to waste manpower by tracking him down officially.' She let her voice harden just a little. Not that she really thought Vickki was giving her a line, but just in case she was, it wouldn't hurt to turn the screw a little.

'Oh heck, don't do that,' Vickki squealed. 'You'll give him a heart attack or something, some big PC Plod feeling his collar. He's a bit of a rabbit, is Timbo. Look, I'll let you know as soon as I hear from him, I promise, all right?'

'All right,' Hillary agreed reluctantly and hung up the phone. Gemma began to pack away the stuff in her handbag.

'Still no joy then, guv?' she surmised.

'No.'

'You all that worried?'

'Not really. I can't see that young Victor Merchant could have been unaware that he'd been cut out of his father's will. I expect his father gave him plenty of warning before-hand, so there's no monetary motive that I can see. And it sounds as if they've been at loggerheads for years — so why up and bash him over the head now? No, I just hate to have loose ends hanging in the wind,' she said, her mixing of metaphors warning her how tired she was. 'And reports of his father's death have been reported in the media now, so unless he really doesn't read the papers or listen to the radio, he must know about the murder. So why doesn't he get in touch?'

'Artistic temperament, guv?' Gemma propounded 'You know, perhaps his gallery showing is more important to him than his old man — dead or alive.'

'Could be.' Hillary sighed heavily. 'Oh hell, let's go home, everybody, and have a good night's sleep.'

Barrington grunted. He had no real desire to go back to his depressing, empty bedsit. He was missing Gavin more than he thought possible, even if he wasn't the best of company right now. 'I'll stay on another hour or so, guv. I might need some time off to attend a funeral, and I want to get in the hours,' he added.

Hillary nodded. 'Are you doing all right?' she asked softly, and Barrington shrugged.

He wasn't sure how to answer that question, and Hillary caught Gemma's look. That Keith Barrington was having a crisis of some kind was obvious. But so far he hadn't volunteered any information, and she didn't feel now was a good time to start probing.

'OK. Let me know when you need the time

off,' she agreed, and watched Mark Chang as he slipped on his coat, and once again glanced nervously out of the big windows into the dark, cold February night.

'Constable Chang, everything all right with you?' Hillary asked sharply, and saw Mark Chang jump. He looked at her with a fleeting expression of guilty surprise on his handsome face, that was quickly replaced with a somewhat blank, all-encompassing smile.

'Yes, thank you, guv,' he said, but inwardly he was wriggling. Everyone had warned him that Hillary Greene was sharp, but he didn't actually expect her to be able to read his mind, which is what she seemed to be doing.

She appeared to hesitate for a moment, then sighed again. 'Fine, I'll see you tomorrow, bright-eyed and bushy-tailed. Or the nearest equivalent.' She slung her bag over her shoulder, and headed for the door.

Gemma shot Chang a quick, frowning look, then followed Hillary out. Tonight, she and Guy were having dinner with Guy's solicitor cousin, an old fogey who thought of himself as 'head of the family'.

He wanted to discuss 'family affairs' which meant stuff probably related to the passing on of the title to Guy, and discuss with them any financial ramifications, or go over whatever quaint little antiquated bits and bobs that needed to be observed. They were going to tell him about their decision to marry as well, and Gemma was feeling just a bit nervous. She was not at all sure that the cousin approved of her. There was something about her being in the police force that set his solicitor's beaky little nose quivering.

Well, to hell with him, Gemma thought. She was going to be Lady Brindley, so he could just go stuff himself.

★　★　★

A floor above them, Superintendent Brian Vane was busy. He was reading, for the second time, the full findings of the inquiry team into the Mallow/Myers shooting.

This time, after reacquainting himself with the facts, he went over it line by line, making himself concentrate on every little detail.

He could find nothing to fault with Janine Mallow's account of how she'd stumbled on the suspect, Clive Myers. He could well see that someone obsessed with her husband's shooting would hang around at the scenes of possible activity. And she'd already been spotted outside Clive Myers's house when she had no business being there. So her story about having nothing to do but kill time and do unofficial stakeouts had the ring of truth.

As did the little detail about her spotting Myers by his ears. That also made some sense — it was an old copper's trick, and he could well see Hillary Greene conscientiously passing it on to those working under her. The story about her tailing and then losing the suspect also held water. There was the interview with Joshua Boyle, the old man who'd been working on the allotments, and who'd seen Janine acting oddly, and his story seemed to back hers up. And he had no reason to lie.

So far there was not a hint of a loose end or anything really bad to worry the inquiry. Of course, Janine Mallow should have been at home with her feet up, but that had already been acknowledged.

Then came the discovery of Myers in the garden shed. That sounded a little far-fetched to Vane, but he also knew that sometimes things like that happened. What was that old saying — truth was often stranger than fiction? OK, so he could go along with that. She'd seen movement, observed the hidden assassin cut a hole in the plastic window of the shed in order to accommodate the barrel of his sniper's rifle.

Yes. So far he could just about accept all that. But why, at that point, hadn't she called for backup? Why go to the shed door at all?

Why risk her life — and, incidentally that of her unborn baby? Weren't pregnant women supposed to be protective of their child above all else?

That was where it began to fall apart, and Vane knew it. And so too, must the inquiry team, although they'd been at pains not to dwell on it.

But pregnant women didn't do such rash things, did they?

He read again Janine Mallow's statement. OK, so she was in a state of high excitement and anxiety. He could even believe that she was genuinely concerned for DI Gregg's safety. He'd been a brave man to agree to act as the tethered goat, and now here he was, within sight of a sniper's rifle, and with the cops guarding him totally unaware of the imminent danger.

Here, the inquiry had also noted that Janine's somewhat gung-ho nature had been the cause of her getting into trouble before. There was Hillary Greene's own account of how Janine, then Sergeant Tyler, had put herself in jeopardy when raiding a canal boat full of suspected drug dealers for instance. So perhaps she did have that have-a-go mentality that Vane half-admired and half-abhorred. And, OK, that might have influenced her decision-making processes.

But even so. To enter a shed where a man with a sniper rifle had set up home was foolhardy in the extreme.

Especially unarmed.

Here, Brian Vane felt the first stirrings of something that told him that things were straying far from being kosher. He'd had the feeling before, many times in the past, and his gut was seldom wrong. And his gut was telling him now that Janine Mallow would not have gone into that shed unarmed. Nobody would — no one with any sense, at any rate. Certainly not a trained police officer, no matter how uptight she was, or how affected by hormones or what the hell ever.

He leant back in his chair and thought it through. Janine Mallow had gone out that day with the idea in her mind that she might have at least an outside chance of spotting Myers. OK, logically, what was she going to do if that happened?

Spot him, then make the call for backup so that she could have the satisfaction of seeing him taken down? But that didn't sound quite right to him. After all, at that point they had no real evidence against Myers. And they'd pulled him in before and questioned him with no results.

OK. Perhaps she'd had a gut instinct that

that day was going to be the day when the case broke. It was a stretch, but he could go along with it. In which case, Janine Mallow might have fantasized about arresting him and getting the glory and kudos of nabbing the man with the actual rifle in his possession.

But she hadn't done that, had she? She'd followed him and waited until the rifle was set up, then confronted him. With no backup and no weapon.

'Hell no,' he said out loud. Quickly he ran his hands through the file papers until he came to the inventory of the contents of the shed again.

Ignoring the domestic list — those items which had all been tracked back to the family that owned the house — he scanned the list of items that had belonged to Myers.

And saw it — the unregistered side arm.

Why would Myers have needed a side arm? He had the rifle and two different kinds of knives. As an ex-army man, he also knew how to handle himself in unarmed combat. Would he really need the handgun as well?

The inquiry saw nothing wrong in supposing that he did. If he was cornered and needed to shoot his way out, a large and clumsy rifle might not fit the bill.

Quickly he scanned the report, and when

he read the statement about the handgun — an old Eastern-bloc gun that had seen better days — he began to smile. Just as he'd begun to suspect, the inquiry had been unable to trace its history.

The sniper's rifle that Myers had used had been traced to a batch of similar rifles that had been due to be destroyed by the army but had subsequently gone missing instead. Likewise, the two knives he had on him had been traced back to a purchase of his in Milton Keynes six months before.

But they had not been able to trace the handgun back to Myers, or to anyone else for that matter. The serial number had been carefully removed with acid, and they had no hits off it in either the police or army databases. So it had not been used in a crime, or any known British conflict.

Vane read the forensic report on it, and his grin widened. The gun was not exactly filthy at the time of its recovery, but it was not in the same spotless condition as was the rifle.

And Vane knew then of what it was that Janine Mallow was so scared. For a soldier, like Myers had been, would have kept all of his armoury in tip-top condition — clean, serviced and ready. Besides, he almost certainly wouldn't have chosen a piece of crap Czech weaponry in the first place.

No, the gun that Mallow had used to shoot Myers screamed of a workhorse piece — something that any gangbanger or piece of shit on the street might carry.

And it was what Janine Mallow had taken with her into that shed.

He read her statement again and knew where the careful lie had been told: she had not seen the gun, complete with a plastic Coke-bottle silencer on the floor. Why would Myers want it silenced anyway?

Mallow had taken the gun with her. She had always intended to kill the man who had murdered her husband.

Vane was sure of it.

OK, the evidence of the medical examiner had corroborated her story. Mallow had said that Myers was crouched on the ground ready to throw the knife at her when she shot him — and the entry point and angle of the bullet that had killed him, backed that story up.

So perhaps it had been genuine self-defence. But Janine Mallow had been ready for him, of that he was sure.

The question was: had she told Greene all of this? Because if she had, then Hillary Greene had covered up for her. If she hadn't, then Greene might still be in ignorance. But at least he could bring down Janine Mallow, and in bringing her down, pile the shit upon Hillary Greene as well.

It might not be enough to finish her though.

Vane slowly gathered the file together and began to reassemble it neatly. His mind raced.

He needed to trace that gun.

So the question now had become, who would Janine Mallow turn to in order to get a gun? She might have taken it from the police evidence stores, but he didn't think so. There would be an entry of her name in the logs if she'd done that, and she wouldn't want to risk leaving a trace. Besides, she would either have had to have the co-operation of the officer in charge of the evidence locker, or think of some way to get around him, all of which compounded her chances of being discovered. Then there was the problem of removing all records of the gun from lock-up.

No. It was simply too risky. Likewise she couldn't simply buy a gun — not without leaving a trace. The gun laws in the UK were too strict for that.

Besides, there was an easier way, and Vane saw it at once. If it had been him in her shoes, he would have asked one of his skells to obtain it for him. Every copper had a network of low-lifes who passed on information and could be used for all sorts of interesting things in a crisis.

So all he had to do was dig through Janine's records and find the likely candidates and sound them out. And once he had the culprit, he could make him talk. Janine was only a DI, and now a dodgy one with a dodgy reputation and future; he was a superintendent, and he hadn't got where he was without learning how to put the fear of something nasty into low-lifes.

Once he had the skell who'd supplied the gun, he'd have Janine Mallow by the balls. Or the lady's equivalent. Only then would he approach Janine Mallow with a deal. He wasn't sure what that was likely to be yet — he would need to get all his skittles lined up first, then see where the best bet lay.

But the goal was simple.

He would be willing to let Janine wriggle off the hook if she would put her old boss firmly on it.

* * *

Barrington heard the desk sergeant call out a cheerful farewell as he crossed the foyer and held up a hand in response.

Outside it was drizzling, and he stepped lively to his car and sank down behind the steering wheel. It was nearly ten, and he was feeling beat. He drove back to his dreary bedsit, parked in the dreary do-it-yourself superstore at the back of the Victorian terrace where he lived, and set off down the street.

He could hear his phone ringing as he put his key in the door and, when he lifted the receiver, felt his heart lift at the sound of the familiar voice.

'I've been ringing you all night,' Gavin Moreland said grimly.

'Sorry. Working late at the office.'

'Do you think they can let you have a few hours tomorrow? We're burying Dad at some hole-in-the-corner place up near your way. Apparently, he lived there briefly as a child, some village in the sticks, and the local vicar's agreed to let us bury him there. We want to keep the jackals at bay if we can.'

'The press still bothering you?' he asked softly, sitting down on the bed and wearily pulling off his boots, the receiver cradled against his face by one hunched shoulder.

'Of course they are. Mind you, not so many now that most of the fuss is over with. Dad's already yesterday's news,' he added bitterly.

'What time is the funeral?'

'Eleven-thirty. It's some place called Cassingford. Out near an old American air force base, I think.'

'I'll find it,' Keith promised.

'Shit, I feel like hell,' Gavin said, the tremolo of tears on the edge of his voice.

'I'll be there for you,' Keith repeated firmly.

'Yeah. But for how long?' Gavin asked, then before he could answer, hung up.

In London, Gavin Moreland replaced the receiver and gave a brief, grim smile.

Tomorrow was going to be another day. And he would prise that red-haired bastard of a lover of his from the arms of the police or die in the attempt. So help him, he'd found love at last, and with his father gone, the future, unencumbered and bright, was within his grasp. Years touring the professional tennis circuit — sunshine, beach, sex and champagne. And Barrington.

That was what he wanted, and that was what he was damned well going to have.

★ ★ ★

Mark Chang counted down the hours to midnight, telling himself that he was not scared.

He partly succeeded.

When he drove the short distance through the dark Oxford night though, he was aware of the coldness in his fingers. He parked near the red-and-white monstrosity that was Keble

College and locked the car.

It was a damp night, but every now and then a full moon peeked from behind the clouds, lending a bright, silvery illumination. Shivering, Chang turned up the collar of his leather jacket and zipped it up to his chin. The jacket was old and thickly padded. Hardly a bullet-proof vest, but he thought it might help deflect a knife, say, if things got really nasty.

He was wearing his best running shoes, and felt as ready as he could be for any eventuality. He slipped a pair of knuckle-dusters into his pocket, along with the short-handled truncheon that was a reminder of his days on the beat.

He walked through the park gates and stopped, looking around. Sometimes, he knew, students liked to use the parks late at night — sometimes for sex, if they were feeling in an outdoorsy kind of mood, but more often to buy drugs.

But it was not the sort of night for hanky-panky, and he knew that most of the dealers didn't like to set up so close to the main entrance. They were too easy to spot and get nicked there.

The moon chose that moment to come out from behind the clouds, and he could clearly see the pale gravelled path leading off left and right. The bare trees looked beautiful against the black, cloud-strewn sky but Chang was in no mood for aesthetics.

Nervously, he began to walk, counting down the park benches as he went. He heard a snuffling sound off to his left, and froze. Then he saw the unmistakable shape of a large, pale Labrador dog retrieve something from the grass and race off back into the darkness, where the sound of his master's whistle could clearly be heard.

Somehow the thought that he wasn't altogether alone, that there were other, innocent ordinary citizens out there in the darkness bolstered his courage.

He counted down six benches and stood uneasily on the path. Large bushes loomed in the borders here, and the moon, according to sod's law, duly nipped back behind a cloud, leaving him in almost total darkness. The street lamps lining the road outside cast batches of light, but that seemed only to disorientate him more.

'You Chang then?' The voice came at him out of the darkness, making him swallow hard.

His hands were thrust deep into his pockets, and he wriggled the iron knuckle-dusters over the knuckles of his right hand.

'Yeah,' he croaked. 'What's this all about then?'

'We paid a little visit to your mum and dad's shop. Did they tell you?'

Chang peered into the gloom but could make out nothing that resembled that of a human shape, and he guessed that whoever was speaking was doing so from behind a bush. Such caution on the other man's part made him feel slightly better.

'I saw it. A brick through the window. Not very subtle, was it?' he forced himself to say, with just a hint of a jeer. Whatever happened, he knew he must not sound afraid. They were like dogs, they could smell fear. Or so an old sergeant of his had once told him, back in his police training college days.

'Didn't need to be, did it?' the voice shot back smartly. 'It got your attention.'

Just then, Chang felt movement behind him and his adrenaline kick-started his flight-or-fight instinct. He began to turn, at the same time, withdrawing his right hand from his pocket.

But he was too late. Whilst the voice in the darkness had kept his attention, a second watcher in the dark had sidled up behind him. Chang yelped as he felt arms that resembled steel bands suddenly wrap around his chest, and his breath left him in a painful, surprised whoosh.

He felt his bowels loosen in sheer fright,

and prayed that he wouldn't piss himself. Or worse.

'Here, get off!' he yelled, and in front of him, a shape emerged from the bushes just as the moon emerged from behind the clouds. The man, about Mark's own height and build stepped closer, and Chang could see that he was Chinese.

'Thing is, copper, we want to be friends, see?'

Chang blinked. His arms were pinioned at his side, and he was being forced to stand almost on tiptoe, so he guessed that the man behind him was much taller than himself, for he was almost holding him clear off the ground. The fact that he did so with easy, quiet strength scared Chang more than anything.

'What?' he asked, puzzled and confused. He felt sick, and swallowed hard once, then again. He felt like he was going to throw up over his sneakers any moment, and the thought was too humiliating to contemplate for long.

He was a detective constable. He was the police. He was the one who was supposed to be in charge. He was the one who did the 'nicking', who got to set the pace and call the shots. To feel so helpless and stupid was almost more than he could bear. What the hell use was his truncheon when he couldn't even wield it?

Suddenly, he felt terrifyingly out of his depth.

'You're going to be our friend, see,' Eddie Lee said softly. 'We like having friends at Thames Valley headquarters, don't we, Ooo Yuck?'

Behind him, he felt a queer sort of movement, and realized the man holding him was nodding his head.

In spite of his fear, Mark Chang found himself wondering. What the hell kind of a name was Ooo Yuck? Were they yanking his chain? Was this some kind of gag, after all?

'See, me and my associates will find it very useful to know what's going on. You know — what raids are planned, who's made it to the top of the big brass's shit list. You know the kind of thing. We might even be able to help.'

Mark Chang blinked. 'Help? What do you mean?'

'You know. Put some information your way. I mean, we're fairly new in town, and we got rivals. Know what I mean? And if you lot nick 'em and put 'em away it creates a vacuum. And we like vacuums. Don't we, Ooo Yuck?'

'My mum's got a Hoover,' a voice agreed helpfully behind him, and Eddie Lee laughed.

'Don't mind Ooo Yuck. He's not got a lot up here,' — he tapped his head — 'but his heart's in the right place. Oh no, wait a minute, it isn't really.'

And Eddie Lee laughed again.

Mark Chang went cold. He was dealing with madmen. He had to be.

'See, it won't hurt your career any, will it, Constable Chang, if you come up with the odd bit of info that leads your lot to putting away some riff-raff,' Eddie Lee continued amiably. 'And in return, you let us know if any operation's going down that we ought to know about.'

'You're a member of a gang,' Mark said, suddenly getting it.

'Give the man a peanut,' Eddie Lee smiled. And then the moon went in again, and the only thing Mark Chang could see was the vague outline and shape of his smiling teeth.

Like the bloody Cheshire cat.

'But I won't have access to information like that,' Chang began to explain helplessly. 'I'm not even part of the team that deals with organized crime. They have specialist task forces for that, led by experienced men. And when they have a specific operation on, it's not as if they go blabbing about it in the canteen. The only times the likes of me know about it, is when they return covered in glory.'

Ooo Yuck might not have been the brightest bulb in the light-bulb factory, but he knew bad news when he heard it, and his grip began to tighten with displeasure.

Suddenly Mark Chang couldn't breathe. He felt himself go hot, then a roaring sound began to pound in his ears.

'We don't like the sound of that, Constable Chang,' Eddie Lee said warningly, then when Mark could only squeak in reply, said sharply, 'Don't crush the constable just yet, Ooo, we want to give him a chance to grow some brains.'

Mark gave a 'whoomph' as his lungs were released and he abruptly drew in a deep, ragged breath.

'Look, you're a bright lad,' Eddie Lee said pleasantly. 'Stands to reason, don't it? A detective already at your young age. The brass must think you're bright. Probably got a university degree or something, yeah? You can figure it out. Ask for a transfer. Find a friendly young gal on the right task force. Butter her up — you're a handsome lad, hey?' Eddie playfully punched Mark on the shoulder — but he did it with real, bruising force, and smiled when Chang bit back a yelp of pain.

'You can take her to bed, give her a bit of tender loving and all that. Pillow talk, that's the ticket. I don't care how you do it — I want eyes and ears in that place, and you're going to be it. Got it?'

Chang could feel the other man's warm breath on his face now, he was standing so close, and it carried with it the stale odour of stir-fry. And once again he had to fight his gag reflex.

'Otherwise, Mom and Pop are going to find their shop burnt down around their ears — with them still in it. Do you get the picture?'

Mark swallowed hard. 'Yes,' he heard himself say feebly.

'Good. That's all then. Oh yeah, one more thing,' Eddie Lee said, and buried his fist in Mark Chang's exposed gut.

Ooo Yuck released him at the same time, and stepped back, as the younger man bent double and began to retch miserably.

'We'll be in touch,' Eddie Lee's voice said cheerfully, from a few feet away, as the two Chinese gangsters walked away.

Mark Chang felt tears slide down his face as he was copiously and painfully sick. He slumped down on to the damp gravel, shaking and aware of a sense of burning shame, fear, and something else. Something hard and nasty, that he eventually traced back to a desire for revenge.

It took him some time to get upright, and walk gingerly back to his car. He drove home at a very careful twenty miles per hour. He was still shaking when he finally managed to get his key into the door. He was as quiet as a mouse as he made his way to his small back bedroom, not wanting to rouse his house-mates and have to answer their questions, or fend off their concern, pity or contempt.

It took him the rest of the night, lying in his bed, to replay what had happened, try to come to terms with what he felt had been rather too much cowardice on the part of a serving police officer, and decide what he was going to do.

At last, at some point, he must have slept.

9

Hillary looked up, slightly startled, as she crossed the lobby the next morning.

'Pssst!'

She paused, saw the desk sergeant give her a quick nod, sighed, frowned and trotted over, not sure that she was in the mood for the latest gossip this morning. Even if it was good. As far as she could see, her case was stalled and going nowhere in a hurry, and she needed to give it a good kicking up the backside.

'Sarge,' she said pleasantly.

'Little Rosie from records wants a word. I'm to give her a bell, and she'll meet you in the ladies loo on your floor.'

Hillary blinked. Little Rosie? She searched her memory databanks, and came up with WPC Rosemary Trubshaw, a fifty-something, ginger-haired mother of eight, who, so legend had it, lurked so often in the windowless vault of records, she would go up in flames like Count Dracula if she ever saw the light of day.

'Oh, right,' Hillary said, thanked him, and thoughtfully climbed the stairs.

She knew Rosie, but not well. A woman with no ambition, content to do her job well, raise her kids and collect her pension at the end of it all. A good enough sort, but what she could want with Hillary, she had no idea.

She vetoed the door to the main open-plan office and carried on through to the far end, where the toilets proclaimed their rather smelly presence. As she pushed open the door, it was clear a cleaner had just been in to do daily battle, because the scent of lavender air freshener almost made her gag.

She walked to the far end and opened a frosted glass window the bare inch that it was able to open. Shrugging off her coat as the radiators, for once, were gurgling with heat, she went to the mirror set over the bank of washbasins and automatically checked her appearance.

She was wearing one of her fawn-coloured two piece suits, with a skirt to just below the knee, and a dark emerald-green faux-silk blouse. A light dusting of matching green eyeshadow was, for her, something of a fashion statement, and she made another mental note to get her hair cut when she could grab half an hour.

A toilet flushed, and a woman DI from Juvenile Crimes stepped out of a cubicle, gave her a pleasant nod, washed her hands and left.

Hillary glanced at her watch. It wasn't yet 8.15. She reached inside her bag for her mobile and checked her text messages. There was just one, from Keith Barrington.

GUV. FUNERAL TODAY AT TEN. NEARBY. WILL BE BACK ON JOB BY LUNCH HOUR. HOPE THAT'S OK? KB.

Hillary erased the message then looked up as Rosemary Trubshaw came in. She was as roly-poly as Hillary remembered her, and she wondered how she managed to pass the police physical, year in, year out. Hillary thought she probably had an examiner who was sweet on her. Either that, or the people in Admin rated her so highly that the examiner got the nod to let her slip through a loophole. She had the usual faceful of freckles that came with her ginger curly mop, and wide, dark-brown intelligent eyes.

'Ma'am.'

'Rosie. Nice to see you again. How are all the kids?'

'Eldest two have left home, praise be. One of the middle bunch wants to be a journalist though,' she added gloomily.

Hillary smiled in sympathy, then watched,

suddenly tensing up as the other woman checked that all the other cubicles were empty. Then she took a breath, and came straight to the point.

'Thing is, ma'am, the little gal who's been training under me for the last fortnight, and is working the night shift, hung around to catch me coming in, and told me something a bit off.'

'Off?' Hillary echoed, not sure she liked the sound of that.

'Yeah. Definitely off,' Rosie confirmed glumly. She had retained just a hint of the West-Country drawl that indicated her origins, and Hillary noticed how it became more pronounced the more uneasy she became.

'Luckily, the gal had enough sense to tell me about it, and cover her arse. Some of them don't, you know. Don't have enough sense to fit on a pinhead some of them.'

Hillary smiled slightly. 'You don't have to tell me.'

''Course not, ma'am. Thing is see, just before the shift changeover, your DS paid a little visit down our way.'

Hillary felt herself stiffen. 'Superintendent Vane, you mean?'

'Yes, ma'am. That's the one.'

Rosie, like everyone else at the station, had heard on the grapevine that Hillary Greene didn't rate him, and everyone also knew he'd made an ass of himself on the afternoon that Janine Mallow took out the cop-killer, Myers. More than that, being in Records and Admin, Rosie knew that definite moves were afoot to shuffle Vane off up north, so Hillary Greene was not the only one who didn't rate him. The top brass didn't like people who tried to rock the boat. Especially when the waters got a touch choppy.

It was a combination of all these three things that had, after careful consideration, brought Rosie to Hillary's door.

Hillary nodded slowly. 'At the shift change, you say?'

'Yes, ma'am.'

Early then, Hillary mused. Much too rarefied a time for a DS to be up and about, normally — unless he was doing something sneaky. And during the shift change was a good time to get up to something. Less people around, more confusion, easier to slip by unnoticed.

'What did he want?' Hillary asked bluntly.

Rosie Trubshaw appreciated straight and direct questions. 'He was interested in Sergeant Janine Tyler's, now DI Mallow's, old cases, ma'am. More specifically, as far my little gal could make out, the sergeant's skell list.'

Hillary felt herself go hot, then cold. She blinked.

Rosie Trubshaw glanced away. Like the rest of HQ, she was aware of Hillary Greene's rep. She had a murder conviction rate next to none and had had a bit of trouble with her ex — who the hell hadn't? She'd also been awarded a medal for bravery after saving her boss, Mellow Mallow's life, only to see her oldest friend gunned down in front of her not six months ago.

Also like the rest of the stationhouse, she believed that somehow or other, Hillary Greene had contrived to cover her ex-sergeant's back on the day she'd stopped Myers from killing DI Gregg. And the moment her little gal had told her Vane had been sniffing around Janine Mallow's (née Tyler) records, a big red flag had waved in front of her face.

And Rosie, like most sensible people, didn't like to see big red flags waving about. They inevitably spelt trouble, and Rosie liked the quiet life. Consequently, she'd wanted to pass the trouble along and so get rid of it at the first opportunity. And everyone knew Hillary Greene was good at handling trouble.

'Did he take any files away with him?' Hillary asked sharply.

'Yes, ma'am. On the Q.T. like. Didn't want to sign anything out like, and my little gal . . .

239

well, she didn't feel as if she could stand up to him. I told her she did right. Best not to get on the wrong side of brass, I always say.'

There was just a hint of a question in the lilt of her voice, and Hillary nodded firmly. 'Oh yes. She did right. I expect the superintendent will want to put the files back the same way when he's finished with them. Just let him. Three wise monkeys, right, Rosie?'

Rosie beamed. Three wise monkeys was her favourite standpoint of all time. 'Right, ma'am. I'll be off then.'

'Yes. Thanks, Rosie. If you ever need a favour . . . '

'Thanks, ma'am. I'll remember.'

Hillary listened to the door close, then walked to the sink, and — just for something to do — washed her hands.

Her mind didn't exactly have to work hard to figure it out. For a start, Vane would have tried to access Janine's old files the usual way, via the computer — and would have found them password-coded. Ever since the Myers shooting, all of Janine's records had been iced, and Vane would have had no reason to be given access to them. Especially after making it clear that he didn't believe Janine's version of events. Hence his need to do an actual foray down into the catacombs, otherwise known as Records.

But it was his choice of reading material that caused her to feel so sick.

Vane had obviously spotted the one weakness in Janine's story and was going for it. The question was — why? He wasn't so thick-skinned or just plain thick that he didn't know the brass wouldn't thank him for it. Of that she was convinced. No, she had the feeling this was personal. He was after *her* hide. Which meant it was all her fault that this was happening, and it was up to her to do something about it.

She didn't need this when she needed all her energy and concentration for her murder case.

Hillary stared at her reflection for a moment, and grimaced. Whether she liked it or not — and she most definitely didn't — she'd have to give Donleavy a heads up. Just in case she fumbled the ball.

She sighed and walked stiff-legged to the door, then climbed the stairs one flight to his office. Detective Chief Superintendent Donleavy's secretary glanced at her in surprise as she tapped and walked in. She knew she didn't have an appointment.

'I just need a bare minute,' Hillary said, then added, 'How goes the quest?'

Donleavy was hoping to make commander,

and his secretary, who was devoted — some said beyond the call of duty — to her boss, would know the latest.

'He's been short-listed, I'm almost sure. I have a friend who's secretary to the committee.'

Hillary held up her hands, fingers crossed. The secretary smiled, buzzed, spoke briefly, and nodded. 'Just a minute, mind,' she warned, as Hillary went past.

Hillary nodded. She wasn't looking forward to this and, if she had her way, would be in and out in a matter of seconds only. She didn't, however, put much faith in that happening.

★　★　★

Geoff Miles fumbled with his packet of fags as he shot up the motorway, leaving London behind. Either side of him, sheer white chalk walls towered above him. He was not far from High Wycombe, and headed for the sticks. That alone was enough to make him crave a stiff drink.

Geoff belonged to that hungry and mostly embittered group of people known as freelance journalists. He had no regular job on a regular paper to cushion him against the rent payments, and was his own photographer, research assistant and bar-room lawyer.

He knew a lot about libel, for instance, on account of the number of times he'd had to defend himself against the charge.

He was nearly fifty, drank too much, smoked too much, and was just a few points away from having his driving licence revoked. He hadn't had a decent story in months, and didn't hold out much hope for the one he was currently pursuing.

The case of the knighted 'sir' ending up in jug and committing suicide had run its course and was over. Still, he knew no hacks were covering the funeral, mostly because it was so hush-hush and rushed, they couldn't be bothered to find out about it. Which meant, just in case he found a titbit, he'd have an exclusive.

Geoff coughed on his cigarette. More likely, they all knew it was a dead duck, of course. But Geoff had nothing else on, and you never knew what might happen at a funeral. Besides, it got him out of London just when Benny the Bright, his bookie, had sent a couple of his lads out looking for him.

He'd find a B&B somewhere and stay the night, before heading back. Perhaps play the gee-gees and win something back to give to Benny.

He glanced across at the map laid open on the passenger seat and swerved across his lane, jerking his head up when the motorist behind honked his horn in warning.

Geoff swore and reached for the mini tape recorder he kept on the dashboard. He pressed play, and listened to his own voice, reciting what he had on the Moreland family.

The only potential for gossip was the son — a gay young spark who fancied himself as a tennis player. Word had it, he'd already put out feelers about selling off his daddy's company. Well, the legitimate part of it anyway; Her Majesty's Revenue and Customs were still fighting over the bones of the most dodgy part of it.

Geoff grunted in dismay. Despite hope springing eternal and all that, the potential pickings looked as lean as a greyhound's haunches.

★　★　★

'Hillary, how's the case going?'

Hillary smiled at Donleavy grimly. 'It's not.'

Marcus Donleavy was wearing one of his trademark silver-grey suits, that went so well with his silver-grey hair, silver-grey eyes, and silver-grey steely personality. Now he smiled. 'Like that is it? Well, I'll expect you'll be able to shake it loose.'

'Hope so, sir.'

'You're not here to talk about the case though are you?' Marcus guessed aloud, one eye on his watch.

'No, sir. I can smell trouble brewing with DS Vane.' She came straight to the point, and Donleavy grimaced.

'It was a mistake to appoint him, I can see that now. But we've already got something in place to move him along, so you won't have to put up with him much longer.'

'It might not be quick enough though, sir,' she said, and told him what Rosie Trubshaw had just told her.

Donleavy's intelligent, narrow face tightened. 'What's the man playing at?'

'I've a good idea, sir. And I'll see what I can do. But I might need you to give me a bit of backup — if I need it.' She knew, even as she said it, that now was a bad time to ask. Commanders-in-hopeful-waiting didn't like to hear about anything that portended a bad smell.

Donleavy leaned slowly back in his chair. 'All right. But I want to know what's behind all this. Exactly what's the trouble between the two of you?' he demanded flatly, and Hillary could see that this time he meant business.

Grassing didn't sit well with her, but she

knew that she could really be up against it this time. So, reluctantly, and with the barest amount of detail, she told Donleavy about her first case with Brian Vane, and how she'd spotted him planting evidence in order to get a conviction. She was quick to point out that the skell in question was undoubtedly guilty, and had served several other sentences since, for the same or similar offences. But she was sure that Vane had realized she'd seen him do it, and wasn't very happy about it.

'And neither was I, sir,' she added in conclusion.

Donleavy rubbed his forehead wearily. 'Just as well he's going, then, isn't it? He can be Hull's problem. OK. Well, if you really need help you can come to me. But I'll need to know the full picture first.'

Hillary sighed. She'd had a bad feeling he was going to say that. And, of course, the full picture was the one thing she couldn't tell him.

'Yes, sir,' she said woodenly and, as she walked back across the office, smiling grimly at the secretary as she passed her desk, admitted forlornly to herself that this time, she was on her own.

★ ★ ★

DC Mark Chang looked up from his desk and watched Hillary Greene enter the main office. It was gone nine and it was not like her to be late. Beside him, Gemma Fordham said softly, 'She's been in with Donleavy.'

She made it her business to know what her boss was up to: she'd found out the hard way that it paid.

'Oh. Trouble with the case?' Chang asked anxiously.

'Doubt it. It's early days yet. And when you've worked with DI Greene for a while, you'll learn that there aren't many cases that get the better of her. So don't worry, we're not going to be yanked from the murder case just yet, Constable, rest easy.'

Her eyes strayed thoughtfully to Paul Danvers's cubicle. 'Besides, she's Danvers's special pet. Didn't you know?'

Chang flushed a little and turned away.

After a restless night, he'd come to two solid conclusions: firstly, he was not quite as bullet-proof as he'd thought. He scared as easily as the next man, and knew when he was out of his depth.

And secondly, that the only person who could get him out of it was Hillary Greene.

He'd got out of bed that morning determined to bite the bullet and confess all to her, but as he watched her approach, he sensed a tension about her that didn't bode well.

Perhaps he'd better put it off for a while.

He turned to his keypad and began to type furiously. Once or twice he glanced across at Sergeant Fordham, considering her thoughtfully. Everyone knew she was a kick-ass sort of woman, who knew martial arts and how to handle herself. Rather ironic that Chang, an oriental, should look to her for protection. But he wouldn't know a martial art from a Picasso.

And that was another thing — he'd have to sign up for some advanced physical combat training courses. He supposed there'd be some martial arts involved in that. One thing was for sure, his ego wouldn't be able to withstand another humiliation like last night. That lesson in vulnerability was still sapping his self-confidence, and that was a state of affairs that he couldn't allow to continue.

But, after a moment's thought, he decided against telling Gemma Fordham what had happened last night.

What he wanted was some sympathy along with the inevitable drubbing, and for some reason he didn't think the striking blonde bombshell (as he'd heard the head of traffic division call her) was the sympathetic type.

No, he'd wait and catch Hillary Greene when she was in a better mood.

★ ★ ★

Keith Barrington found the church with some difficulty. As Gavin had warned him, it was well off the beaten path, on the outskirts of a village so small it was almost a hamlet.

As he parked, he saw only a scattering of cars that told him that for such a high-flying and wealthy man, Sir Reginald Moreland was going to have a very quiet send off.

He climbed out of his car, glad to see that the grey day was clearing, sending a few odd shafts of sunlight down to earth. As he stepped into one, he had no idea that the flaming colour of his red hair had attracted the attention of a man standing in the concealing shelter of a bunch of trees.

Geoff Miles took a couple of snapshots of the tall, lanky redhead in the ill-fitting black suit, just because he didn't seem to fit. He was not a member of the Moreland family, of that he was sure. Nor did he look like a wealthy businessman type, which comprised the small number of other mourners.

Geoff sucked on another cigarette and glanced at his watch. As soon as the hearse arrived, he'd sneak in the back of the church and see if any of the grieving women looked good for a touch-up.

But even if he stumbled across a secret mistress, he doubted miserably that any hack editor would be interested. It wasn't as if Moreland was royalty or anything.

★ ★ ★

Hillary gave her team their day's orders, then grabbed her bag and headed outside. She wasn't going anywhere other than to the car-park, but what she had to do now called for privacy.

She sat in Puff the Tragic Wagon's front passenger seat and got out her mobile, then dug into her bag for a large, leather-bound phone-book that was her lifeline.

She knew Vane had worked up Birmingham way for a while, and ran through her mental database for someone she knew who might be able to help.

She trawled slowly through the back of her book, where she kept her regular updated list of retired coppers.

Her finger lingered for a while over the name of Kevin Bachelor, then walked on. She remembered now hearing that he had cancer, and she didn't want to give him any more hassle.

Then she gave a little grunt. Robin Ryce. He'd worked at Thames Valley for years before marrying a Brummie. Got to her rank, DI, before retiring three years ago. They'd worked together as young sergeant and even younger WPC, and she'd made sergeant herself before Robin had been promoted up. She rang directory enquiries, got a number for him, added it beside his name, and rang the phone.

She felt tense and forced herself to relax.

'Hello?' It was a woman's voice, with a broad Birmingham accent.

'Hello. Can I speak to DI — sorry, can I speak to Robin please?'

'Oh yeh, just a minnit, will'ya?'

Hillary heard the phone clank noisily as it was put down, then the same female voice yell, ''Ere, our Robbie, it's for you. One of your old lot. If they want yer to do some cold cases, you tell 'em to sling their 'ook, y'hear?'

Hillary couldn't help but grin. The popular BBC detective series called 'New Tricks' had a lot to answer for. In it, retired coppers got to work old cases under a regular officer. Nice thought, but Hillary couldn't see it catching on.

'Hello?' The voice was cautious, and Hillary mentally crossed her fingers that he remembered her. And fondly.

'Hello, Robin? It's Hillary Greene.'

'Hill? Hey, shit, it's been nearly ten years. What do you want?' he added, with a mock growl, and Hillary laughed, remembering anew his lively sense of humour.

'What makes you think I want something,' she shot back, 'and how soon can we meet up so I can ask you to get it for me?'

'You don't change. Hey, I heard about your troubles up there. I was sorry to hear about them. I knew Mel a bit. It was bullshit what happened.'

Hillary swallowed hard. 'Yes. Look, Robin, it sort of touches on the whole Mel thing — this problem of mine, I mean. Do you know a Brian Vane? He's superintendent now.'

'Oh yeah, I know Vane all right. He was in my nick in Solihull when I first moved north,' Robin interrupted. And something in his voice made the tension in Hillary suddenly subside. It was only then, when she felt the unexpected rush of tears come to her eyes, that she realized how truly frightened she'd been.

'I need to see you, Robin. Any chance we can meet in neutral territory?'

'You know Leamington Spa?'

Hillary didn't, but could find out. 'This afternoon?'

'Sure. You'll need to find a pub called the Gosforth Arms on the far south of town — nearest your end. Any cabbie can take you to it. You coming up by train?'

'Probably not, but I'll find it. Say two-thirty?'

'OK. You're buying the Scotch.'

'You bet,' Hillary said warmly and hung up. She leaned back in the seat and took a few deep breaths, then told herself to get back to bloody work.

* * *

Geoff yawned as the mortal remains of Sir Reginald were laid to rest. As far as he could see, there were no secret mistresses ready to throw a wobbly, and all the mourners wore that furtive look that said they only wanted to get away as quickly as possible.

Geoff guessed there'd be no wake, and any chance he might have had of a free lunch, whilst letting his ears wag, was well and truly scuppered.

The widow stood at the gateway, shaking hands with the departing mourners. She seemed to have only a cold smile for everyone except her son, whom she kissed warmly, and the lanky redhead, who got a real smile instead of a fake one.

253

Geoff, parked up under a cedar, watched them go gloomily. Finally, the widow stepped inside the only hired black limousine, whilst the son and heir stood talking to the lanky redhead.

He watched Gavin Moreland, a good-looking, dark-haired boy, lay a hand on the other's sleeve, and something in the movement screamed of possessiveness.

'Ah, the boyfriend,' Geoff muttered. 'Nothing in a gay relationship these days,' he added, speaking out loud, a habit of his when he was bored or scared. Or both.

Nevertheless, some streak of stubbornness made him start the car and follow, not the son, but the redhead. Perhaps he was simply unwilling to write the day off as a total loss. Or perhaps some little spark of near-dead journalist instinct made him decide to follow his nose. Either way, he found himself following the nondescript hatchback towards Oxford. Whoever the boyfriend was, he wasn't as well-heeled as the tennis ace, obviously.

He followed his quarry doggedly to the large village of Kidlington, then swore and laughed aloud as the car in front indicated to turn into the entrance of the Thames Valley Police Headquarters.

The building itself wasn't of much

architectural merit — it looked like a sixties monstrosity to him, but Geoff could have got out of his car and kissed it.

Because why was the lover of Sir Reginald Moreland's son going into the car-park of a major cop shop? It wasn't the sort of place where you reported crime; it was the sort of place you visited with information on a major case, or because you worked there.

And either option was all right by Geoff.

Suddenly, he could smell a story. Or the potential for a spot of lucrative blackmail, anyway.

★ ★ ★

Hillary, too restless to go back inside HQ, rooted around for something else to do to kill the time before she had to set off for Leamington Spa.

When in doubt, re-interview the witnesses, was a favourite saying of one of her old tutors and, with a sigh, she turned the ignition in Puff's engine and picked one at random.

Perhaps the continued non-show of Victor Merchant, their vic's only child, was still rankling her, because she found herself heading towards the firm of solicitors that Barrington had discovered. She wasn't sure why. It was not an obvious line of inquiry, after all. Finding out that the missing son had an independent trust fund he was about to come into was a reason *not* to suspect him, since it removed money from the list of possible motives.

But the moment she was ushered into Robert Linfield's office, she scented blood. The solicitor, young and pleasant, nevertheless seemed a touch jittery.

'DI Greene, sir,' Hilary showed him her card. 'Thank you for agreeing to see me at such short notice.'

'Oh, think nothing of it. That's fine.' He waved a hand vaguely at the seat in front of his desk, and Hillary sat down. 'I take it you're here on the same business as your colleague?'

'Concerning the trust fund for Victor Merchant. Yes, sir.'

'I thought so. I took the opportunity of getting out the Merchant file when my secretary told me of your arrival. But really, I can't add much to what I already told the constable who came the other day.'

Hillary nodded. 'Something seems to be bothering you, sir,' she said pleasantly, making the younger man start. He was fiddling with the file, which he now opened up and pretended to read, but Hillary could see she'd disconcerted him.

As she'd meant to.

'I don't know what makes you think that, Inspector,' Linfield lied. For, ever since the redheaded copper had spoken to him, Linfield had been in close contact with the trustees, and he, like they, were beginning to get distinctly cold feet about the whole business. The longer it went on without the police making an arrest in the David Merchant case, the more likelihood there seemed to be of all of them all getting dragged into a very nasty mess indeed.

Hillary, who was very good at reading upside down, reached for her notebook and quickly jotted down the names of the trustees noted in a list in the opening page of the file.

'Well, this is a murder investigation, sir. It would be natural to feel a certain amount of nerves. And your client, Victor Merchant, as the son of the victim, is obviously going to come under close scrutiny from us.'

The young man gulped audibly, and Hillary said softly, 'Are you sure there's nothing you want to tell me, sir?'

Robert Linfield smiled tightly. 'Obviously, I can't reveal the affairs of my client without the proper documentation,' he prevaricated.

And Hillary smiled. Because that told her all she needed to know. Namely, that there *was* something worthwhile knowing about Mr

Victor Merchant's trust fund.

'Well then, Mr Linfield, I'll just have to see about acquiring that documentation, won't I?' she bluffed.

As things stood, she was not at all sure that she could get a judge to see things her way. Still, now that she had the names of the other trustees she could contact — hopefully trustees who had no legal training — who needed a warrant anyway?

She could just bluff the truth out of them.

10

Mark Chang stared at the small mobile phone in his hand and swore softly at the text message. He simply couldn't believe their cheek.

The package had come through the mail, right into Police HQ. At first, when he'd opened it, he'd thought it was some sort of promotional gimmick on the part of the phone company. He saw that he had a text message waiting and accessed it, expecting the hard sell. It annoyed him, because he was perfectly happy with the mobile he already had.

The text was simple and to the point — and definitely not from a phone company.

KEEP THIS MOBILE. USE NUMBER IN MEMORY TO CONTACT US.

But it was the listing beside the phone number in the Contacts menu that really made his gorge rise. Right beside the saved number, in place of a name, were three words.

His master's voice.

'No damn way,' Mark Chang said viciously.

And when he looked up, it was to see Hillary Greene walking towards him, heading for her desk. 'Ma'am,' he said, standing up and making Gemma, who was surprised by his sudden formality, look up from transcribing her notes.

'Guv, I've got all that background work you wanted finally done,' she said.

Hillary nodded. 'Good, you can leave it on my desk. Constable?'

'Ma'am,' Mark Chang gulped and, before he could loose his nerve, launched into his tale, leaving nothing out. Gemma turned her swivel chair around the better to watch his face — and that of her boss — as she realized just how juicy this was becoming.

By the time Chang finally stumbled to a halt, Hillary was sitting behind her desk, her face tight and grim.

She didn't like low-lifes putting the bite on coppers. Or trashing legitimate business owners' premises.

'Do I really need to tell you just how stupid you've been, Chang?' she asked quietly. 'I thought someone who has the brains to get a degree would know better than to meet unknown suspects alone at night.'

Chang nodded miserably. 'Yes, ma'am. But I wasn't sure if the situation was really serious or not.'

Hillary raised an eyebrow, and Chang tried again.

'That is, I thought I should find out more before coming to you with it, ma'am. What with a murder case on and everything.'

Hillary understood at once what he was getting at. And could even, in a way, admire it. He didn't want to bring any time-consuming foul-ups into his own nest. And the fact that he attended the meeting at all showed he was made of the right stuff. His mistake was understandable, and something many a green young DC might make. Still, it showed he had guts.

'Did they hurt you?' she asked abruptly, and saw Chang blush.

Mark tried to ignore the dull ache that still cut across his stomach whenever he straightened up or bent over. In the films, heroes took many punches to the gut and seemed to shake them off; Chang now knew from experience just how bloody ridiculous that was.

But he shook his head firmly. 'No, ma'am,' he lied.

Gemma shot Hillary a knowing look, but she too, like Hillary, was vaguely impressed. Obviously, they must have given him a bit of gyp, just to show him who was supposed to be boss. But the handsome new boy had shown some backbone, it seemed.

'All right. Here's what we do. You call them back — seeing as they were so nice as to provide you with communication and all. You tell them you have something for them tonight — same meeting place. Don't take no for an answer. You wear a wire. Me, Gemma and some uniforms will back you up. We'll have the buggers for trying to pervert the cause of justice, blackmail and whatever else the CPS can throw at them. Gemma, get me someone in Gangs,' she said, referring to the team whose job it was to tackle gang activity. 'They'll want to be in on this. Sounds as if Constable Chang here has stumbled across a wannabe Chinese connection.'

'Guv,' Gemma said, her heart pounding at the thought of some real action at last. Perhaps these two jokers who were trying to put the pincers on Chang knew some kung fu. It was a long time since she'd had a real workout. Fighting at the sports centre was OK, but was hardly a real substitute for the real thing.

Already she could feel her adrenalin pumping.

'Gemma, you need to set up the equipment and run DC Chang through the procedure. You ever wear a wire before, Chang?'

'No, ma'am.'

'Guv.'

'Guv,' Chang corrected, feeling happier now he'd been given permission to stop calling her ma'am. It meant he was out of the doghouse. For now.

'All right. I've got to run this past Danvers. Mark, leave a text message, don't ring the number. Talking one-to-one gives them a chance to try and set the agenda. Once you've sent the text, turn the phone off,' Hillary ordered firmly.

Gemma grinned. 'They won't like that, guv,' she agreed. 'They want to think they have our Chinese detective here under their thumb.'

Hillary grinned. 'Well, it's about time they learned differently then, isn't it?' she said. And although she spoke softly, there was something of a smiling cat in Hillary's eyes.

For the first time in a while, looking at the two women beaming confidently at one another and in perfect accord, Mark Chang felt happy. Once again, he was part of a team — a winning, supportive, powerful team.

★ ★ ★

Paul Danvers looked up as Hillary Greene knocked on his door. In his hand was confirmation of his transfer papers, and he

263

began to automatically turn them over when he saw who was at the door, then hesitated.

He needed to tell her he was going sometime and now seemed as good a time as any. He beckoned her to come in.

'Sir. It's about DC Chang,' Hillary said, the moment she was through the door, just in case he thought she'd come to update him on the case. Danvers listened without interruption as she told him what was happening, a tight little tic in his lower jawline the only indication that he shared her outrage at the blatant attempt to suborn a young officer.

'Right. Make sure you take plenty of backup. And make sure they get the message.'

Hillary smiled grimly. 'Right, sir.'

'Oh Hillary, before you go, sit down a minute,' he added, as she moved back towards the door.

Hillary felt a sudden sharp sense of foreboding as she sat down. There was something in Danvers's tone that she hadn't heard before, and for some reason it made her feel just slightly sick.

'I thought I'd better tell you I applied for a transfer a month ago, back up north, and I've just got confirmation. I'm heading for Leeds at the end of next month.'

Hillary blinked. It was the last thing she'd expected to hear and for several long seconds, she literally had no idea how to respond. Finally, she shifted in her seat. 'Family reasons, sir?' she asked cautiously. But now the nasty feeling in her stomach shifted again, telling her even before he spoke that it was nothing so benign.

Paul Danvers looked at the woman in front of him, and smiled sadly. 'No. Not really, Hillary,' he said softly. 'The thing is, I just don't think we should be working together anymore.'

Hillary felt herself blush. Shit. He still didn't fancy her, did he? Surely he must be over that by now.

'It's what happened on the afternoon Janine shot Myers,' Danvers went on, making her feel foolish suddenly. 'Oh, I'm not saying that I don't back you up on, well, whatever . . . ' He held out a hand, then let it fall back. 'It was what happened when Vane came in, trying to throw his weight around that got me thinking. You announced you were going to make an arrest, and implied that I knew all about it. Remember?'

Hillary did vaguely. She frowned. 'I don't see the problem, sir. The arrest was kosher.' All right, it hadn't resulted in a conviction, but only because the killer had died before being brought to trial.

'Yes, I know,' Paul said. 'But I didn't, at the

time, have the faintest idea what you were talking about. I had no idea who you'd be bringing in, or what evidence you had, or anything. Oh, I trusted you to get it right, but that's not the point, don't you see?'

Hillary didn't. She wasn't usually so dim, but, as she sat in Danvers's office, she got the sudden, dreadful feeling that things were slipping away from her.

'Not really, sir,' she said flatly.

'I backed you up, blindly, on faith. I'm not sure that I'd have done that for any other officer,' Danvers said, sounding exasperated now. 'Especially not with a superintendent around, looking for blood. I realized then just how much you affected my judgement. And it worried me, Hillary,' Paul Danvers said softly. 'It worried me a lot.'

Hillary felt herself chill. 'Ah,' she said softly. Now she got it. And understood. And Danvers was right: she'd jammed him up. Without even realizing it, without even thinking about it. Taking him for granted. It was something she'd never thought she'd be guilty of doing. Jamming up your colleagues was something other coppers sometimes did. And now here she was, guilty of it herself.

'I see, sir,' she said softly. 'You must know, I'm very sorry. I never meant to . . . ' She stopped. Whining would not help.

'It's not your fault,' Paul Danvers said flatly. 'But it's time I went. I'm not sure who they'll get to replace me, but both myself and Donleavy will go out of our way to make sure it's someone you can work with. All right?'

Hillary nodded mutely, got up and walked away. She felt stiff and tired and suddenly old.

★ ★ ★

Keith parked the car in front of the café in Summertown and climbed out, looking around. He didn't notice Geoff Miles pass him and park a few cars down.

He walked into the café and looked around. At nearly two o'clock, it was fast emptying of the lunch crowd, and he spotted Gavin at once. He went to his table and sat down.

Geoff Miles took up position a few tables away and turned on his mobile phone, pretending to talk to someone, but, in fact, engaging the photographic gizmo that allowed him to take discreet snapshots of the unsuspecting couple.

'What's so urgent, Gav?' Keith asked wearily. 'Couldn't we have talked about it at the funeral?' It was only a matter of two hours since he'd last seen him, and Keith was beginning to feel a little hunted.

'No. Sorry, it wasn't the right time or place,' Gavin said, eyeing Keith almost with hatred. What was it about this lanky, red-haired bloody copper that was so vital to him? He felt his palms sweat as he went for the final gambit. 'I just sold the business. Next weekend I'm flying to Japan for the Carlington.' He named an important amateur tennis championship. 'It's my last one as an amateur. After that I turn pro. I'm finally going for it. Better late than never, right?'

In his heart, he doubted he'd ever give Andy Murray cause for concern, but he could be good enough to at least make his presence known. With luck, and hard work.

Keith felt his heart sink.

'And I want you to join me on the circuit,' Gavin said, taking a deep breath. 'Permanently. I want you to be my manager. You can take a PR course, accountancy, whatever you want or need. I know how you feel about money, and I'm not asking you to be a' — here Gavin pulled a face and made quote marks in the air with his fingers — 'dare I say it, 'kept man'. I know you'd need a proper career. You could take on other sportsmen and women, become a proper agent. Just think, we could have a great time — travel, fun, relaxation. We're still young, and we have everything ahead of us. I can't stand this hole-in-the-corner stuff any more. Shit, Keith, do you realize you're the only one I know still in the closet?'

Keith stared at Gavin helplessly for now he could feel it coming: the ultimatum. He'd been expecting it for days now.

'I want you to quit, once and for all, Keith,' Gavin said softly. 'Come with me. We could even get married. Your parents know about us, right?'

Keith nodded automatically.

'Well then, it's time you chose. The cop shop or me. Because this time, when I walk away, I'm staying away. You either come with me. Or don't. Do you understand?'

He got up and then reached down and suddenly kissed him. Geoff Miles got the perfect shot and grinned behind his coffee cup. That was the money shot. If only he could figure out how best to use it.

'Don't let me down,' Gavin whispered, then turned and left.

Keith Barrington sat in the café for a long time before slowly getting to his feet and walking back to his car. For once, he hadn't even bothered to look around, embarrassed about the kiss, and worried about the possibility of hostile eyes watching him.

Geoff Miles also left, but went in the opposite direction. He needed to hit the internet and get an ID for Gavin Moreland's cop lover. Then he could start to write the story.

★　★　★

Hillary found the pub in Leamington Spa with relative ease. Her sense of things slipping away from her was getting worse. She'd seen Gemma shoot her a surprised look when she'd told her she had to leave the office for a few hours, and Hillary couldn't blame her. With the murder case still in full swing, and the added complication of sorting out Chang's Chinese gangsters, now was hardly a good time for the boss to be absent, as Gemma's accusing eyes had told her.

But she had no choice. To make up for it, she'd given Gemma the list of trustees overseeing Victor Merchant's money, and told her to get contact details for them, plus any facts she could dig up. Something about the whole set up struck her as being somehow important. Although at the moment, she couldn't have said why.

Gemma had seemed slightly mollified and a little intrigued at this hint of a new lead, but had still watched her boss depart with surprised, and even slightly concerned, eyes.

She'd told them Danvers was leaving with a terse announcement that gave nothing away, but could tell that Gemma hadn't been convinced that Hillary was feeling as sanguine about it as she tried to make out.

She sighed and left her car in the pub car-park. The Gosforth Arms was dark, poky and, despite the smoking ban, smelled curiously and strongly of cigarettes, although Hillary could see no one actually smoking. She saw Robin immediately, sitting at the back, near a noisy game machine. He'd probably done it automatically — seeking to use the noise of the machine for cover against any earwigging natives.

Not that she suspected anyone would be interested in them.

She went to the bar and ordered a large Scotch for Robin, but only a pineapple juice for herself. She was driving and needed a clear head.

'Robin,' she placed the drink in front of him, and seated herself. 'You haven't changed.'

Robin Ryce patted his round stomach and smiled. 'Ten years of the wife's good cooking. But you now, you really haven't changed. If anything, you look even better than ever.'

Hillary smiled grimly. 'Got rid of Ronnie

and got promoted,' she said flatly. 'That'd buck up any girl.'

Robin laughed. 'Your old man was a piece of work,' he agreed.

'Like Vane?' Hillary asked, with not much subtlety, and getting right to the point.

Robin took a sip of his Scotch and looked at her thoughtfully. 'Oh I wouldn't say that. I mean, not to such a degree anyway. Your ex, sorry, Hill, but let's face it, was as bent as a corkscrew. Vane . . . well, he's not lily white, but nobody's gonna say he's on the take.'

'No. I never thought he was,' Hillary agreed. Whatever Vane had done, he'd done to advance his career, but since that involved taking down scumbags, nobody would begrudge him that.

'Just likes to sail close to the wind sometimes,' Robin agreed cautiously.

Hillary nodded, glanced around, then told the ex-copper about her own experience with Vane. She was taking something of a chance, she knew, since nobody liked a copper who grassed on coppers — even on the QT in an out-of-the-way pub to an old, retired friend.

When she'd finished, Robin pursed his lips. 'And the skell was guilty?'

'Oh hell yes,' Hillary said at once.

'You kept schtum?' he asked, and Hillary shot him a quick, hard look. 'Sorry, sorry.'

Robin held up his hands in a peace gesture. ''Course you did. Right. So what's the problem then?'

'The problem is, this time Vane's looking to take down another copper,' Hillary said flatly.

'You?' Robin asked, obviously surprised.

Hillary hesitated. Strictly speaking, she should have said yes. But she knew that it wasn't herself who was first in the firing line.

Robin, as wily a bird as any, saw the dilemma in her eyes, and rapidly put two and two together. 'Your ex-sergeant, the pregnant widow vigilante,' he quoted the name given to her by one of the less upmarket rags with a wry twist of his lips. 'We heard on the grapevine Vane made the wrong move concerning her.'

Hillary took a sip of her drink and said nothing.

Robin slowly took a sip of his own drink, in no hurry to talk now, and Hillary let him get on with his own thinking in peace.

She understood his position, after all. Hillary was an old acquaintance, a good straight copper, and all of that, but hardly a bosom pal. And she came seeking something nasty on a serving officer — a superintendent no less. He had to be careful.

'I had a word around, like,' Robin said at last, and reached into his jacket and brought out a plain A4 sized brown envelope. 'I ain't gonna tell you the name of the man who gave me this — he's still serving. And I won't tell you the story behind it, neither,' he added firmly, as Hillary glanced around carefully before opening the flap and sliding out a single photocopy of a photograph.

On it, Brian Vane was on a residential street somewhere, and it looked as if he was arguing with the woman in front of him. She was a forty-something redhead, who might have had the air of a tom about her. Hillary didn't recognize her, and there was no reason why she should. She'd never worked Vice.

Hillary glanced at Robin curiously.

'Like I said, no background. But I've been assured that if you show that to Vane, and threaten to go public with what lies behind it, he'll back down.'

Hillary shifted a little in her seat.

'I don't know, Robin. It's a bit . . . ' She held her hand out and shook it from side to side in the universal 'iffy' gesture. 'Vane's going all out for trouble, and he's not going to want to back off.'

Robin nodded. 'I heard you always stood by your team, Hill,' he said softly. 'And I made some assurances to the guy who gave me that. His name would never be mentioned. So you know about loyalty.'

Hillary did. She nodded, slipped the photograph back into the envelope and reached for her drink.

'I don't like flying blind, that's all,' Hillary said. The sick feeling was back in her stomach. Once again, she had the feeling that she was losing her grip on things. But this time, the feeling was much, much stronger.

'I get you,' Robin commiserated. 'But you can take my word for it. That'll cover your back,' Robin nodded down at the photo. 'Vane can't afford for that to come out.'

Hillary smiled. 'I don't doubt your word, Robin,' she said wearily. 'It's just that I'll be bluffing if I have to use it. And if Vane even gets a whiff that, I am, well . . . ' She shrugged her shoulders.

Robin Ryce smiled. 'Come on. The day when Hillary Greene can't handle the likes of Brian Vane, they'll be holding snowball fights in Hell.'

Hillary forced a smile and raised her glass. 'Cheers,' she said. But inside, she felt something jar loose.

Later, she knew, she'd have to dig deep and find out what it was. And she had an idea that she wasn't going to like it when she did.

But for now, she had a murder inquiry to solve.

So she thanked Robin, left, and drove back

towards Oxford. But before heading back into the office, she made a quick detour to Cowley.

She needed to see Vickki again. She might know something about her errant boyfriend's trust fund.

⋆ ⋆ ⋆

This time, the weird, wiry little blonde was wearing a long dark-blue velvet skirt that swept well past her ankles, and a white, billowing shirt with a string-tie neckline and billowing sleeves. It was the sort of shirt you'd expect to see an actor wearing in a costume drama if he was playing Byron, or Shelley, or someone like that. With it she wore a curious choker, a white velvet band so broad it reached practically from her chin to her collarbone. On it was a large, awkward, pale-blue cameo. Hillary guessed Vickki herself had probably made it at a ceramics or pottery class, for the cameo was the face of a punk rocker, with full Mohican, and holding up two fingers.

Nice.

'Oh it's you.' Vickki sighed heavily when she answered the door and reluctantly let her in. 'Sorry, still no sign of him, I'm afraid.'

Hillary nodded. 'Then I'm going to have to

put out a search notice on him,' she warned flatly, and saw Vickki glance quickly across at her. She had her hands stuffed into the pockets of the skirt and Hillary thought she saw the other woman's hands clench into fists behind the material.

She was, as usual, wearing layers of make-up, this time leaning towards creating a starving, elfin look.

'What can you tell me about Timbo's trust fund, Vickki?' she asked sharply.

'His what?' She gave that little-girl, high-pitched giggle that Hillary found so false and annoying, then blinked. 'You mean it's for real? He wasn't shitting me?' She grinned then shook her head. Her mass of blonde hair bounced wildly. 'Well, well, well. He told me he was going to come into money from his dear dead very rich grandparents when he finally hit twenty-five, but I thought he was just spinning me a line. You know? I mean, look around,' Vickki tossed her head, but didn't remove her hands from her pockets to gesticulate, as Hillary would have expected her too.

It made Hillary wonder if she was holding a flick-knife or some other weapon in one of those pockets, and she took a careful step backwards, without making a big thing of it.

'So, Timbo really is coming into dosh then?

Well, the little cherub,' Vickki laughed. 'I thought it just something he said to get into my knickers. I'll have to be extra-nice to him from now on, won't I? When he gets back, that is,' she added hurriedly.

Hillary nodded. There was definitely something off about this woman. She gave off a tense, jittery vibe, and Hillary didn't think it could be put down to the usual reason either. She knew junkies the moment she spotted them.

'Have you heard from Timbo? Did he ask you not to say? Is he scared about something?' Hillary asked abruptly, and Vickki jumped.

'Oh no. No, I swear.'

Hillary sighed. She was wasting her time here, she could tell. If her boyfriend had been in touch, now that she knew he was worth some money, she'd be even less inclined to do anything to make him mad at her.

'OK, Vickki,' Hillary said, deciding not to push her. Best let her stew for a while, and probably come back tomorrow for another try. 'Remember, I'll be putting out an all points bulletin on him. We'll probably pick him up in a matter of hours.' It was a bluff, but she hoped Vickki wouldn't know that. Although she would indeed set it in motion, and throughout the UK his details would be passed on to other forces, the likelihood of a foot patrol or a couple of bobbies in a panda car spotting him were slim to none.

She left the house thoughtfully. Although she didn't think Vickki had a knife on her, she was careful not to turn her back until she heard the door close behind her.

Vickki leaned against the door, and began to bite her nails. Perhaps Timbo should make an appearance? Just show up at the police station and be interviewed and get it over with.

But just the thought of it brought Vickki out in a cold sweat. Surely, if she was just patient, it would all blow over? The cops clearly didn't have a clue.

*   *   *

Outside, Hillary climbed into her car but didn't turn on the ignition. Instead she thought about Leamington Spa, Robin Ryce and the photograph of Brian Vane.

Would it be enough to save her and Janine if Vane came across some hard evidence that proved Janine's version about how Clive Myers met his death was false?

She didn't know. And that was part of the problem. Normally, she'd never go into a situation without having all her ducks lined up in a row. 'Never pick a fight unless you know you're going to win,' her father had always told her.

But this time she had no choice. She had to hope Robin was right.

And that was what was bothering her.

The feeling that things were spiralling out of her control intensified.

And Hillary didn't like it. She didn't like it one little bit, because she knew she couldn't live with it for long. Or, more importantly, do her work.

Before she could seriously spook herself, she turned the engine and drove back to HQ.

★ ★ ★

Gemma looked across as Hillary slumped down into her chair, and reported her background findings on the trustees of Victor Timothy Merchant's trust fund.

Chang was still downstairs, experimenting with the wires he was to wear later that night, and Barrington was, as was becoming usual these days, AWOL.

'Guv,' she said softly, and Hillary glanced across at her, a 'what now' expression briefly crossing her face. It made Gemma wonder what other bad news had been winging her boss's way just lately.

She looked almost scared, Gemma thought in real surprise. She smiled cautiously. 'Nothing bad, guv,' she heard herself say. 'In fact, just the opposite. Well, I think so. I just thought I should tell you — Guy and I are going to get married.'

Hillary let out her breath in a long, slow, relieved whoosh.

'Oh? That's great, Gemma. You set a date yet?'

'June. We're going to the Maldives for the honeymoon.'

Hillary grinned. 'All right for some. When did he pop the question?'

'Oh, ages ago,' Gemma said airily. 'I've been making my mind up for some time, I suppose. Thing is, guv,' she added, glancing around, 'Guy's cousin and his son died recently. I think I said, didn't I?'

Hillary nodded.

'Well, see, Guy's family has a title. A baron, which made his cousin a lord. Now, though, Guy's had to inherit it, so I'm going to be Lady Brindley. Isn't that a hoot?'

Hillary Greene stared at Gemma Fordham for a moment, and then forced herself to smile.

'It sounds marvellous,' she lied carefully.

11

Mark Chang coughed nervously as he went through the iron gates and into the park. Then he hoped that whoever was listening with the headphones on in the Ops Van hadn't been blasted out of his seat by the noise.

He knew that there were several people recording his every movement and it made him feel clumsy, as if he was suddenly wearing diving flippers or something. He kept expecting to fall over at any moment. Having knees made out of jelly didn't help either. He kept telling himself that it must be normal to be nervous in such circumstances. After all, this was his very first time doing something like this. After a while, he was sure, he'd be able to do it without his heart sounding like the percussion section of the London Philharmonic. Then he wondered. Could those listening on the other end of the microphone attached to his chest hear it? Did they all know how scared he was?

The thought was enough to make the back of his neck go cold, and he cleared his throat nervously. He winced, and gave another mental apology to whoever was listening in.

He approached the same park bench as before slowly, looking around cautiously. He knew that Hillary Greene and Gemma Fordham had come hours earlier to pick their spots, and he could only hope they were close. But not too close to be spotted. Obviously they must have hidden themselves well, since he'd had the call twenty minutes ago that the two marks had entered the park and were sat on the bench, chatting. They had made only a token reconnaissance, arrogantly taking it for granted that Chang had been too cowed to set them up for anything.

'Marks are still behind the big tree about fifteen yards to the right,' he heard a faint tinny voice say in his earpiece, and felt his mouth go dry.

The two Chinese gangsters must have seen or heard him coming by now, and it reassured Chang to know that he had a whole team dispersed around him. Hillary had briefed the officers from Gangs thoroughly just a few hours ago, and the sight of the predominantly male, fit and competent squad was something Chang kept firmly to the forefront of his mind.

He reached the bench and hesitated. There were no clouds tonight, and the moon, though hardly full, seemed to provide more light. Chang stopped and glanced around. As he did so, he saw movement behind him, and turned, as two figures approached from the tree.

'Let's get one thing straight,' Eddie Lee's voice came quietly hissing through the night. 'We set the agenda. We call the meets. Don't ever summon us like we were a pair of dogs again, copper, or you'll be eating through a straw for the next six months. Got it?'

'No,' Chang said, launching straight into the scenario that Hillary had devised for him.

Since this was a largely 'conspiracy' related case, they needed to get as much on tape as they could, she'd explained. And Hillary believed the best way to do this was for Chang to play hardball. She'd been straight with him, and told him that this was also likely to end in something physical. But they'd be there in seconds, and it would mean they'd be able to add charges to the list.

At the time, Chang had nodded and agreed fulsomely. He wanted the bastards behind bars for as long as possible. Now though, he felt himself shiver. But he was damned if he was going to let fear get the better of him. He had colleagues all around him. This was what he'd joined the force for. If he couldn't hack this, he might just as well hand in his notice.

'D'yah-wha?' it was Ooo Yuck who spoke,

slurring the sentence into one word.

'I said no,' Chang repeated, hoping his voice wouldn't tremble. 'I've been thinking it over, and I've decided to tell you to take your offer and shove it.'

Eddie Lee sighed. He'd half expected this, of course. Nobody liked to be bullied and forced into doing something they considered beneath them. As an Oriental, he knew all about saving face. And this copper was new, young, and all fired up. It had been more than he could hope for that he wouldn't put up some resistance.

'You need to reconsider that,' Eddie Lee said, stepping on to the gravel path and looking around. There were no parked vans nearby on the road that he could see, no ostentatious dog-walkers, or 'courting couple'. But he was feeling a little tense. This might be a set up.

'I don't think so,' Mark Chang said, gaining confidence. 'See, the way I see it, it's like this. We both belong to gangs — but mine's bigger, stronger, and ubiquitous. You do know what that means, right?'

From her position sitting down behind a bush in the large and thankfully well-packed border, Hillary gave a mental nod. Good, the lad was needling him now, getting him pissed off, just like she'd coached.

When she'd found her spot nearly three hours ago now, she'd made herself comfortable. She'd advised Gemma to do the same. Squatting down, hunkering down, or even kneeling down, didn't do the human body any good after a while. It would become almost impossible not to move about. Also, muscles that aren't used much in a daily routine, tend to cramp more easily than most. And the last thing you needed, when suddenly springing into action, was to find your foot had gone to sleep, sending you sprawling.

So she was sitting comfortably, flexing her ankles, making sure she was ready to move when Chang needed her. She could only hope Gemma had taken in her lecture and was doing the same.

''Course I know what it means, you little shite,' Eddie Lee hissed. 'But knowing big words won't help your mum and dad when they wake up and find themselves roasting, will it? Live over the shop, don't they? Firetraps, them places. Hope their fire-escape isn't blocked.'

Chang gave a mental clenched fist of triumph. Yes, he'd got the first of it on tape. His instinct was to press on, and say something to egg him on. Like, 'But you wouldn't really murder innocent people would you?' But Hillary had warned him against this.

Skells nowadays were wise to being caught on tape, and they might get suspicious if he tried to get them to spell things out. Besides, Hillary had said, juries were more sensible than a lot of QCs thought, in her opinion, and didn't need all I's dotted and T's crossed. Just make sure it's obvious what's what, she'd told him, and leave it at that.

So Mark moved on.

'You talk big, but how do I know you can even pull it off?' he challenged. 'I had a quiet word with this mate of mine, who's in Gangs, and I don't reckon they've even heard of you. You probably don't have the muscle or know-how!' he jeered.

Ooo Yuck hissed. It took a bewildering second or two for Mark to realize that he was laughing.

'He don't think we can do it, Eddie,' Ooo Yuck fairly danced with glee, his big bulky body shimmying.

'We might be new, Chang, but that just means we're even more keen. Now do you really want to risk it?' Lee asked, ignoring the lumbering giant beside him.

'Suppose I tell my parents to go back to the old country for a visit,' Chang said, his voice gaining in confidence with every moment.

'And suppose I tell my guv'nor about you lot. How would you like that?' he derided.

'Let me hurt him, Eddie,' Ooo Yuck said, his voice whining. 'I can bust his kneecaps. I like doing that. I bought the little balpeen hammer.'

Yes! Mark just stopped himself from grinning. Another gem for the tape. Threatening a police officer in the line of duty. Or something along those lines. Who knows, other nicks might have unsolved knee-cappings on their lists that they'd be able to link to this big thug, which would help with clear-up rates.

'Nah, that might get him invalided off the force. And we want him to be right where he is, don't we? We just need to make him see sense, that's all,' Eddie said softly, turning to glance behind him.

Had he heard movement?

Just then, a fox trotted across the path further down, glanced at them with yellow eyes, but didn't break trot.

'Bold bastards, aren't they?' Eddie said with a smile. 'Bet they can bite. What do you think, Chang?'

There was something in Lee's voice now that was making the jelly return to his knees.

'Probably,' he agreed, somewhat feebly, sensing he'd momentarily somehow lost the upper hand, but not sure how. 'But I ain't scared of foxes, and I ain't scared of hyenas like you either,' he said, in an attempt to get things back on track.

Behind the bushes, Hillary Greene rolled very carefully to her left, where she'd already cleared the ground of any dry leaves, the rustling of which might give her away, and got on to all fours. Any moment now, she could tell, things were going to hit the fan.

'And if you think I'm going to tell you squat about what raids are planned, or help you remove any of your rivals, you can think again,' Mark Chang said flatly.

'Yeah?' Eddie Lee said, almost smiling now, and beside him, he could feel Ooo Yuck begin to quiver. The big, dim-witted man loved violence, like other men loved women or dogs.

'You bring your pliers, Ooo?'

'Sure did.'

'Ever tried dentistry without anaesthetic, Chang?' Lee said. 'Ever watch the Marathon Man? You know, that film, where some poor sap gets his teeth drilled. Well, this is our version, right, Ooo? Only in our version, they get pulled, not drilled. Should we go for the front ones, and spoil Detective Constable Chang's good looks, Ooo, or do we go for a back molar?'

'The back ones. They're tougher to get out,' Ooo Yuck said at once. 'They scream more.'

'OK then. Back it is,' Eddie said, and suddenly launched himself forward.

Chang gave a squawk of surprise, then started yelling 'Mexico, Mexico!'

For a second, Eddie Lee wondered what the hell Mexico had to do with anything, and then he understood: it was a code word. The bloody copper had been wired after all!

'Run for it!' Eddie Lee yelled to his confederate, immediately veering off and heading for the open grass. But Ooo Yuck had become too primed, and was already grabbing Chang by the throat.

Mark Chang brought his knee up sharply, hoping to connect with the thug's groin, but Ooo Yuck was far too wily for that, and twisted to the side.

Dimly, the gangster saw something shoot out of the bushes and take off after Eddie, and heard a woman's voice shouting instructions. But the next moment his head exploded with pain as something landed with a sickening thud over his right ear.

He dropped Chang and spun around, one hand going up to his face. His jaw dropped comically as he looked at the woman in front of him. Slender, dressed in black with well-made, steel-capped boots, she had short spiky blonde hair and was wearing a grin so wide the Chinese thug could actually see her teeth gleaming.

'Ow,' he said belatedly, and lunged towards her.

Gemma danced back, twisted, turned and landed a steel toe-cap right to his gut.

Ooo Yuck doubled up and grunted, then lifted his head to stare at her under lowering eyebrows.

Ooo Yuck had watched every martial arts movie ever made, but had never, much to his chagrin, been able to get anyone to teach him any of the moves. He was too clumsy, too thick, too muscle-bound to be of any use at it, or so they told him. Now he clenched his fists and roared. It wasn't fair. Here was this white chick, a little stick of a girl, landing her feet on him! Without straightening up, he charged forward. He wanted to land his head in her own gut, bulldoze her into the ground and stomp on her. He might not have been taught any Bruce Lee moves, but his masters had been more than happy to teach him back-street dirty fighting.

Hillary Greene raced through the night, wondering how long her wind was going to last. She'd taken off after Lee the moment he'd bolted, but he was fast out-pacing her.

Not that she was seriously concerned. And even as she wondered where the hell the others were, a large shape appeared from behind a big brass sculpture and rugby-tackled Lee to the ground.

Hillary slowed to a jog and bent down, resting her hands on her knees and taking a deep breath. Her eyes, though, never left the struggling pair on the ground until she saw the man on top handcuff the man beneath him and haul him to his feet.

'OK?' she called. She wasn't sure which member of Gangs it was in the dark, but a hearty male voice quickly answered.

'All right, guv.'

Hillary nodded. This was her operation, since Chang was her officer, which made her everyone's guv tonight. But she knew the DCI in charge overall was back in the van, listening in.

'Right. Take him to the van, book him, and your guv'nor can have first go at him if you like.'

'Thanks, guv,' the voice called back.

Eddie Lee began to swear, first in English, then in something Hillary thought might be Mandarin, then, of all things, in French.

It was nice to nick multi-lingual skells every now and then, she thought, trotting back towards the park bench. It gave you hope that not all standards were slipping.

As she approached the bench, she noticed two things: the first was the sound of roaring and grunting, that made her think of a bear fight. The next was that a small ring of Gangs officers was standing around, doing nothing.

It was puzzling, until she came up behind them and, realizing who she was, the broad line of masculine backs parted to let her through. And she saw Gemma Fordham land an edge-of-the-hand blow to the thick neck of a Chinese man, built like a brick outhouse.

He yelled and shook his head, and backed off a step, panting, and staring at Gemma with a puzzled, aggrieved look.

'Had enough, fatso?' Gemma asked cheekily, bouncing around on her feet lightly.

'My name's Ooo Yuck. Not Fat So,' Ooo Yuck said, and then frowned, wondering why everyone was suddenly laughing at him. He didn't like being laughed at.

Gemma shook her head. 'Why don't you just give it up, hey? These nice men will take you to the police station, and give you a cell to sleep in, and a cup of tea. What do you say?' In truth, she felt ashamed at having to keep on poking away at him. It was like shooting fish in the proverbial barrel.

'Cell?' Ooo Yuck said with a lilt of interest.

'That's right. You know the drill, right?'

Gemma encouraged. 'Nice warm cell, some food. Get to talk and have people listen to you, for a change.'

Ooo Yuck sighed heavily. 'Can't,' he said, almost regretfully. 'Not 'less Eddie says so.'

'Eddie's already on his way to a cell of his own,' Hillary called out drily, and when Gemma glanced across at her, Ooo Yuck lunged forward.

Quick as a flash, Gemma leapt into the air, twirled, caught the man under his jaw with an audible 'crack' that made several of the officers around her wince, and landed back on her feet.

Ooo Yuck sat on the ground and contemplated the blood on his shirt front.

'I think you may have just broken his jaw, Sergeant,' Hillary said flatly.

Gemma sighed. 'Sorry, guv. He must have a glass one. Can someone call the ambulance?'

★   ★   ★

In his flat, Keith Barrington, who hadn't returned to the office that afternoon, and so didn't know about the operation, sat at his desk and opened up his laptop.

If he'd known what was going down in the park, he'd have been annoyed to miss it. But even though Hillary could have called him on his mobile and ordered his presence, she'd already decided that Keith's head wasn't where it ought to be right now. And operations such as the one they'd just carried out, needed to have everyone on their toes.

But then, if he'd gone to the park, he'd have missed Gavin phone's call.

At first, he couldn't take in what his lover was saying. But Gavin soon made it clear. Some flea-bag journo had taken pictures of them kissing, and was trying to blackmail him for five grand. If he didn't pay up, he'd publish.

Gavin had snorted, and quoted Wellington. Barrington hadn't been sure what he meant, so the Eton-educated Moreland had enlightened him.

And whilst *Publish and be damned* was all very well for Gavin, Keith knew that for him it would be a whole different thing. If the local rags published his picture, his working life would be made ten times harder.

But Gavin had been too angry to care, and Keith didn't have the heart to argue.

Which meant, really, that his decision had been made for him.

Keith didn't know it, but, as he began to type the most important letter of his life so far, his boss had already decided that they needed to sit down somewhere and have a serious heart-to-heart chat.

And Hillary didn't know it, but she'd already left it far too late.

★   ★   ★

The next morning, Gemma parked and walked into the lobby to ragged cheers from the desk sergeant and the uniforms milling about.

Her face flushed with pleasure, she ran a similar gauntlet through the main office, with colleagues going out of their way to tease, jeer, congratulate and pretend to quail in fear of her.

Hillary watched her triumphal procession, and wondered if her sergeant realized that she ought to make the most of it while she could. Because Hillary doubted she'd have other opportunities.

Hillary knew how the top brass still thought — even in this so-called classless society of theirs. And once it became known that a serving officer had come into a title, things would quickly change for Gemma, of that Hillary had no doubt. For a start, her promotion to DI would be assured. And so would a move on to a high-profile, low-risk committee, squad, or task force. Since the PR department would throw a hissy fit at the idea of Lord or Lady Copper getting wounded in the line of duty, Gemma's days working the streets, or any real cases for that matter, were going to become a thing of the past.

She wondered if Gemma knew that, and thought that she probably didn't. She knew Gemma was ambitious, though, so perhaps she wouldn't care. As Lady Brindley, her chances of a top-flight career were infinitely higher. Not that anybody would ever admit the reason, of course.

'Gemma,' she said, as her sergeant sat down. 'No aches and pains?'

'Oh please,' Gemma laughed. 'He never got to lay a finger on me.' She reached for her phone as it rang, then leaned forward, her smile fading as it became sharp with concentration.

'You're sure? OK, Barrington, go and bring him in.' As she spoke, she cast a quick look at Hillary. Strictly speaking, of course, she had no authority to tell him any such thing, but Hillary caught her eye and nodded. She didn't know what Gemma had, but knew she could trust her judgement. Which was just as well, if she was all set to become the first female Commissioner of Police!

'Barrington, guv,' Gemma said, hanging up. 'You know he got all pally with that secretary of Martin Scraggins?'

Hillary nodded. 'Our vic's business partner at the publishing works?'

'Right. Well, apparently the takeover deal that David Merchant was fighting so hard against has just gone through. And according to the girl, guess who now owns the whole company? And will, as a result, get the whole profit from the takeover?'

'Scraggins.'

'Right. According to Barrington, he's set to get at least a mil five for signing on the dotted line. Now is that a motive, or is that a motive?'

Hillary smiled. Her sergeant was pumped up, scenting blood of a different kind now. She was going to miss all this, when she was sitting behind a large desk with a secretary of her own, and shuffling paperwork.

'OK. Let me know when he's downstairs, and we'll see what he has to say for himself. While we're waiting, go around and pick up our witness. Ask him if he'd mind popping in. Arrange for him to be taken to the viewing room, and see if he can recognize Scraggins.'

'This would be the old man with the dog?'

'No. He saw a blonde woman. This is . . . ' — she consulted her notes — 'Stan Collins I'm talking about.'

Gemma consulted the murder book quickly and frowned.

'Didn't he describe the man as tall and fair? According to this, Scraggins is a little runt of a man.'

'I know,' Hillary said. 'But you've been around long enough by now to know what witnesses are like. They'll tell you the man they saw was a one-armed black man who spoke with a broad Geordie accent, until you show them a whey-faced bodybuilder with a lisp, and then they'll nod happily.'

Gemma laughed. 'Right, guv,' she said, and reached for her phone to make sure Collins was at home.

Hillary turned to her in-tray and began to sort through the usual pile.

One letter, typed and addressed with a single line — her title and name — stood out. Usually, internal mail consisted of memos or cheap circulars in brown envelopes. This envelope was long, stiff and good quality white paper.

As she opened it and read it, she felt her mouth go dry.

It was Detective Constable Keith Barrington's official letter of resignation.

★ ★ ★

In his small cottage near Tackley, the artist Francis Whyte began to gather his belongings

299

together. He hadn't heard back from the cops, and he sure as hell didn't particularly want to.

If he legged it, surely they wouldn't bother tracking him down, even if they did have any more questions for him?

He could always use the excuse that he thought he needed to vacate the cottage. After all, what did he know about probate or his rights? A bit thin, perhaps, yet it would have to do. He simply couldn't stand it any longer, waiting to see if the axe would fall and wondering with every knock at the door, or ring of the telephone, if this was it.

He could disappear for a couple of months, easy. Maybe even go abroad. It would all blow over and if not . . . well. Francis wasn't sure what the penalty would be for what he'd done, but prison seemed a pretty sure bet.

And he certainly didn't fancy being an old lag's lace doily.

★   ★   ★

Martin Scraggins arrived at Kidlington HQ with a solicitor in tow. It didn't particularly surprise Hillary, but it added to the aggravation.

As she walked into the interview room with Barrington, she knew Gemma was watching from the viewing room with Stan Collins.

'Thank you for coming in, Mr Scraggins,' she said, but it was the thin, dark-haired man beside him who spoke first. Not much taller than Scraggins himself, he had the wiry look of a long-distance runner. Protruding teeth and chin gave him a distinct and rather unfortunate profile.

'My client is pleased to help; Inspector Greene, is it?'

Hillary nodded, shook hands with the man who introduced himself as Terrence Morgan and set the tape recorders going.

Beside her, Keith Barrington shot his boss a quick look, wondering if she'd read her internal mail yet.

'As you know, we're investigating the murder of your business partner, David Merchant.'

'Yes. I still can't believe he's dead,' Martin Scraggins said piously. 'I think I'm still in shock.'

'But your shock hasn't prevented you from taking advantage of Mr Merchant's demise to go ahead with a takeover deal that you know he was bitterly opposed to?' she said smoothly.

Scraggins flushed. 'Business can't grind to a halt because I lose my partner, Inspector,' he said stiffly. 'Especially in the current financial market.'

Hillary nodded. 'If Mr Merchant had been alive, I take it that he would profit by half of the proceeds?'

'Yes.'

'And what would his share have been?'

She saw Scraggins glance across at his solicitor, who nodded gravely.

'About eight hundred thousand,' Scraggins said reluctantly.

'And who gets his share now?'

Scraggins gritted his teeth, and Terrence Morgan said smoothly, 'As I'm sure you already know, Inspector, my client had a legal agreement with Mr Merchant. On the death of either partner, the other man assumes full control of the business — and the profits therefrom.'

'Bit hard on relatives, isn't it?' Hillary asked mildly.

'I have no children,' Martin Scraggins said stiffly, 'and David had no wish to see his only child profit by so much as a penny.'

Hillary nodded. 'Why was Mr Merchant so opposed to something that would make him so much money? Was he afraid that there'd be no job for him in the new company? Was he one of those men who struggled hard against retirement?' she asked curiously.

'Not really,' Martin said. 'David's objections were mostly moral. He was a very moral man. He objected to the other company's publishing list.'

'It must have been annoying to work with someone so straight-laced,' Hillary smiled.

'My client has provided you with an alibi for the time Mr Merchant was killed, I believe?' the solicitor interrupted.

Hillary smiled. 'He was in his office, working.'

'Which his secretary confirmed?' the solicitor pressed.

'He may have slipped out when she was taking a break,' Hillary said, but without much enthusiasm.

The other man smiled grimly. 'Really, Inspector,' he chided.

And although Hillary went at them hard, she could make no dent in Martin Scraggins or his solicitor. After a fruitless hour, she had to let them go.

She went into the viewing room, which was empty, then walked back upstairs. Gemma had probably returned to the office after sending the witness back home, seeing for herself that Hillary was getting nowhere. She was sure that Collins must have nixed the ID, or he'd still be there. But it had been a long shot at best.

Beside her, Barrington moved silently.

'I've read your letter, Constable,' she said

quietly, once they reached the top of the stairs. 'Are you sure?'

'Yes, guv. It's no good. It's been coming on for some time.'

'You've got other plans, I presume?'

'Yes, guv,' Keith said, but had no intention of discussing Gavin or his private life.

'All right then. Well, you don't need me to tell you that you'd have made a good officer, Keith. But if you're sure . . . ?' She gave him once last chance, but already knew it was pointless.

'Yes, guv,' Keith Barrington said firmly, and Hillary had to leave it at that.

12

Ronald Buscott smiled at them and indicated the chairs opposite the fireplace, where a real fire crackled merrily. Of all the trustees for Victor Timothy Merchant's trust fund, only Buscott had sounded even remotely helpful. The others Gemma had called to try and book an appointment with had fobbed her off, and the sergeant knew she had no real muscle to flex in order to get them to change their minds.

'If you ask me, that solicitor chap, Linfield, has told them to keep their lips buttoned,' Gemma had complained to her boss, when Hillary returned from her unsatisfactory interview with Martin Scraggins.

Now, as they sat down in Ronald Buscott's small front room, they eyed the elderly man warily. 'So, Mr Buscott, how is it you're one of the Merchant trustees?' Hillary decided to tread softly.

'Oh, I knew Victor's grandparents. Went to the same school as the old man — oh, many years below him, of course. I'm not quite as ancient as I look. After that we went into the same line of business. So when they set up the trust fund, they asked me, the local vicar, and one or two other worthies to oversee it for them.'

'I see. I have to say nobody else seemed keen to talk to us,' Hillary said carefully.

Buscott, a fairly lean, tall man with a completely bald head and dark-brown eyes, smiled faintly. 'No. Linfield thinks we may run into problems.'

'Oh?'

'Victor's father, David, was trying to stop his son coming into his money,' Buscott said, making Gemma perk up and take notice. 'Linfield didn't think he'd manage it, but he persuaded the others to drag their feet. And now, of course, there's this murder business.'

Hillary smiled wryly. Obviously, Buscott was not the sort of man to be overly impressed by mere homicide. 'And I take it Victor Merchant wasn't very happy about this?'

'Oh no. Livid,' Buscott confirmed. 'But like I said, Linfield was handling it. Had scheduled some sort of conference, proposing something or other. I think, in the end, young Victor would have got his way though. Nowadays the old-fashioned ideas of the older generation don't count for much, do they?'

Hillary smiled. 'Knowing his father as I'm

beginning to, I take it the problem he had with his son had something to do with sex?'

Ronald Buscott's dark eyes distinctly twinkled. Evidently, something was amusing him. 'Well, technically I suppose, I'd have to say yes — but probably not in the way that you're thinking. But here' — he held up his hands — 'I have to draw the line and tell you that I can't really discuss it. Young Victor's affairs are his own, until you have the proper documentation that says otherwise.'

Hillary, sensing that pushing the man for more information would only make him become obstructive, rose to her feet.

'Well, thank you, Mr Buscott. You've been very helpful.'

The old man rose to his feet with a rueful smile. 'No doubt I shall be hearing about that from Linfield. But I'm old enough and mean enough to make up my own mind about things. And I've always felt it a duty to help the police in any way possible.'

Hillary, sensing that he and the solicitor probably clashed wills often, was simply grateful for the fact that Buscott's antipathy to being told what to do had loosened his lips as much as they had.

She shook hands politely and outside, back in the car, Gemma smirked behind the wheel. She headed quickly back to HQ.

'Well that's put the cat amongst the pigeons,' she said. 'Now we know the son and heir has a motive after all. You want him found, right?' she added rhetorically.

'Pull out all the stops,' Hillary agreed shortly. 'See if you can find a picture of him, and get on to the PR department. I want his face in all the newspapers. Play it low key for now — we're growing concerned that he hasn't contacted us so long after his father's murder. We need him to sort out some legal affairs. You know the drill.'

'Right, guv. But the public might be more alert if we slant it towards the suspected murderer-on-the-run angle.'

'And if he is our man, that'll only be sure to make him bolt,' Hillary pointed out. 'Don't forget, Buscott seemed to think that he'd be getting his money sooner or later, so unless he needed the money urgently, there would still have been no real reason for him to resort to murder.'

Gemma sighed heavily.

Once back behind her desk, Hillary went through the latest reports, but had trouble concentrating. Forensics, interview reports, house-to-house, she'd read it all before. But something about what Buscott had said kept nagging at her. 'Technically speaking', he'd said — the reason their victim had been trying to stop his son coming into money had had to do with sex, but not in the way she was probably thinking.

But how many ways could you think about sex? Men and women, women and women, men and men. Threesomes? Worse?

But as far as she could tell, Merchant's son hadn't even been gay — he was shacked up with Vickki. Perhaps he'd led a very promiscuous lifestyle before the steady girlfriend?

But Buscott had said the problem wasn't the obvious one. So what else could it be? What was 'technical' about sex?

Well, there was the actual gender of course, Hillary mused, doodling idly on a pad. The male sex. The female sex. Hermaphrodites . . .

Suddenly she froze. Something she hadn't even been aware of that had been fermenting in the back of her mind suddenly reared up and screamed at her.

'Oh for Pete's sake,' Hillary yelped, making Chang jump. Barrington and Gemma, who'd seen the phenomenon before, also looked up, excited.

Hillary shook her head. 'What a bloody idiot. Gemma' — she glanced up at her — 'go and bring in Vickki.'

'You think she knows where the boyfriend

is, guv?' Gemma asked excitedly, already reaching for her coat. 'What if she doesn't want to come in?'

'Drag her in,' Hillary said ominously.

'Barrington, start the paperwork for an arrest warrant.'

'Right, guv. Who, what, where, when?'

'Victor Timothy Merchant, for the murder of his father. I've got to see Danvers and lay it out for him.'

Chang blinked from Keith to Gemma, then stared at Hillary's retreating back. Barrington smiled at him wryly. 'Don't worry, Chang. You work around here long enough, you'll get used to it.'

★　★　★

Half an hour later, Hillary faced Vickki across the table in interview room one. Beside her she had Chang, deciding he needed the experience, although Gemma had been chafing at the bit. But her sergeant had had to content herself with watching in the interview room, along with Danvers and a member of the CPS, who happened to be in the building and was curious.

Since she hadn't had a chance to fill Gemma in, she wondered if her sergeant had twigged it yet.

'For the tape,' Hillary began, and went into the usual routine. When she was finished, she looked across at Vickki and nodded. Today, she was wearing an army-style green, high polo-necked sweater, that reached to just under her chin. With it, she was wearing a pair of Ali Baba style trousers in pink and orange silk, and wore a silver-fox fur muff in front of her, into which she had tucked her hands. Bizarre as ever, she was wearing almost clown-white make-up, with blazing red lipstick.

Now that Hillary understood that the absurd clothing was more of a disguise than a fashion statement, she couldn't believe she'd been so blind before.

'Right then, let's get started. For the tape, can I have your full name and address.'

Vickki giggled nervously. 'Oh all right. My name is Vickki . . . '

'No, your full name please,' Hillary interrupted.

Vickki rolled her eyes. 'Oh please! Do I have to? All right, I'm Miss Victoria Margaret Maltravers, and I live at — '

'Please don't lie to me, Vickki,' Hillary interrupted again. 'Your name is Victor Timothy Merchant. Do I really have to call in the police surgeon and have you stripped and medically examined?'

In the viewing room, Gemma gasped, then began to laugh. Danvers shot her a quick look and she abruptly shut up. The man from the CPS leaned forward in his chair.

Beside Hillary, Chang managed to keep a perfectly straight face, but he felt vaguely shocked. His eyes ran over the girl, man, whatever, in front of him and tried to see past the weird clothes and heavy make-up.

Vickki herself tensed visibly.

'I noticed, every time we met, Victor, that you were wearing something that totally covered your throat and your hands,' Hillary explained, as Vickki continued to stare at her silently. 'Obviously, you needed to hide your Adam's apple, which was a dead give away, but also your hands. A man might have shapely legs, or trim ankles, or very creditable fake boobs, but a man's hands can never really pass for those of a woman, can they?' she asked sympathetically.

Vickki blinked, then shrugged. 'No,' he admitted.

'You're transsexual, rather than merely transvestite, I take it?' Hillary continued softly.

'Yes. I've gone through the counselling and all the psychiatric rigmarole you have to agree to before they'll seriously consider you. I had to go private, but I've had some of the ops,

312

but not all. Not the big one. For that I needed serious money.'

Hillary nodded. 'And your father disapproved, didn't he?'

Vickki snorted. 'That narrow-minded, hard-hearted, dried-up bastard wouldn't even discuss it. He thought of me as an abomination. You know, he actually said that to my face once? Just because I'm a woman trapped in a man's body.'

Hillary noticed that the little-girl voice was gone now, and through the pale make-up, his face was becoming flushed.

'He tried to stop you inheriting your trust fund, right?' she said gently. 'And that was the final straw. You went around to his house to try and get him to change his mind, I expect?'

Vickki threw off the muff, revealing large-knuckled, definitely male hands, with nails painted incongruously candy pink. 'He wouldn't even discuss it! He was ruining my whole life, trying to interfere as he always did — he made me so raging mad.'

Hillary nodded. In the interview room everyone tensed as they sensed Hillary was moving in for the kill.

'I can imagine it did. I'm not surprised, in the heat of the moment, that you reached for the first available thing and bashed him over the head.'

313

Vickki nodded. 'It was the poker I think,' he said, and beside her she heard Chang give a very faint sigh of audible relief.

'Yes,' she agreed quietly.

'And once I'd started, I think I hit him again. I can't remember. It was all a blur,' Victor Merchant said.

'And then you burnt all his things,' Hillary prompted, and Victor laughed, then began to cry, then finished up laughing again. 'All his goody-two-shoes stuff. I hated it. He loved them more than me. Can you imagine it — his own flesh and blood? Since Mum died . . . ' He shrugged, then leaned back, wiping the tears from his face. It smudged his make-up and left him looking truly pathetic.

'I just wanted to see it all go up in smoke. Then, at some point, my mind seemed to clear. I was beside his body, and realized he was dead. Really dead. And that I'd killed him. I just panicked and ran.'

Hillary nodded, but he was going too fast. She'd have to take him back, get him to add detail. This she did, getting him to admit that he was dressed as a woman when he called, confirming the time of the call, and going through their short, final conversation as close to verbatim as she could get it. Until, almost at the end, they reached an unexpected sticking point.

'And when did you decide to drag him outside and burn him on the bonfire, Victor?' she asked, careful to keep her voice neutral and any hint of horror or judgement out of it.

'I didn't,' Victor said, staring down at his ugly hands. 'That's what shook me up so much, that first day you came to talk to me. And told me he'd been burned. I thought at first you meant that the whole house had somehow caught fire.'

Hillary felt a jolt go through her as she remembered for herself how surprised and aghast 'Vickki' had been when she'd mentioned the state of David Merchant's body.

'But that doesn't make sense, Victor, surely you can see that?' Hillary began carefully. 'You've admitted to hitting and killing your father and burning his things.'

'Yes. And if I'd dragged his body to the fire and tossed it on, I'd have admitted that as well,' Victor said flatly, his bitter, defeated eyes glaring out from behind a fringe of thick mascara. 'But I didn't do it. I told you. I just suddenly came back from the daze I'd been in, saw his body lying there on the carpet where I'd left it, and ran for it.'

And from that, Victor Merchant would not be moved.

★ ★ ★

315

Afterwards, in the pub celebrating the closing of the case, they mulled over the reasons for it.

'I think he just couldn't face what he'd done, guv,' Barrington said. 'You know, his mind just blanked it out. Perhaps he really can't remember doing it.'

Danvers nodded. 'Could be. The CPS chap didn't seem to think it really mattered, anyway.'

'I got the feeling he thought the victim had more or less brought it on himself,' Gemma put in. 'You know, by being such a narrow-minded religious fruit cake and all.'

'Bollocks,' Hillary said flatly, before anyone could agree. 'David Merchant was entitled to his religious beliefs. And he sure as hell was entitled to live out the rest of his lifespan in peace. If you really want to contemplate what having a narrow point of view does for you, think about Victor. He wanted his sex change op, and nothing and nobody was going to stand in his way. He's a self-obsessed killer. And anybody who has more pity for him than his victim needs their own head testing,' she added firmly.

And Mark Chang, who'd been sitting and absorbing things in silence, found himself nodding. This had been his first murder inquiry and he'd found it fascinating.

Danvers, Gemma and Barrington, who were aware of her feelings from cases gone by, said nothing.

Then Barrington chose that moment to announce his resignation to the rest of the team. Gemma wasn't surprised, and Chang wasn't sure how to react. Only Danvers tried to talk him out of it, but eventually gave up. Barrington left first — he wanted to talk to Gavin and be reassured that he'd done the right thing.

Hillary watched him go with sad eyes. In her own mind, she thought he was making a mistake, but who was she to give advice?

Danvers left shortly afterwards, and Gemma, who had a date with Guy to interview wedding planners, quickly drank up too.

When it was just herself and her newest recruit left, Hillary nodded at his half a shandy.

'Drink up, Constable. We've a man to see about a cremation.'

★ ★ ★

Francis Whyte was slinging his last case into a taxi when he heard the car draw up. He stared in dismay as Hillary Greene and the good-looking Oriental constable got out.

'Going somewhere, Mr Whyte?' Hillary

gave him a small, hard smile. 'I think we'd better have a little chat first, don't you?'

Inside the cottage, sitting facing them on a large overstuffed sofa, Francis Whyte sighed heavily. 'You know, don't you?' he said, and Hillary nodded at Chang, indicating she wanted him to take notes.

'Yes, I think I do,' she said. 'You went to see David Merchant that morning didn't you? We have a witness who saw a tall, blond-haired man leaving the premises.'

Francis nodded glumly. 'I wanted to tell him to lay off my model.' Then he burst out laughing. 'Poor choice of words, considering the man was probably celibate since the death of his wife. But you know what I mean?'

Hillary nodded. 'The door was unlocked?'

The artist nodded. 'I went in. I called out, then found him there, on the floor,' Francis swallowed hard. 'So much blood. But when I bent down and checked his pulse he was still warm. Very warm.'

'You thought there might be a chance you could revive him,' Hillary prompted him. 'Lori Dunne told us you knew first aid, and could do CPR and all that.'

Francis shrugged, then shuddered in remembrance. 'I tried everything I could. Heart massage, mouth-to-mouth, you name it. The poor sod just looked so . . . crumpled.

I tell you, afterwards, when I was sure it was hopeless, I just sat back on my heels beside him and cried.'

Hillary nodded, and felt her heart stir. At last, somebody who actually mourned him. Even if only out of a sense of shared humanity.

'And then you began to think,' Hillary said. 'And you got scared.'

Beside her, Chang scribbled away furiously.

'Right. Here I was, with a dead body, and my DNA and clothes fibres and who knows what would be all over him,' Francis shrugged helplessly. 'We were known to have quarrelled and I'd made threats against him and, well . . . I just panicked. And the poor bastard was dead. He was just so very dead, do you see?'

Hillary, in a strange way, did.

'So you took him out to the bonfire and put him on?'

'I saw it going through the living room window. I couldn't figure out why he'd lit it but it seemed like fate. You know. As if it was meant to be.'

Hillary sighed. 'You'll need to come in and make a statement,' she said flatly and Whyte shot her a quick, scared look.

'Will I go to gaol?'

'I'm not sure,' Hillary said truthfully. 'The charge of interfering with a dead body probably doesn't carry a custodial sentence, but tampering with evidence, hindering a police inquiry — that might earn you some time. Depends on the CPS.'

Francis Whyte laughed bitterly. 'What is it they say? Let no good deed go unpunished?'

Hillary smiled wryly. 'I'll put in a word for you.' He might still get time, but perhaps in an open prison.

The artist nodded glumly.

★ ★ ★

That night, Hillary poured herself a glass of wine and sat in her narrowboat, next to the woodburning stove. It was dark, and she'd had a long, tiring and eventful day.

But it wasn't over yet. She had some serious thinking to do. And now, with the case successfully solved, she could put it off no longer.

First, her team had disintegrated around her: Danvers was transferring back up north; Barrington had quit, and Gemma, whether she was aware of it herself yet or not, would soon be promoted and transferred away. And Mel was still dead. Mel would always be dead.

Even Donleavy was leaving her, for if he got his promotion — and Hillary couldn't see why he shouldn't — he'd not have the time for her he usually did.

If she'd been the kind to believe in signs, she'd have said someone was giving her the message in letters sixty feet high.

But that was not all: there was Vane. And her need to spend precious amounts of her time in thwarting him, that should be dedicated to solving her cases. That was bad. Very bad. The decisions she'd made in her past were coming back to haunt her, and who knew where that might end up?

But even that was not the worst of it.

Taking a long drink of her wine, she thought back to Leamington Spa, and the feeling she'd had when talking to Robin that something momentous had happened to her. It didn't take her many moments, sitting in the dark, listening to the life of the canal going on outside her window, to explore and realize what it was.

She was becoming a liability. To Donleavy, her ex-sergeant Janine, her current colleagues and the police force as a whole.

And Hillary had always had an uncompromising view of what coppers who became liabilities should do.

As she finished her wine, Hillary Greene faced her demons head on.

It was time to go.

We do hope that you have enjoyed reading this large print book.

Did you know that all of our titles are available for purchase?

We publish a wide range of high quality large print books including:
Romances, Mysteries, Classics
General Fiction
Non Fiction and Westerns

Special interest titles available in large print are:
The Little Oxford Dictionary
Music Book
Song Book
Hymn Book
Service Book

Also available from us courtesy of Oxford University Press:
Young Readers' Dictionary
(large print edition)
Young Readers' Thesaurus
(large print edition)

For further information or a free brochure, please contact us at:
Ulverscroft Large Print Books Ltd.,
The Green, Bradgate Road, Anstey,
Leicester, LE7 7FU, England.
Tel: (00 44) 0116 236 4325
Fax: (00 44) 0116 234 0205